June Zeller

Herbert's Mountain

Twenty-One Tales of Transformation

John Slade

HERBERT'S MOUNTAIN
Twenty-One Tales of Transformation

ISBN 1-893617-03-3

Library of Congress Catalog Number
99-93598

FIRST EDITION

Front cover photograph by the author.

Back cover photograph by the late Detective Dirk Hardarme.

"Ol' Mossyhorn" reprinted by permission of
Adirondack Life, December 1990, Vol. xxi, No.7.

"Ol' Mossyhorn" and "Frederick on the Fourth of July" reprinted
by permission of *blueLINE*, SUNY at Potsdam, Potsdam, New York.

WOODGATE INTERNATIONAL
P.O. Box 190
Woodgate, New York 13494

315-392-4508

This book is for my grandmother,
known in these pages as Milly,
who gave me my one true home,
and who, in September of 1998,
celebrated her One Hundredth Birthday.

CONTENTS

The Ballad of The Lonesome Fireman

Once there was a fireman, who was not a fireman at all. He lived in a brick firehouse, and at least once a day the big brass bell clanged and he jumped into his fire truck and raced through the city to save a burning building. Sometimes a house was burning because children had been playing with matches. Sometimes an apartment was pouring flames out through its window because someone had been smoking in bed. And sometimes the fireman had to race in his fire truck outside of the city, with his siren screaming up to the stars spread over the countryside, until he reached a barn that some angry person had set on fire. While giant flames raged into the sky and tried to burn the moon, the fireman chopped open the locked door with his axe, then ran into the hot smoky blazing barn and brought out eight frightened horses and a goat before the roof collapsed.

But this was not what the fireman really wanted to do. What he loved were the quiet hours at the firehouse, when he could sit in his chair by the potbellied stove and listen to a strange, faint, beautiful music that he heard in his mind. If he listened carefully, and long enough, he could begin to play bits and pieces of the music on his guitar. Slowly, he discovered the chords waiting for him to find them. The pieces of music fit together into a song. First he would find the music, and then, if he closed his eyes and listened to his music very carefully, he would begin to hear the words that went with the song. He loved to practice each new song, polishing every note, until it was perfect.

But often the big brass bell clanged while he was hearing his music, and the fireman had to put down his guitar and jump into his tall black rubber boots. Then he raced in his fire truck through the city to an old building where frayed electrical wires had started a fire and now the business offices were burning.

Between fires, the fireman wrote a dozen songs. Some were about the moon and stars spread over the sleeping countryside. Some of his songs were about children playing in the city park. Sometimes he wrote a quiet and especially beautiful song about the loneliness that he felt in his heart. He had to work for many years before he had finished his twelve songs, because again and again the big brass bell clanged and the fireman had to race in every direction through the city to put out somebody's fire. Sometimes there were two fires at the same time, and once the fireman had three fires calling to him from three different parts of the city. But slowly, slowly, during the quiet hours, he listened to his strange beautiful music and wrote his twelve songs.

Now the fireman thought that he would sing his songs for other people, so they could enjoy them too. He put up a sign outside his firehouse and invited people to come in and look at his shiny red fire truck, and then to sit with him in the back room beside the potbellied stove, where he would play his guitar for them and sing his songs.

But almost nobody came. People rushed past his firehouse, walking quickly to wherever they were going, riding their bicycles to wherever they were going, driving their cars to wherever they were going, and most of them never even saw his sign. Only when their houses were burning did they need the fireman. So he sat alone in the back room beside the warm potbellied stove and sang his songs to a small gray mouse who scurried across the floor and gathered tiny pieces of cheese that the fireman had set down on a saucer.

Late one night, when the fireman was driving his fire truck back to the firehouse after he had put out a fire, he began to hear the saddest, loneliest music he had ever heard. He parked his fire truck beside the curb in front of a dark grocery store, then he closed his tired eyes and began to sing. He did not have his guitar. He did not have even his little gray mouse. He had only the song that he sang in his deep beautiful voice. Tonight he had poured water from his fire hose onto leaping orange flames until he had saved a house, but the tears that poured down his cheeks could not put out the flames that burned in his heart.

The fireman drove his fire truck back to the firehouse. He sat beside the potbellied stove, then he played his new song on his guitar. And he decided that he would not put out any more fires, he would not save any more houses and apartments and stores and barns, unless the people who called him had listened to his songs. So he put up another sign in front of his firehouse, which said, DO NOT RING MY BELL UNTIL YOU HAVE LISTENED TO AT LEAST ONE SONG.

The next time the big brass bell clanged, the fireman kept playing his guitar. He could not hear his guitar because the bell was so loud, but he kept playing it anyway. Finally the bell stopped ringing. The fireman stopped playing his guitar. The firehouse was very quiet. The fireman thought that maybe he was doing something terribly wrong. Maybe children were trapped in a burning house. Maybe horses were trapped in a burning barn. But he did not jump up from his chair. He did not put on his tall black rubber boots. He did not race in his fire truck through the city, and he did not fill the night with the rising and falling scream of his siren.

He waited. And sure enough, people began to gather in front of the firehouse. Angry people, shouting at him, asking why he had not come to put out their fire. More people gathered in front of the firehouse, for they had heard the shouts of the angry people and they wanted to know what was going on. A man from the newspaper arrived with his notebook and camera. A man from the radio arrived with his tape recorder. The mayor arrived. The city councilmen arrived. The chief of police arrived. They talked with each other and shouted at the fireman and made a great deal of noise, while the fireman sat on the shiny chrome bumper of his shiny red fire truck and played his guitar.

The chief of police learned from a very angry man that the man's little boy had been playing with matches and that the boy had burned down a garden shed. Nothing had been lost but the shed and a rake and a shovel and a hoe inside the shed.

No children had died. No horses had died. No office buildings had burned down.

While the crowd shouted and talked and argued and took pictures, the fireman sat on the shiny chrome bumper of his shiny red fire truck and played his guitar. He sang a song about an orange crescent moon hovering on a warm summer night above rolling black hills, as if the hills were really children sleeping beneath a huge black blanket and the moon were a face peering down and singing a lullaby to them.

While the father of the boy who had been playing with matches demanded that the chief of police take the fireman to jail, the fireman stood up with his guitar and walked over to the sign that said, DO NOT RING MY BELL UNTIL YOU HAVE LISTENED TO AT LEAST ONE SONG. He sang another song, about children playing in the city park. The man from the newspaper took his picture. The man from the radio held out his microphone and recorded the song. Slowly, one by one, people stopped shouting, stopped talking, stopped demanding that the fireman be taken to jail. They listened to his song. They read his sign. And then, one by one, they went home.

The very next morning, the picture of the fireman appeared in the newspaper.

The very next afternoon, the radio played the fireman's song. Several people phoned the radio station and requested that the song be played again. The station played the song four more times that day.

On the following day, the mayor and the city councilmen visited the fireman at the firehouse and asked him if he would give a concert in the city park on Saturday evening. The fireman said yes.

On the following day, an announcement about the concert appeared in the newspaper. An announcement was repeated several times during the day on the radio.

On Saturday evening, while the fireman stood on a stage with his guitar and sang his songs into a microphone, he looked out at thousands and thousands of people in the audience. They sat on benches, they sat on picnic blankets, they sat on the park swings. Above the people, lightning bugs blinked. Above the people, a breeze whispered through the maple trees. Above the people, stars twinkled and a crescent moon peered down.

After his concert, the fireman sat on the shiny chrome bumper of his shiny red fire truck and played his guitar in the morning and in the afternoon and in the evening for people who gathered on the sidewalk to listen.

The big brass bell almost never clanged.

Six months later, the newspaper printed an article about some astonishing news: fires in the city had become so rare that not a single person had been hurt. Not a single horse or cow had been lost. The mayor announced during an interview on the radio that the Fire Department had saved so much money that now the city could buy a new ambulance for the hospital. The city councilmen invited the fireman to give a concert once a month in a school auditorium during the winter, and once a month in the park during the summer. The radio broadcast his concerts to families who lived on farms far from the city, and to children who were sick in bed, and to old people who sat in their wheelchairs and listened to the fireman's songs about an orange crescent moon that sang a lullaby to rolling black hills, and about children laughing as they played on the swings in the park, and about a little gray mouse.

OL' MOSSYHORN

Way up in the Great North Woods it was, where the white pines grew so tall that a shaken-loose pinecone became a five-foot sapling before it hit ground. And a long time ago it was, when snowflakes in January often stopped and hovered in mid-air, shivering so fierce they didn't know down from sideways.

Three varmints we were in our timberlog cabin. Pa, descended of a bullsnake so long it fell in love with its tail one moonless night, was an intelligent critter, for his schoolmarm was the wilderness itself.

"Pa," I would ask with keen admiration and youthful uncertainty while we split wood for the winter, "when will I ever be as wise a man as you?"

He'd cock an eye at me, his grizzled beard filled with wood chips. "You hear a bear about a mile away?"

"Yup," I answered confidently. "First heard it half an hour ago."

"It moving or put?"

"Put."

"Picking berries?"

"Nope, slapping for trout."

"Any luck?"

"Two."

Pa nodded with paternal satisfaction. "So far equal." Then his eyes glinted with a challenge. "That bear male or female?"

"Pa, how could a body determine that?"

He stood up from the chopping block and deeply growled, "Rrraaaawwwwwww."

No answer.

Pa filled up his lungs and growled again, "Rrraaaawwwww!"

Still no answer.

"Male," said Pa. "He don't answer."

Brother Luke was a lad who never concerned with things going on. He'd perch on a stump in a fern patch and you couldn't see higher beneath the drooping brim of his old black cowboy hat than was he grinning or grimacing or gnashing his teeth. His buckskin pockets were full of books, and he wouldn't have known had that he-bear sat down beside him.

"Luke!" I would holler at dinner, fourth time, "you be eighteen and of staunch build and ought to be able to pass me that platter of chicken legs." But he'd poke me a plate of rabbit ribs and go right on reading. When a child he learnt to make out the words on liquor bottles, then he discovered Shakespeare at the schoolhouse and he ain't given up since. He was so stirred one day, pacing back and forth in front of the cabin while declaiming some dialect about a king caught out in the rain, that he never realized when the real rain began. Drops averaging half a gallon apiece came pouring down, lightning struck so close that Pa's woodpile was turned to charcoal, and thunder boomed so loud the ground was still shaking like a scared dog three days later. But Luke, he never knew. He stretched his arms up to the heavens and bellowed, "Blow ye winds! Crack your cheeks!". His drooping hat dripped like a waterlogged mushroom.

Me, I was there, the only one with any sense at all. And you too, while I recall the facts.

We were three for a while, and happy . . . for a while, content with two to cuss at, and a forest so broad a rainbow once slipped in the wet and tumbled in, lost forever, though I've seen bits and snatches of it peeping out in the waterfall spray. Yonder from our cabin glimmered Lilypad Pond, water sweet and clear, where me and the snapping turtles would laze in the hot sun on the roof of a stage coach that strayed off the road one foggy night. I knew the raucous rattle of the kingfisher, the high "Keeeheeeeeee!" of the hawk. I could follow with my ears a puff of wind waltzing through the spruce boughs. And I listened to silence so deep, it seemed every bird and leaf was holding its breath, waiting for the loon's first yodel at dusk.

But more beautiful than all else was our meadow deep in the forest, where butterflies flitted and flirted, and wildflowers danced and drowsed. On August afternoons, us and the bears would call a truce and pick huckleberries, the bunch of us with purple mouths and daisy chains around our necks. On October evenings, we'd sit in the frosty grass and listen to the rumble of last May's thunder, still an echo bouncing between the mountain peaks. Twas there in that meadow, on a rise overlooking the pond, that Pa years ago built our home.

Wintertime, however, turned our cabin into a prison, a dungeon, a tomb. Snow drifted so high over the roof, we knew day from night only by taking apart the stovepipe and peering up at the sky. The cold was so fierce, our fire froze one night; we dried our socks on a poker suspended in the flames. Every morning I'd awake to the same two uninspiring faces and wonder if I'd even slept at all. Rolling over with a groan, I'd cocoon myself in the six wool blankets and dream of Beaver Crick, the town two miles down the road. There was Sam McClinnic's Catalogue Outlet, (sweetcorn and wives the establishment specialities when in season,) fifteen cabins, fifteen barns, and the Bald Vulture Saloon, (this last supported faithfully by those gentlemen leaning against both sides of its moss-grown walls). Townfolks were friendly if you'd been born local, didn't pry overmuch, and spat toward the door. Us three would sit on Sam's porch them good summer evenings, each in his chair worn to fit, Pa always in the middle while we passed a quart of huckleberry wine up and down the row and waited for the women. They'd come downstairs around dusk, looking fat and fine, and Ooooooo, I'd lay abed all winter dreaming about them girls. I ain't no more than held hands by then. Most were taken with Luke with his poesie, and others were taken by Pa back upstairs, but there were always one or two who would kiss my cheek and talk sweet. A lonesome lump beneath my blankets, I bayed more miserably the winter long inside those four log walls than the starving timber wolves outside.

Spring awoke at last when Bronze John smiled down through the cracks in our sodden roof. A week later we stood on chairs to stare out the upper window panes. Day by day we watched the great sea of snow lower by inches, releasing now and then a pine branch that sprang into the April warmth. Finally, with a run and a three-shouldered heave, we cheered "Hello!" in the light of the opened door. Birds, blue sky, bright mountains! We lost our socks in the melting flames.

Into town we bounded, light as jackrabbits. A week later, home we trudged, grinning but miserable. For we owed our land, humble possessions, and a year's hard labor to the stablemaster for nightly lodging, to the barkeep for spirits and crackers, to anyone in town with the slightest wit at poker, and to the sheriff for fines and bail resulting from indisputable charges of uncivilized conduct. Not a woman in town would deign to even scowl in our direction.

Luke sat on a stool beside the cold stove, wagging his head at the floor. "Wherefore art thou, voluminous tart?"

I lay abed; already I could taste oatmeal at dawn with Pa and Luke, corn cakes for lunch with Pa and Luke, boiled bullhead for dinner with Pa and Luke, oatmeal at dawn with Pa and Luke. We needed to extend the family. A new face, a warming voice, a fresh opinion on the porch after dinner, beyond Pa's "Rained today, sure enough. Yup." Somebody to bide the time with us at home, and to keep a close watch over us in town on Saturday nights.

Who?

It was the old man who knew who.

After he'd climbed into the middle bunk and dropped his boots, his drawers, his woolen underdrawers and his underneath woolen underdrawers over the edge, he lay back and declared his choice: "A moose."

I turned to face the sagging lump above me. "I prefer a soft-footed delicate doe of a lady, Pa. I know you like them big, but—"

"A brawny, bounding, bellowing moose, striding head high through the forest, sturdy in battle for his favorite cow."

I queried with dismay, "You're talking about a real moose?"

"There's sure to be a bull moose about, wallowing through bogs, lunching in the quagmires."

"Pa. I don't mind a moose in the distance—"

"We'll have to think of a name for him."

Luke hung over the top bunk like an ostrich, its head engulfed in the black hole of his hat. "Behold the noble horns o' Sylvan's grand beast," he intoned.

"Flies," I said.

"Harken to its hooves along the mossy trail." Luke and the bedsheets began to waterfall over the edge.

"Dirt and dung," I said.

"Mossyhorn," whispered Pa, winnowing the syllables through shared poetic instinct. "Mossyhorn. What ho, Luke!" He bounded out of bed into the darkness. "In spring, their antlers be covered with moss. Thicker'n on a stump." A flaring match lit the room. Pa stood potbelly to potbelly beside the stove, grinning at the thought of our new next-to-kin.

Luke hung clutching his wolf-skin blankets as in the abyss he swung, mumbling iambic pentameter two or three inches above the nightpot.

Turning to our patriarch, I inquired, "Pa, why not a mountain lion, a polecat, or a porcupine?"

He affirmed, "A moose be a thoughtful and compassionate beast."

Though his wisdom had wandered irretrievably from the matter at hand, I asked nevertheless, "How—though I honor you deeply, O father—but how does anyone catch a grown-in-the-wilds moose?"

"Son, to attract a moose," he held the match before his lips, "I simply whwhwhwhistle." The room went black.

As did my hopes for any womenfolk before the snows of the coming winter.

* * *

We stood as miniature creatures beneath the giant pines, hushed upon command to a faint breathing. Pa held a wet finger to the wind, searched for broken twigs, shaved bark, uncrusted dung. Then he bent over and sniffed the trail. I recall thinking that if I were a moose, I'd surely be close enough so's not to miss a moment of this folly. Luke was busy carving a sonnet into the bark of a birch, but had to mutter the couplet while he sucked his bleeding thumb.

Pa threw his proud man-o-the-woods look at me, sucked in, wheezed out, sucked in and let loose one such whistle blast that I had to step back off the tracks. "Hold ye still," he scolded, "or ye'll scare him away."

I held still, staring down at the pinecones at my feet. "I think I heard a chipmunk, Pa," I smirked. "Though it might have been the twitter of a chickadee."

"Sam. "

"Hush, Luke," I scolded. "You'll frighten the wild creatures."

"Sam!"

I realized it was the first intelligible thing my brother had said in eleven years, so I looked up. Yonder among the mammoth trunks stood one-half ton of fuzzy brown, thundering-large beast, its moss-covered antlers reaching so high they nearly grabbed the sun. Pa gave sound once more, and in cordial reply that bull moose flashed a foot-wide grin and bugled a grand how-de-do. To me, why me?, mouth hung open and couldn't have whistled a peep, it came a-trotting. I stumbled backward, found every log in the forest and crashed to the ground in a huckleberry bush. The moose straddled its five-foot legs over my body, lowered its peninsular nose to my face and snorted with amusement.

My senses overwrought, I fainted.

Hours later, I awoke in bed, roused by sawing and hammering on the other side of the log wall. I opened the door and looked out. Happy-Hoofed-One stood munching horsetail sprouts at the edge of our porch while Pa and Luke built him a stall downwind from the cabin.

"Afternoon, Sam," called Pa. "Grab ye a tool and start swinging."

"Yessir, Pa." The moose snorted with apparent impatience at my dereliction, so I snorted back. It snorted again, then Pa loaded a board into its antlers for Luke up on the roof.

The stall was finished by sunset, as Pa likes to say, (it finished us, as I like to say,) and the old man found fitting an initiation ceremony. He had me and Luke stand gentleman-like by the sagging door while he introduced Red-Eyed Filthyfur to its new abode and the men of construction.

"Moose," Pa growled, "pay attention. We ain't here for you to nibble at the window ledge."

The moose stripped off a last piece of succulent birch bark, then laid its wet nose on my shoulder with a moist sigh and much heavy breathing. Luke whispered the immortal words, which Pa repeated with his booming voice, "Welcome O King of the Forest to our honored family. Like a brother do we embrace thee. Henceforth shalt thou be known to one and all as the esteemed and most noble Mossyhorn Moose." I twisted my boot in the dust while the prose flowed like soup. Grunts of agreement and approval rumbled in my ear.

Finally Pa concluded, "And the authority invested in me by the grace o' me being most aged and wise." He wrapped up the dedication with a sort of baptism: solemnly he dribbled a cup of spring water down the nose of Ol' Quagmire. The moose sniffled, grimaced, held its breath, and the ceremony was over in a volley of moose mucus. Pa called for a towel.

* * *

Our dumb beast was awful intelligent. Pa took the moose into town to get acquainted. With antlers spread like an oak tree on Main Street, Mossyhorn looked each man eye to eye as the names were called. Pa talked and slapped backs and kept talking and signed papers. Storekeep Sam McClinnic hung a leather sack from an antler, filled with groceries and dry goods, then he read a list as to what was to go where, and offered a carrot. The barkeep hung the Wells Fargo mail pouch on the opposite antler, filled with letters for those who hadn't been by the saloon during the last month. The sheriff deputized Mossyhorn, then showed him a sheaf of Wanted posters. Mossyhorn memorized a dozen mugs, and nodded he'd keep an eye out. Then he pushed through the crowd toward a widow with twelve children tugging at her skirts. Our majestic moose soon pranced down Main Street to accomplish his appointed rounds, with six younguns riding in a row on his back, and six more up in his antlers, two of them hanging by their knees.

It wasn't long before we'd squared all debts with folks who no longer herded the cows to the barn, fretted over mountain lions, or mulched the vegetable patch. And the church at last had what passed for the bass pipes of an organ.

I wondered if Pa had known beforehand about the women. Mossyhorn's cavalier grin, and his long-lashed eyes half closed, soon brought ladies with bulging wicker picnic baskets knocking at our door.

Mossyhorn has been with us one full summer when the Great Disaster happened. Now don't get a-feared, because it ain't that Mossyhorn got shot at by a no-good squirrel hunter last seen catapaulted from an antler toward Suckmuck Bog. I'm not going to bore you with how Mossyhorn took to reading over Luke's shoulder, sometimes snuffling with tragical sadness, sometimes grinning and guffawing and nudging impatient if Luke took too long to finish the page. The story here isn't that Mossyhorn kept us awake one balmy summer night because he stomped in his shed and bugled like he'd blow the roof off. When we opened the door to see what was wrong, Mossyhorn burst out and galloped for the woods . . . but home he came an hour later, nose drooping nearly to the ground. He wouldn't eat, wouldn't talk, but bellowed mournful from a broken heart. Pa, moved to commiserating tears, scratched with sympathy behind the ears.

I lay abed one evening of early autumn, listening to a bull-frog that cherumped in the pond, a big frog known to snag geese with its tongue if they circled too low. Its lady cherumped back from a lilypad. I heard a splash like a horse had jumped in, and knew he was swimming over. A tree frog peeped, a green frog garunked, and soon the pond hummed with a low rubbery rhythm. They must think it's spring, I mused, for evenings had been chilly lately, but this was a warm one.

"Awful warm," I muttered with amazement as I tossed off my blankets. I looked to see if someone had closed the window, but my eyes were drawn to where flames were blazing out of the stovepipe and across the ceiling.

"The cabin's a-fire!" I roared as I jolted the lump above me.

"Fire!" hollered Pa. "She's a-fire, Luke!"

Luke hung over the edge, head-down in the hole of his hat, a gesticulating oratorical ostrich.

"Hush, Luke," I scolded as I jumped out of bed. "This part of the story is true."

We tried brooms, blankets and that evening's dishwater, but when the old man lost his Fruit of the Looms to cinders falling from the ceiling, we burst out the door with buckets and the nightpot to fetch water from the pond.

Looking back as we ran, we saw that flames had engulfed the stall!

"Mossyhorn!" cried Pa. But he hadn't taken a step toward the stable door before the door began to come toward him. What had once swung in the portal now rose to the sky on the charred antlers of a three-quarter-ton thundering smoldering moose who bellowed so loud the trees leaned back. Mossyhorn galloped past us, blazing like a meteor, as he headed straight for Lilypad Pond.

"Forgive us!" called Pa, but the apparition spewing sparks was indifferent to apologies as it plunged into the pond, then dunked its head so even its incandescent antlers disappeared. Smoke bubbled to the surface. Frogs exploded onto the shore in every direction, leaping clear of the water before they were scalded. A snapping turtle scampered faster than any hare across the meadow, clambored up a tamarack tree and peered down from the peak, its massive jaws chattering with fright.

Mossyhorn boiled up the bank, clouds of steam billowing above him, lilypads dangling from his antlers. He charged headlong into the forest, bugling as if he'd been struck by a bolt of lightning. "Mossyhorn, come home!" shouted Pa, but our scorched moose headed due north, apparently determined not to stop until he sat his haunches in a tundra snowdrift.

Forgiven or not, we still had our cabin to save. We sprinted back and forth with buckets and tossed water in through the door, but the flames began to creep down the walls and we knew the roof would fall in shortly.

"Sure was a fine shack," I lamented.

"Mighty sad," mourned Pa.

"Speak not defeat," quoth Luke, racing past us in his nightshirt with a hatful of water. Still hanging from a peg beside his bed were his buckskin britches with a book in every pocket. "Wail not thy plaints bereft of hope, but thine ardor augment, for save we must the eternal bard."

We hove in our bucketfuls, but knowed that Shakespeare should have called for rain tonight.

And then, while we were dashing and puffing and struggling and staggering once more across the meadow, our arms aching with the weight of laden buckets, we began to hear distant voices . . . faint, becoming louder: the cries of a clamoring throng approaching through the forest. A flock of startled crows rose up and flapped across the moon.

A motley tribe of pajama-clad townfolk emerged from the trees, frothing inhuman screams and bearing brooms, clubs, muskets, hay forks, and a sword glinting in the moonlight. Just ahead of the mob trotted an enormous sooty creature: twas Furryfellow.

The vigilantes came to a sudden silent halt as each man and woman stared with horror at the burning cabin. Our Hairy Hero looked back over his shoulder and snorted as if to say, I told you so.

Forming a proper bucket brigade, we doused the flames quicker than the shake of a burnt tail. Luke stepped through the steaming door, then reappeared, grinning triumphantly as he held up his buckskin library, slightly singed, slightly damp.

Then in the meadow we gathered, to piece together the tale of the valiant moose who had roused its fellow citizens in time of desperate need.

"Mossyhorn galloped up Main Street like a demon of the apocalypse," recounted Sam McClinnic, his arms raised over his head, fingers spread lifelike. "I leaped from my chair and threw open the door on a bugling phantom that drove ahead of it a tumultuous herd of wings, claws, hooves and tails straight up in the air, every fleeing creature from the forest bleating with stark terror. As I turned with a shout to the wife to get the children in the cellar, I was bowled over by a yowling saucer-eyed bobcat that dove beneath the bed."

"Mossyhorn burst in through the saloon's swinging doors," gasped the barkeep, still in shock. "He toppled the poker table, kicked the spittoons, swept his horns down eight octaves on the honky-tonk piano, antlered up the barmaid (gently) into a chandelier, galloped the entire length of the bar, brew spewing from his hooves, then crashed again through the swinging doors. Shots rang out, and fifteen bottles of beer blew their corks."

"Back out in the street, the moose charged head down into a tinker's wagon and sent it arching toward the stars, spinning clouds of silverware and tea sets in the moonglow. The tinker himself sat on the buckboard seat, blinking down at the world and shouting 'Whoa!'"

"Mossyhorn circled beyond town, clattered through the village graveyard, then sailed once more down Main Street, a wreath of roses in his antlers, and every ancester twelve generations back sprinting one step ahead of him, ashen-gray and gape-mouthed with long silent screams. Cows whinneyed and horses mooed, and chickens laid an even dozen eggs, down to their last primordial yolk the size of a dried pea."

"Along the road toward home Mossyhorn galloped, great whoops bugling from his uplifted muzzle as he led a hundred mustered flustered clanging banging citizens of town to the very spot where a timberlog cabin was burning down."

Well now, in the midst of such testimonial praise, any humble moose would have snuck off to some hidden corner of the forest. But Mossyhorn stood square in the middle of the crowd, moss hanging from his antlers in tatters and ashes as he nodded left and right and grinned his foot-wide grin.

The government wrote and said they needed a senator, the church wrote and said they needed a saint. A feller wearing a white hat and a mask walked into town and said Hi Ho and that his silver had run out and did we still have that moose? But folks shook their heads and said No, they were sorry, but Mossyhorn was last seen heading down the road into the Great North Woods.

That wasn't anything unordinary, they didn't say, a moose striding down the road with Pa, Luke and me riding in a row, the four of us singing old love songs to the moon as we trotted through the misty meadows toward home.

MILLY

We were heading south in late September, wings beating steadily over forests clad with crimson and gold, when we heard, from far below, a goose call that sounded like no goose I knew. Wary of hunters, I anticipated we might rise a few hundred feet for safety on our undeviating course toward Chesapeake Bay. But the lead goose, cutting the cold clear autumnal air at the point of our chevron, honked over his shoulder to the flock, "That's Milly." This was my first trip south, so I had no idea who Milly was. A discussion traveled up and down the two branches of our V, as to whether that lone honking was truly Milly—an almost invisible pink figure sitting in an Adirondack guideboat, her call the beckoning voice of a well-fed and contented gander—and if it was, should we stop so early in the afternoon? Several of our members were determined to fly until dusk; and a few, veterans of many flights who knew to take advantage of good weather, honked vociferously that we should cruise on through the night, the stars our infallible guides, for further south we might meet with storms or fog or adverse winds. We had a good norther behind us, crystalline air from Canada streaming south on which we rode like canoes on a river, so those who advised holding our course had the elements in their favor.

And yet, as the lead goose argued, those who did not know Milly and who therefore passed her by were missing a most important experience on this journey. For Milly, ninety-one years old, could speak a dozen dialects of duck, as well as crow, turkey, chukar, chickadee, hawk, blue jay, kingfisher, and of course Canada goose, better than most who spoke these as their mother tongue. She carried no shotgun, never fired a shot, certainly never lured waterfowl down from the skies if hunters were on the lake. She simply liked to converse, and more, to exercise her expertise with a knowledgeable and appreciative audience. With Milly, explained the lead goose, a cylindrical wooden goose call became a Stradivarius, and foolish and unfortunate the goose who did not spend an afternoon with her, to share a bit of conversation and to enjoy the rarified limits of the honker's language. Thus it was that the lead goose, despite opposition, convinced our flock to drop from the blue skies down toward a pocket of the long black lake in order to feed and rest and savor what would prove to be an extraordinary afternoon, and an even more exceptional evening, with Milly.

Millicent Smith sat in her guideboat, snug in her pink L.L. Bean parka, and pointed her P.S. Olt black walnut goose call not toward but forward of a flock of fifty geese winging overhead. She hoped that a few of the honkers had spent an afternoon with her the year before, or the year or years before that, so they might be acquainted with her. Each autumn since she was ten or twelve, in 1910 or 1912, she forgot which, she had raised her nasal trumpet and sent skyward her invitation, with the hope that the aerial plow might hesitate and circle and come to a decision and then glide down and flap as disparate geese, each honking with uninhibited heartiness as they circled once more around her bay. Her ancient heart thumped when the big birds set their wings and descended against the wind, splayed their webbed feet and splashed into the black water near enough to her boat that she could continue the conversation. Her simulated honks and hoots, unintelligible in human terms, communicated nevertheless from her heart, a heart which had weathered nearly a century of autumns and so which had, in the endless articulations of goose talk, much to talk about.

No, her goal was not a goose dinner. Having outlived most of her generation, brothers and sisters and brothers-in-law and sisters-in-law and best friends and distant friends and even two of her children, her goal and heartfelt need was companionship. For though human life waxed and waned in sixty or eighty or ninety or more years, while the maple leaf waxed green and red and then fell and waned brown and vanished in one year, still the human lifespan was so much less than eternal. Thus she looked to the eternal, or to the eternally seasonal, embodied in a flock of loquacious geese, for infallible companionship. Milly loved those big black and white birds, and after eighty years of practice—since her grandfather had taught her way back before the Great War—she could talk to them better almost than the geese could talk to each other. For she spoke with a lifetime of wilderness in her heart, and so expressed nuances which the younger geese had yet to learn. She had not the lung-power and so not the volume she had possessed in her forties and fifties and even in her sixties, yet her call, modulated by throat and tongue and hands cupped around the walnut cylinder, was clear, true-to-life, and unabashedly reverent. Reverent as if she called to angels not of a church god, but a god of thunderstorms and waterlilies and blueberries and the extraordinary unexpected unnecessary unneeded and wholely impractical blazing red and orange and yellow and maroon of autumn, undeniable proof of a god's satisfied laughter in a chilly forest before its winter sleep; yes, angels of a god who loved his geese, or he wouldn't have bothered, busy as he was, to create them.

From where I floated among the lilypads, I saw she was a small woman with white hair, her hands cupped around her goose call, her eyes sharp with excitement. The lead goose honked hello, and she, able to distinguish his call among the jabbering of a dozen others, turned immediately to him and honked hello in return. She did not merely replicate our enunciations, but rather elaborated on them with refinements and flourishes. She was a musician with a keen ear, who, when given a theme, developed and recapitulated that phrase into a dozen dexterous variations. The adolescent squawk of a gander whose adult feathers were but weeks old became, when rendered through Milly's goose call, the croonings of the queen of geese.

As the sun arched west over the glittering lake, Milly singled out and spoke individually with every goose in our flock. Even the most skeptical, reluctant or taciturn were eventually melted by Milly's overtures. Perhaps in her younger years she had been a teacher, skilled at addressing every student in her class, no matter how wayward or unruly some might be.

When a flock of crows flapped in their ragged non-formation over the bay, she set down her goose call, took up a crow call and cawed with such familiarity that I understood this flock must reside nearby. She chattered with a chipmunk on shore, scolded and barked with a squirrel in a spruce tree. "Kee-heeeeeee" she called to a broad-winged hawk soaring high overhead.

Paddling over to the lead goose, I suggested that next spring, on our way north, we must be sure to visit Milly when the frogs would join our concert.

But the full range of her repertoire became evident at dusk, when a hush settled over the lake as we geese, our bellies full, now turned to pruning and preening our feathers in preparation for the long flight tomorrow. The air became frosty once the sun had dipped behind the hills; wisps of mist drifted over the water. Stars pierced the violet sky. An owl hooted in the darkening forest; Milly hooted "good evening." Or was it Milly who hooted first, and the owl who answered?

And then from out on the lake came the wail of a loon. Now even the wisest old goose will pause in his ruminations when he hears the wail of a loon. No matter how many times I've heard that eerie, mournful cry, it still makes the feathers along my back stand on end. I waited for Milly to answer, paused in my preening and held my breath in anticipation of her attempt—for who could more than attempt—to replicate the ghostly lamentation of a loon. But Milly did not answer. She set down her goose call, turned her face toward the bay, cupped her hands—in mittens now—behind her ears, and listened.

Milly heard the call of the loon as a lamentation, filled with mysterious sadness, and as a cry of celebration, filled with mysterious joy; but the sadness and joy were her own: joy from the many summers, stretching back eons it seemed, which the loon and other loons of generations before had shared and enriched and blessed, and sadness that soon this loon would leave for its winter home in the south, bequeathing to her the frozen black-and-white silence of half a year, relieved only by the occasional raucous cawing of crows, the dependable twitter of chickadees, and by the cracking of the ice on the coldest nights. Every wintry month seemed to her like a year, the song of the peepers an eternity away.

So she listened, and savored, and stored up in her soul the sound of the soul of the lake, given utterance through this wild and privileged bird. Only after it had called a half-dozen times, without answer from another loon, did she slip off her mittens and raise her cupped hands. Taking a deep breath of air pungent with damp fallen maple leaves, she intoned a pure and prolonged wail, not in simulation of what she had heard, but rather giving voice, after ninety-two summers and more than forty winters in the woods, to her own wild and privileged soul.

Putting her mittens on, and tying a scarf beneath her chin, she reached for the oars and paddled toward the mouth of the bay with the slow but steady rhythm of an old but experienced paddler. The flock of murmuring geese swam in the swirls from her oars. She rowed to the belly of the lake—the Dipper was reflected upside-down as if the lake did its best to mimic the heavens as she had mimicked the loon—where she shipped the oars and drifted. The loon, at the far end of the lake, wailed again to her, and she wailed in return, her calls three and four and five times longer than the loon's, for she knew that he with these geese tomorrow would be gone.

She could not only wail, this small woman in her guideboat with starlight on her hands and face, her hair as white as a halo. She could also laugh like a loon; sets of tiny waves rippled out from her boat and washed around us as the hull shook with her rising and descending tremolos.

And she could shriek like a loon. She seemed to understand the threat to a nest, for her high-pitched undulations were not frantic, but a cry of feisty defiance.

In one respect, as the loon progressed through its litany of calls, its shriek but brief before it laughed again, Milly outdid the loon. Yes, her grace notes were her own, her embellishments as unique to her as honk or caw or wail of any bird is to itself. But more than that, Milly outdid any bird I'd ever heard . . . in calling forth an echo. She seemed to speak not only to the loon, but to the lake itself, and the lake was glad to answer. An owl can hoot and hear a hoot in return; a loon can laugh, and hear from the opposite end of the lake the ghost of a loon laugh back. But when Milly laughed, the lake itself laughed with hearty agreement. And when she wailed, the lake wailed too that winter was coming.

Her guideboat upside-down in its shed, Milly often stood by day and by night on her dock, an ice-locked promontory from which she beheld snow blowing across the frozen lake, or wands of sunlight beaming down through grey clouds, or, upon occasion, Orion striding and his great hound leaping as together they hunted whatever it is the living must eternally pursue. She would call names across the lake: her mother's, and her father's, and the names of brothers and a sister, of a husband, of four children, of their six children, and of three of their children. And the opposite shore, white and green, or white and black, would call these names back to her, muted and muffled, so that never, though her heart often ached, never was she alone.

The Monster of Bullmoose Bog

FLASH: Sheriff Gerrit Entwistle announced today during a press conference at the Woodgate Constabulary Headquarters that he had "cracked the case" involving the disappearance two weeks ago of Professor Phillis Thorne-Bottom from Muskrat Lake. Thorne-Bottom, a world-renowned botanist who had summered for the past fifty-six years in the Adirondacks, vanished on Tuesday afternoon, July 15, while collecting pitcher plants from Bullmoose Bog at the northern end of the aforesaid Muskrat. When she failed to return to her camp that evening, neighbors notified a park ranger, who organized an immediate search. With the help of a helicopter's searchlight, Professor Thorne-Bottom's straw hat (her neighbors conclusively identified the hat by virtue of its wreath of pink plastic begonias) was found on the bog. Near the hat was a black muck-hole, the sphagnum edges of which showed signs of a struggle.

The following morning, three New York State Troopers trained in underwater search and rescue donned their Scuba tanks in order to investigate the waters beneath the bog. Only two returned. Both men, apparently suffering from shock, have been unable to describe their experiences beneath the bog. They are presently recuperating at Marcy Psychiatric Hospital until such time as they are able to talk, stated a New York State Trooper spokesman.

Sheriff Bentwhistle contacted Navy divers at Norfolk Beach, Virginia. Naval authorities spent twenty-four hours evaluating the evidence of the case as presented to them by Sheriff Tentthistle over the phone, then they responded by telefax: "Sorry, we are strictly saltwater. That's not a job for us."

The Woodgate Chamber of Commerce, concerned that Muskrat's reputation as "as pretty a lake as you'll ever find in the Adirondacks" might be affected by adverse publicity, offered a reward of a two-week free vacation at the local Rifle and Rod Club camp at the southern end of Muskrat, (an idyllic three-bedroom cottage with fireplace and recently repainted outhouse, just two doors from Professor Thorne-Bottom's own hemlock-sided camp,) for information leading to the whereabouts of the vanished-without-a-trace-except-for-her-begonia-straw-hat Thorne-Bottom.

That advertised bounty brought a private detective from the Bronx to the Woodgate Constabulary Headquarters on Saturday afternoon, July 19. Detective Dirk Hardarme assured Sheriff Rentfizzle that he would "crack the case by Monday noon". "Not counting Sunday," he said. "I'm a church-going man on Sunday." And indeed, Detective Hardarme was present for services in the Woodgate Chapel on Sunday, July 20. Parishioners noted a bulge under the left side of his black-and-red checkered sports coat.

At 6:30 a.m. on Monday morning, July 21, Detective Hardarme was motored by Sheriff Ventsizzle in the latter's (Bentnozzle's) Constabulary Search and Rescue Watercraft, otherwise the Rifle and Rod Club's fishing boat, to Bullmoose Bog at the northern wetland end of the now-notorious Muskrat Lake. The detective came well-equipped with fingerprint powder, a laptop computer capable of global Internet communication, a pair of handcuffs jangling at-the-ready from a belt loop, and his camera. Despite the sheriff's admonition that a walk on a bog required rubber boots, (as recounted by Sheriff Nozzle-Bottom at his Constabulary press conference,) Detective Hardarme insisted that his Nike fuel-injected hightops were "better for pursuit on foot". Schnozzle-Wobble, recipient of the WOODGATE WELCOMES THE WORLD award in 1952 for his impeccable courtesy toward visitors to the North Woods, did not further contest the issue with his guest.

He did note, however, (as he recounted to reporters packed

shoulder-to-shoulder in the pine-paneled sheriff's office, directly adjacent to the cobblestone-walled jail,) that Detective Hardarme's Nikes disappeared "more than once" into the soft sphagnum moss while the detective examined the site of Professor Thorne-Nozzle's as yet unexplained disappearance.

Woodgate's sheriff pointed out the spot where the straw hat was found. (He had brought with him during this investigation the very hat itself.) He placed the hat on the bog beside the black muck-hole.

Detective Hardarme photographed the straw hat as Piece of Evidence Number One (1).

Sheriff Throttle-Nozzle then pointed out the black muck-hole and the signs of struggle: two scars where someone had ripped two chunks of sphagnum moss right out of the bog, as well as splotches of dried black muck splattered on the otherwise reddish-green moss to a distance of (Sheriff Bottle-Nozzle carefully measured with his combination U-Weigh-'Em Scales and Tape Measure that he keeps in his tackle box) eleven feet, eight and three-quarter inches.

Detective Hardarme was about to photograph the black muck-hole and signs of struggle when Sheriff Bottle-Bottom heard a hermit thrush "as pretty as you please" in the spruce woods flanking the eastern side of the northern end of mysterious Muskrat Lake. Turning toward the thrush, the sheriff, born and bred in Woodgate, cupped his hands to his ears—"as my grandfather was wont to do"—so as to better hear the bird's purling liquescent warble.

At that moment, he heard behind him three simultaneous sounds: a thunderous inhuman roar, a piercing very human scream, and the click of a camera.

As he ran in his rubber boots toward his Search and Rescue Watercraft, he heard behind him a fourth sound: a man's frantic breathing, as if the aforesaid man were engaged in violent struggle; a fifth sound: three shrieks of increasing volume, "NO! NO!! NO!!!"; and a sixth sound: (the sheriff at this point was leaping into his boat,) "a deep brief sucking sound." The sheriff added, "like flatulence in reverse."

He returned to Bullmoose Bog on Monday afternoon with twenty-six deputized members of the Rifle and Rod Club, each man armed for bear. Stepping onto the bog in their rubber boots, they found Professor Thorne-Bottle's straw hat lying precisely where Sheriff Spentwhistle had placed it that morning, Monday, July 21. Near the hat with its unmistakable wreath of pink plastic begonias lay Detective Hardarme's auto-zoom auto-focus mini-macro Nikon camera, apparently where he had dropped it. Several chunks of moss had been ripped out of the bog, indicating a severe and protracted struggle.

The sheriff and his deputies concurred that the hat and camera should be retrieved, and that the film in the aforesaid camera should be developed at QuikPix in Utica in order to ascertain the possible presence of photographic evidence which might be conducive to the solving of this baffling case.

The men returned at once by boat to the Muskrat Rifle and Rod Club, and thence to the Woodgate Constabulary Headquarters. Accompanied by three armed men in his Constabulary Jeep Eagle, Sheriff Entwistle drove, with siren at full volume and red lights flashing, directly to Quik-Pix.

At his press conference, the sheriff distributed copies of a photograph which he feels "cracks the case".

When asked by a reporter from the *Seattle Times* what further steps would now be taken, the sheriff nervously fingered his badge and announced, "I consider this case to be closed."

YOU ARE MY SUNSHINE

The windshield wipers whish-whacked back and forth against a downpour so fierce I wondered if I shouldn't pull to the side of the road until the worst blew over. But a teenager appeared in my headlights: standing ten yards in front of the Thruway ticket booth, his white arms hugging his wet T-shirt, he held out his thumb as I approached. So I determined *not* to stop. No sir, I'd read too many articles about Good Samaritans who'd picked up a hitchhiker, and then had been found dead in a ditch a day later. For a moment, as the wiper swept the window clear, we looked at each other. He was a skinny kid no older than sixteen, his face half-hidden by long black hair plastered over one eye. His other eye squinted into the rain. He didn't appear dangerous, but pathetic: one of life's lost waifs without the means to purchase a car, a bus ticket or even a raincoat. I'd worked long and hard during my seventy-one years for what I'd earned, and had little patience with the ne'er-do-wells, druggies and dropouts who seemed to feel that America's bounty was theirs for the taking.

And yet, as I passed him, relegating him to the storm and darkness that would teach him a lesson, I recalled a night over fifty years ago: hadn't I once been caught out in the rain, equally forlorn, during my courting days when I thumbed every weekend on old Route 5 to see Irene? Maybe this guy had a sweetheart in Albany, and like any dumb kid in love, he hardly knew it was raining. What the hell, I was going only as far as Utica, then I'd head north into the Adirondacks. I could leave him fifty miles closer to the love of his life, and if he tried any funny business, he'd learn right quick what an ex-Marine could still do.

So I pulled to the side of the ramp and tooted the horn. Then I flicked on the dome light, for I wanted to get a good look at this character before we went any further. If he was drunk, his ass was back out in the rain.

The first thing he did was, he didn't get in. He leaned down and opened the door a few inches so not to let the rain blow inside, then said through the crack, "Thanks. But I'm gonna get yer seat wet. You gotta towel?"

"It's vinyl," I said. "Get in."

"Thanks." He jumped in, shut the door and ran his hands over his face to wipe away the water and push back his hair. I noticed the grease-stained fingers of a mechanic, and his pasty-white face, though today was the twenty-third of August. This kid hadn't seen ten minutes of sunshine all summer. When he smiled at me, I was struck by both his eyes and his teeth: his gaze was far more personable than I had expected, but his teeth were lousy. "What time ya got?" he asked.

I pointed to the clock on the dashboard. "Eight oh five."

"Dynamite. I gotta be in Albany by two. How far ya going?"

I was right about Albany, and might be right about the girlfriend too. "Utica."

"Dynamite." He snapped on the seatbelt. Then he held out his hand. "Name's Zeke."

"Chuck," I said as I took his cold wet hand. He had an earnest look, not so much glad for the ride, as glad to meet me. Yes, I could see a girl taking a shine to this fellow, a girl who knew little more than inner-city Albany.

I flicked off the dome light, stopped at the booth and as I reached out the window for the ticket, I heard Zeke call to the attendant, "Thanks fer the coffee!" The big-bellied man on a stool gave him a sleepy nod.

I felt a little more at ease. A Thruway attendant always had the option of calling the Troopers, but Zeke had apparently been offered a cup of coffee. "You from Syracuse?" I asked as I followed the curving ramp to the highway. I studied the rain-veiled string of headlights for a spot to merge; Friday night, and everybody was heading somewhere for the weekend.

"Naw, Buffalo. Ain't ever been in Syracuse. Been past it 'bout a thousand times. Ain't never been in Utica either. Nice place?"

I merged behind a piggyback semi, saw my mistake when even my wipers at high speed failed to clear his spray off the windshield. But a glance in the rearview mirror showed headlights close behind me, so I couldn't drop back. I gripped the wheel, kept a steady distance from the blurred red lights of the truck, said nothing. Could have tried to pass—other cars were passing me and the truck—but I hadn't come seventy-one years by taking risks on a rainy night. Irene had huckleberry pie waiting, whether I got there at ten-thirty or quarter to eleven. So I waited for the car behind me to finally pull out and pass, then I dropped back far enough that the next guy to pass pulled in between me and the truck. I had good tires—never rolled on a set of bad tires in my life—and held a steady fifty-five. Lightning flashed overhead and for a moment the median strip was green, the car ahead of us red, the Chevy's hood bright blue. Thunder boomed on the roof, and I regretted I wasn't sitting with Irene out on the screened-in porch, watching what she called a "crack-and-dazzle" storm over the lake: angled sheets of rain silvered by the flash, the spruce on the opposite shore green for an instant, windswept water slapping the dock. The canoe would need bailing tomorrow.

I thought I might drive out of the worst of the storm, but it was moving east, same as I. My hitchhiker sat quietly, staring straight ahead, still hugging himself with his thin white arms and I could hear his teeth chattering. I had a dungaree worksuit in the trunk; I put it on whenever I had to change a flat. But it was too damn dangerous to stop in this rain. If a semi pulled off too, he'd never see me until I was meat on the road. Besides, by the time I got the trunk open, *I'd* be drenched. And was I going to ask for my dry worksuit back before I dumped this Zeke out in the rain again? So I let his teeth chatter; if they shattered to pieces, maybe a dentist would give him a new set and the kid'd have a real smile, not those black and yellow stumps with gaps between them.

My two grandsons had orthodontic braces on their teeth, and Charlie said Suzy would too, soon as she was old enough. And of course those kids had sun on their faces. Boys got a regular haircut. Full rain gear and rubber boots the day I hiked them into the woods to look for funguses. This Zeke, well, I'd known a lot of boys like Zeke when I'd been a sergeant, looking out for my men. What they needed was discipline, and a purpose in life, and—

That's when he started singing, and the darndest song too in the middle of a rainstorm. I wouldn't have believed a kid like him could have such a voice, a warm steady voice, even though he was singing quietly, like a good singer in a church choir. "You are my sunshine, my only sunshine, you make me happy when skies are gray." I glanced at him, still hugging himself, his whole body shivering and I realized what a thoughtless ass I'd been; I turned on the heat full blast. The ol' sarge would've turned that heat on the moment the kid got into the car. "I hope you know, dear, how much I love you. Please don't take my sunshine away." Zeke sang a second verse, still looking straight out the windshield, not singing for me, that was for sure, and I was all the more certain he had a girl either getting off a factory shift at two in the morning, or finishing up as a waitress in some all-night truck stop, and he wanted to be there, maybe he'd even sing to her as she drove him home to some seedy apartment. Funny that a kid with such bad teeth could sing.

"You are my sunshine, my only sunshine, it's you I'll love, dear, forever more. No matter what, dear, don't you forget, dear, it's only you who I adore."

"Gotta girl in Albany?" I asked.

"Naw, a brother. Ezer stole my bike. Gonna skin 'im alive."

"Oh." He kept right on singing, "The Tennessee Waltz". Sang for about twenty minutes, and not a song in the dozen was any of this modern rock and roll you'd expect from a kid. They were all old timers, the kind of songs Irene would sing sometimes in the kitchen. And another thing, Zeke had his own words to a lot of them. Mostly the first verses were the same, but then he'd go on and make up his own, and never missed a beat.

It must have been about ninety degrees in the car, but his teeth weren't chattering anymore. The sarge in me started thinking, You gonna dump this kid out in the rain? That how you take care of your men? But he ain't one of my men. He's just some stray mixed up in who-knows-what. Ay-yuh, and half the strays you used to kick into shape, no, better than half, a good three-quarters: they straightened out. Flew right. You never were no war sergeant, you were a people sergeant. Irene told you that, second week she knew you.

So, I'm going to take this character with me up to Camp? Drive him down to Utica in the morning and put him back on the highway? With dry clothes and a raincoat. Some pancakes in him. Ay-yuh, but what would Irene say, you show up tonight with a teenage grease monkey, hippy hair? Camp wasn't the house in Syracuse. Camp was for family, and old friends.

UTICA, 10 MILES.

"Where'd you learn all them old songs?" I asked.

He looked at me, half his face lit by the faint green dashboard lights, and he wasn't just interested, but almost delighted, that I'd asked. "My Pop used to sing 'em to my mother. I was only about ten, eleven, eleven and a half at the end, but I can remember the words like he was singing yesterday. She . . . " Never saw a face change so fast, from delight to devastation. This kid wore his heart on his sleeve. He looked straight out the windshield. "She loved his singing."

It wasn't my business to ask what happened. Zeke stared ahead, silent, no longer hugging himself. His face was dry. T-shirt still wringing wet.

"Say, I'm turning off at Utica, like I said. Heading up into the Adirondacks. You gotta get to Albany tonight? Maybe you'd like to come up to the cabin, put on some dry clothes, have a piece of Irene's huckleberry pie. She picked the berries herself. I could bring you down to the Thruway in the morning. Whadya say?"

He stared out the windshield. He was either right there with you, his face as open as a book, or the next moment he was a thousand miles away . . . or six, eight years ago when something happened to his mother. Well, I'd given him the choice. If he wanted to stand back out in the rain, that was his business.

"Ezer ain't going nowhere," he said. "I gotta be back to Buffalo Monday morning. No problem, if he ain't sold the bike." Zeke looked at me, apprehensive. "I ain't never been in the Adirondacks. They got bears up there?"

I laughed, and thought for a moment I'd tell him about the tracks I'd seen near Camp last winter. "Well, you might see some chipmunks. Irene feeds them peanuts."

"I'm not putting ya out?"

"I wouldn't have asked if you were."

When I paid the toll in Utica, and drove around the loop onto 12, Zeke still in the car, I wondered if I should phone Irene, tell her I was bringing company. She'd been down in the dumps lately. Maybe she didn't want a late-night surprise, not that she'd ever make a guest feel uncomfortable. I could have stopped at a gas station to phone. Probably would have if it hadn't been raining like someone was pouring Lake Ontario on the roof of the car.

"Say, you can turn down that heat," said Zeke. "You look like yer sweating."

Irene held open the screen door so the stranger and I could run from the car into Camp. "This is Zeke," I said as we stood in the glow of a kerosene lamp; as usual during a thunderstorm, the power was out. "He was hitchhiking and half-drowned out there. Zeke, this is my wife, Irene."

Though he even bowed a little as he smiled and shook her hand, I was embarrassed by his teeth. I hadn't brought home a lost wet puppy, I'd brought a misfit. I wanted to tell Irene I'd be taking Zeke back down to the highway first thing in the morning. But of course I said no such thing with the boy right there. Instead I asked her, "Got a spare piece of huckleberry pie?"

"Well, I should say. But first we've got to get him into some dry clothes! Take him up to the loft and see what's in the old dresser."

With a flashlight, I led Zeke up the steps to the loft where Charlie and Suzanne had spent their summer nights while they were growing up. I lit the lamp on the dresser, then opened the bottom drawer, filled with old sweaters and sweatshirts and wool socks, mostly stuff Charlie had outgrown, though still, thanks to a yearly dose of mothballs, in pretty good condition. "Hey, Zeke, there's even a pair of jeans here, if you don't mind patches on the knees. What's your waist?"

"Here's a towel," called Irene from the top of the stairs. "We'd offer you a hot shower, Zeke, but without power, the pump's off."

He seemed a bit dazed by all our attention, so I told him to put on anything that fit, and to bring down his wet clothes and we'd hang them on a line on the porch. Then I headed down the stairs, ready for a scolding. But the old girl was humming in the kitchen.

When he came down the steps and walked shyly into the kitchen, yes, he was still Zeke with the pasty-white face and oily hair and bad teeth, but for a moment there was a pull at my heart, because suddenly a teenager in Charlie's red plaid Camp shirt and patched jeans and moccasins walked into the room. For a moment, I could feel who we were back then, those happy summers, when Charlie and Suzanne and their mother swam across the lake and back every afternoon. Charlie often wore that red shirt when we'd go out in the canoe after dinner to cast a plug for bass.

Irene set out three pieces of hot fresh huckleberry pie. And I remembered even further back, to the old days on the base when I'd bring one of my men home for Thanksgiving dinner and she would go all out to make a homesick Marine feel he was almost one of the family. When Zeke finished the first piece, she offered him a second, and when that disappeared too, she gave him a third. Milk for Zeke, peppermint tea for me. She drank her Sanka and told us about sitting on the porch to watch the storm. "Lightning hit a tree across the lake. The whole Camp shook! I thought the thunder was going to bowl the roof right off." Zeke said not a word, though his gaze rarely left her face.

She made him up a bed in the loft, and through the pine board ceiling over the kitchen, I heard him say, "Good night, Irene." Sleep good, kid, I thought. But I wasn't ready for what happened next. As she came down the stairs with the flashlight—I had stood up from the table and was gathering the pie plates—we heard him singing, "Good night, good night, Irene. Good night, Irene. Thanks for your pie, oh my, oh my. Good night, Irene, good night."

She called up through the ceiling, "Good night, Ezekiel. Sleep tight."

Irene and I lay in bed out on the porch, my arm around her as we listened to the rain and the wind buffeting the trees, and to the deep rumbles of thunder skulking off further and further to the east. But for some reason I couldn't get out of my head a recent week in July, one of the worst we'd ever endured in our family. Charlie and Rachel and the three kids had arrived from Chicago in one of those big boxy fifty-foot recreational vehicles that Charlie said were "selling like hotcakes" in the Midwest. The first thing he wanted to do *wasn't* to jump in the lake, as he'd always done before. No, the vice-president and general sales manager for Holiday Wheels took his parents on a tour through his pride and glory: beds for five (Suzy's over the cab with pink curtains), a microwave, alarm clock coffee-maker, television, video console, electric popcorn maker, stereo tape deck and fifty-five cassettes in their own little closet. Mobile telephone. All-weather carpeting. "You want heating, you got heating. Air-conditioning? You got it!" Behind the van was a boat on a trailer. More horsepower in the engine than I had under the hood of the Chevy. "Going to teach the gang to water ski this summer," Charlie announced.

And so around and around and around the lake they went for a week. Charlie gunned the boat again and again as Sammy and then Steve and then Sammy and then Steve got up and fell, got up and stayed up a few seconds and fell again, and finally got up and stayed up for fifty yards, a hundred yards, and by the third day, all the way around the lake. Rachel, in the boat, took video movies of each son's progress. Irene and I watched from the dock. Charlie brought the television and video console from the RV into Camp so we could all watch the zoom-close-up expressions on the boys' faces and the big splashes they made. But after Rachel's film had been played and fast-frozen and replayed a dozen times, that wasn't the end of it. The television stayed on all evening with reruns Irene and I had left down in Syracuse for the summer. She and I made popcorn and tried to get a game of Scrabble going, but no go. "Miami Vice" in Camp, loud. Charlie was proud of himself, for he'd wired the antenna on the RV to the TV in Camp, and the reception was "great!"

It was Irene who put her foot down the second night, while drug enforcement agents in a helicopter were machine-gunning a car below them on the Los Angeles freeway. After some tension and dark looks, Charlie carried the television and video back out to the "Waldorf on Wheels," and there the five stayed until they came into Camp around ten to say a brief and slightly offended good-night.

The three inner tubes I had bought for Steve, Sammy and Suzy never got wet. Suzy had her own little skis, and once the boys got up, she had her turn too. "Ready?" called Charlie. "Gun it!" shouted the kids. "Ready? Gun it! Ready? Gun it!" The canoe thumped against the dock with the incessant wash from the boat. Irene made some beautiful dinners to entice her son and daughter-in-law back into the Camp, but the bunks upstairs stayed empty. One rainy day, the "Gang," as Charlie called themselves, drove to the Enchanted Forest, and Irene and I sat out on the porch and listened to the sweep of rain on the lake, and to the lovely silence.

A sad silence, for after the gang left for Montreal and Bar Harbor and Mystic and Boston and back to Chicago (they promised they'd phone us on the mobile telephone when they passed by on the Thruway), Irene and I felt we'd never really been with our family.

And Suzanne, well, she never showed up this summer at all. Got a job with a bank out in Santa Monica. "Not Los Angeles, Daddy," she tells me. "Santa Monica." All right, I call it Santa Monica. But two, three times a year now, she flies to Japan on banking business. Ay-yuh, Tokyo's not too far away, but Syracuse? Not this summer. And, well maybe it's a prejudice I find hard to shake, but let me tell you that after fighting and sweating and watching my buddies bleed on island after island up that South Pacific (when I personally wanted to pull the trigger on Tokyo Rose,) it kinda made my guts crawl when Suzanne sent us a postcard of the Imperial Palace. Sure, I'm glad she's doing so well, successful career-woman and all. She and Charlie trade business cards every time one of them gets a promotion. But it would have made their mother a whole lot happier just to have a little noise up in the loft this summer.

I could tell from Irene's breathing that she was still awake. "You should hear Zeke sing 'You Are My Sunshine'," I said.

She did not answer. I thought perhaps I was wrong, that she was asleep. Then she said with a whisper I could hardly hear above the rain, "I bet he can eat a dozen pancakes."

He slept until after ten, came down the steps in that red plaid shirt, looking a little embarrassed. The power was still out, though the rain had stopped, so I took him down to the dock to show him how to kneel and cup his hands and wash his face from the lake. But he didn't kneel when I did; he stood looking back and forth, up and down the gray lake, the clouds still heavy in the sky, and that look of wonder on his face was just the look I loved to see when we brought friends from Syracuse up to Camp for the first time. He asked with amazement, "Are we still in New York?"

During breakfast (Irene and I both counted fourteen pancakes, and a hefty side order of Canadian bacon,) Irene suggested that Zeke and I bail out the canoe.

"You gotta get to Albany right away?" I asked him.

"The Green Lantern closes at two. Ezer'll be on his stool till they throw him out. I gotta get my bike and ride back to Buffalo by Monday morning, eight o'clock sharp. I s'pose if you took me down to the Thruway this afternoon, it'd be all right."

"How can you ride a bicycle from Albany to Buffalo?" asked Irene.

"Oh," he smiled, and I thought even braces couldn't fix those teeth, "it ain't a bicycle. It's a sixty-eight Harley Hog, hums like a bee. I fix 'em up and sell 'em. Ezer rode this one right out of the shop soon's I was done with it.

"Easer?" I asked.

"Ebenezer. Gonna skin him live."

We bailed the canoe, put an orange life jacket on Zeke, then practiced in front of the dock until he got the hang of a paddle. The sun was burning through the clouds as we headed up the lake to where the channel narrowed and then opened into a lovely little pond wrapped by spruce and maple and a few giant white pines. Here, on opposite sides of the pond, the beaver had built a pair of houses. "The beaver come out at dusk," I told Zeke, my voice hushed. "Just before dark, that's when they go to work. We won't see them now."

"Can we go up close to a house?"

"Sure."

I paddled so that Zeke in the bow sat right beside a dome house. He reached out, touched several sticks with his white, grease-stained fingers.

"That branch there with the leaves still on it," I said, "they probably cut that one and added it to the roof last night."

He reached out further (the canoe wobbled and I had to lean against his off-center weight) and brushed his fingers over the alder leaves. Then he picked a leaf and put it into a pocket of the plaid shirt.

"They're in there right now?" he asked, wobbling the canoe as he looked over his shoulder at me.

"Sound asleep, about four feet from where you sit."

We crossed the pond to the second house, with fresh mud on the roof. Zeke asked, "Would they mind if I took one stick?"

"Go ahead. They'll just cut down another."

Well, he picked the right stick all right, just the one I would have chosen, about four feet long, tapered at both ends, teeth marks real clear in the wood. "Wait till the guys at the Texaco take a look at this!" he marveled. "They'll think I been all the way to Alaska."

We took our shoes off and climbed carefully out of the canoe onto a spongy bog. I showed Zeke the flies down inside a pitcher plant. He just about jumped a back summersault when a big ol' snapper slid into the water. I tried to teach him how to catch a frog, but he wasn't too slow, he was too gentle.

Irene met us at the dock and admired Zeke's beaver stick. After lunch on the dock in the sunshine, I fetched the three inner tubes and we showed Zeke, still in his orange life jacket, that a tire could do more than roll along the Thruway. The lake was chilly from the rain, but even after his teeth started to chatter, we couldn't get him out of the water.

That evening, after Zeke had eaten half a meatloaf and more potatoes than I thought could fit into even a teenage boy, he and I canoed (careful not to bump our paddles against the gunwales) back to the beaver pond. As we passed through the narrows, I whispered, "Now just sit still. Don't paddle. Look for a silver V going across the black water."

Well, there wasn't any V, nor any chewing along the pond's edge. I took us slowly across the pond and then looped back again, the brighter stars of the Dipper just appearing in the purple sky. Not a darn beaver anywhere. We circled a couple more times, heard a green frog's Garunk!, and I heard a distant owl, though I doubt Zeke heard it. But no beaver. I whispered, "I guess they're on vacation."

Nothing from Zeke. Not a nod, not a word.

I guided us out through the narrows and down the channel, the water so black and smooth that my paddle dipped like a spoon into the stars. After the fury of last night's storm, the lake was now hushed; not even a whisper of wind in the pines. Then suddenly, KaPoosh! A beaver's tail slapped so close to the bow that Zeke stood straight up, paddle in his hands. I thought we'd topple over, or that he'd fall overboard while I steadied the canoe, but he stood up so straight that the canoe hardly more than shivered. Not a sound from him. Then he sat right down again and turned to me, his pale astonished face lit by the stars. "I thought they weren't any bigger than a squirrel"

He helped to paddle now, couldn't wait to get back to the cabin to tell Irene. "Look!" he exclaimed in the kitchen, pointing at his wet jeans as if to convince her that such an extraordinary event could really happen. "The splash came right into the boat!"

Sitting later out on the porch, each of us with a bowl of popcorn in our lap, I asked him if he wouldn't sing "You Are My Sunshine" for Irene. And for the next hour, as that boy filled the Adirondack night with song after song, I saw a happiness on Irene's face in the candlelight, a delight in old remembered verses, a fascination in Zeke's ability to recollect such treasures, an admiration for the warmth, even more, the love, in his voice, that reminded me why I had built the Camp in the first place. I wanted to ask, I ached to ask, what had happened to his mother. And whether his father still sang these old songs. But I remembered that look of helpless grief on Zeke's face in the car, so of course I never said a word, but sang along as best I could, while I fell in love all over again with the girl for whom, after I had come back in '45 from the Pacific, I built this Camp as a wedding present. And if Zeke, his shoulders too thin for that red plaid shirt, could make the Camp tonight what a Camp was supposed to be, then, I decided right then and there, he was damn well welcome to come back anytime and sing with Irene.

As we drove down Route 12 on Sunday morning, he was wearing the shirt, and about half of what had been in that bottom drawer (sweater, jacket, rain gear, wool socks) was in a duffel bag on the back seat. His beaver stick was in the bag too, because I told him, "Nobody's going to pick you up if you stand beside the road with a pointed club." Irene had packed him a lunch that would feed a platoon. And she'd made him a nicely written cardboard sign that said, ALBANY, PLEASE.

He stared straight ahead as we drove down out of the mountains, out of the forest, through farmland, toward now the buildings of downtown Utica clustered in the hazy Mohawk Valley. "My mother woulda liked it up there," he said. He didn't look at me, just stared through the windshield. Didn't say another word until I was driving the loop toward the ticket booth. "Hey Chuck, take Irene out tonight in the canoe to see a beaver."

"All right, I will."

"Yeah, when I'm riding back to Buffalo on the Harley, if Ezer ain't sold it already, I can think about you out there in the canoe."

And that's just what we did that night, and there were silver V's crossing the black water two and three at a time, while down on the highway, roaring west among the trucks and the Troopers and the recreational vehicles, was a pale-faced kid with an alder leaf and our phone number in the pocket of his shirt.

STEPPING OUT

DISCOVERY

Bert the burnt-out biology teacher, (that's me), sat in a teachers' meeting on a Friday afternoon, aware that he was feeling "ornery," as my wife called it when I got this way, and so he was cautious about what he said. We were discussing problem students, currently Susan Bloomingdale, "performing poorly in English," according to Hazel, "nearly flunking algebra," said Fred who hates to flunk anyone, "poor attitude in physical education," says Harriet, who measures performance only by attitude, never by physical ability. I know Susan well; a year ago, just before Christmas, I left the microscopes in the cabinet, and instead attempted to read from the Book of Scrooge in order to bolster the holiday spirit. Susan had heard no more than a paragraph before she interrupted my reading, "C'n I go?" "Go?" I asked, annoyed that the atmosphere I'd hoped to create of Dickens' England had been so quickly shattered. "But we just got started." "I already seen it on television," she said. "You did? But this is different. Now we're reading from the original--" "I seen the Mister Magoo cartoon." She stood from her desk. "C'n I go?" Given the choice between trying to put the images of a classic tale into her adolescent mind, or allowing her to leave so the others could concentrate without interruption, I hesitated . . . tired as we neared the end of the semester, frustrated at the ever-growing disparity between my original dreams as a teacher and the reality in the classroom, and, deep, deep down inside, volcanically angry at the televised rot I was forced to contend with. I heard myself say, "Yes, please go." I didn't bother to add, 'to the library.' I simply cast her out from the garden of Dickens' Eden, to smoke a cigarette in the girls' bathroom for all I cared.

A year later, Susan was failing nearly every course in the senior year curriculum, and she was now in serious danger of not graduating.

"Bert, what do you recommend?" I heard Frank ask. "You've worked with Susan, met with her parents, tutored her after school."

I looked up from the doodling on my notepad. "Strangulation."

I sat for another two hours while we went through the list of teenage cadavers; three hours of discussion on the nutritional pros and cons of macaroni and cheese, artificial grape juice, and fruit cocktail Jello; and four hours of professional debate on how often to empty the pencil sharpeners. Suddenly, through the funereal gloom, I remembered, vividly, a moment from sometime this week when I was driving home: I had glanced from the car at kids ice skating on the lake. The early winter had been unusually cold, though the snow had as yet held off, so the lake was frozen to what appeared to be a perfect sheet of ice. I hadn't been on skates since I was a young man courting Helen. As a kid I'd been a whiz on the blades. Aching ankles, a frozen nose, the whole gang playing crack the whip. A bonfire on the shore, my mother with a thermos of hot chocolate.

I wondered how many more days we would have before the snow came and covered that perfect lake. Then I heard Frank ask, "Well, any other business before we finish?"

"Yes," I said, looking around the table at my colleagues. "Does anybody have a pair of men's ice skates I could borrow? Size ten and a half."

My daughters, Rebecca and Ann, sixteen and fourteen, both have figure skates from Christmas a year ago, when skating had been all the high school rage. This year, their skates gather dust, their feet grow, and the rage is the video shop in town. My wife, Helen, has skates, somewhere in a box at her mother's house. But Helen tells me at dinner that she has grocery shopping on Saturday morning, church auxiliary Christmas charity guild planning committee in the afternoon, and we have a dinner party at the Lewises Saturday evening at seven. She reminds me that I have promised for weeks to clean the garage: the newspapers for recycling are stacked almost to the ceiling, the lawnmower has been leaking oil since August.

Friday evening, I load newspapers into the trunk, into the back seat, into the passenger seat. I spread newspapers under the lawnmower.

Friday evening, Helen balances our check book, orders Christmas presents from Bean's, writes her monthly letter to our congressman. Our daughters and several friends, who are sleeping over with Helen's consent (though I was never asked) spend the first hours of their slumber party watching ax murders, car explosions, drug busts, machine gun massacres and borderline pornography while they sit in the darkened living room in their pajamas, each with a bowl of popcorn in her lap.

On Friday night, out in the tidy garage, I sharpen Frank's skates, size eleven.

Despite Helen's concern during breakfast at my plan to go skating alone on a remote lake, I was determined to do just that. I did not want to see other people, except (were any willing to come) members of my family. I did not want to see camps along the shore. I certainly did not want to see traffic on a highway. I wanted to see ice, and trees, and sky, and if no one was smart enough to come along with me, then phooey with them.

"You're just being ornery," she scolded me.

Ornery I was, and ornery I stayed until I had dropped off the piles of newspapers, filled the car with gas and finally rolled, skates on the seat beside me, out of town. Suddenly, another feeling came back from boyhood: that delicious exhilaration of playing hooky from school. Though the sky was gray, portenteous of snow, I knew I'd get in at least one afternoon on the blades. As I cruised along beloved and beautiful Route 28, I scanned the lakes beside the highway: each a perfect sheet of ice with its own unique shape, and islands and narrows and beckoning bays; I should have been out every day last week, exploring. Which day had it been so gorgeous? Wednesday, that day of sunshine and blue sky without a cloud. What a day *that* would have been on the gleaming ice! Instead I'd been proctoring an exam, and when I opened a window the students complained of the cold.

Forget it! Forget all that! Today, by golly, I was stepping out. Breaking out. Bustin' free.

At Crow Lake I turned left, then forked left again past Little Turtle, and now I saw not another car. The dirt lane cut through forest; the trees were dark green and gray and black, drab with winter's dreariest colors, ungarnished by snow. But neither did snow block the road.

Plenty of parking in the rectangular clearing where on many a summer's day I had scowled at the crowd of cars. With a skate in each hand, rucksack on my back, I followed the path along which I usually carried a canoe. As I descended to the strip of beach, I saw keel marks in the frozen sand, left by the last paddlers of the season. But when I looked out at Lake Camilla, allowed my eyes to roam and wander across that unencumbered expanse of black ice, I discerned not a trace of human existence. Alone and aloof stood an island, a tuft of feathery green, where Helen and I had conceived our first child.

I stepped warily in my boots onto the ice: though cracked and buckled along the beach, it was clear, and I could see by the captured bubbles that it was nearly a foot thick. Brimming with anticipation, I sat on a log and laced up the skates, snugly, but not to tightly—didn't want my feet to ache—then I stood (the blades sank into the sand,) crossed the beach and stepped hesitantly, with the awkward determination of an infant learning to walk, onto the ice. And now I gave a little push.

The blades made that lovely dry gliding sound which I knew from years ago. Another push, and I was on my way; I leaned forward, began to swing my arms with the old remembered rhythm. Gaining confidence, I headed toward the island.

Oh, how my mind cleared out on that open lake! I circled the island, or rather, I ovaled it, with a sprint past the off-shore rocks on which we had often baked in the August sun . . . and a smooth-cruising turn, the sharpened skates cutting perfectly . . . straightened into a sprint along the boulder-strewn shore, tufts of white pines towering above me . . . another turn as tight as I could cut it . . . and now the homestretch (pushshsh hard, pushshsh hard, pushshsh hard), arms swinging, breath even and deep, eyes locked on the rocks near the island's end: the finish line.

As I sailed past those rocks, I remembered lying with Helen on a blanket beside a campfire that summer night seventeen years ago. The flames lit her sweat-glistening body and her eyes filled with happiness as she shared with me our mutual dream of engendering a child here in the heart of wilderness, where the water we drank came from cupped hands dipped into the nectar of springs and streams, and the air we breathed had brushed the mountaintops and sifted through the fragrant forest, and where the wandering moon and tail-slapping beavers and a yodeling loon were invited to mix their magic into the making of the soul of a human child.

Yes, I envisioned Helen's joyous and passionate and peaceful face; but then as I stood, breathing hard, and glided in a straight line with diminishing speed past the end of the island toward the middle of the lake, opening my jacket to the cold air, I recalled Rebecca's expressionless face the night before as she sat on the couch staring at the TV screen, a waxen image of my beautiful child.

I skated the entire periphery of the lake, in and out of bays, around other islands, keeping a careful distance from the Otter River outlet. Stopped twice to put bandaids on incipient blisters. Sat on a branch of an ancient pine that had toppled, and ate my lunch while I looked down at the bone-white crown of the tree in and beneath the ice; the sun was breaking through and I could see the trunk quite far down into the chilly gloom.

A breeze picked up, from the north, and I could tell that crystalline winds, Canada's finest export, were going to push away the cloud cover and bring a starlit night to Lake Camilla, a night that should not be missed. But I had to be at the Lewis's dinner party. If I wasn't home by seven, Helen would send out the Forest Rangers. Ornery didn't begin to describe how I felt as I skated, beneath a clearing turquoise sky, past our island and toward the beach.

THE RHYTHM

Like a man who has been at sea all day and still feels the rocking of the boat though he stands on steady shore, I felt, in the shower, at the table eating Hazel's ratatouille, in bed that night beside Helen (who fell immediately asleep) and even in church the next day while I stood singing a hymn: the swinging of the arms, the steady purposeful push of the legs, the twin rocking and racing of the body. The rhythm of the blades would not leave me.

Had a stack of exams to correct on Sunday; decided to feed them to the lawnmower. Tried to get Helen and the girls to come with me to Lake Camilla; their excuses I don't remember, my disappointment I do. The sun was beaming outside, the thermometer had dropped to a crisp fifteen, and the calendar showed a full moon tomorrow night. But we could have a foot of snow by then, so as I packed a brown bag dinner, I told Helen I probably wouldn't be home before midnight.

"Midnight!" she exclaimed, turning in her pink apron from the sink, her gloved hands dripping with soapsuds. "Bertram, you have to work tomorrow. And we have a PTA meeting tomorrow night. I *won't* have you falling asleep in your chair."

"If it hasn't snowed by tomorrow night's full moon," I declared defiantly, "I am neither a P nor a T."

Mrs. Duck was still clucking as I disappeared out the door.

Deep, deep, deep into the forest I drove, delighted that not another car was parked in the clearing. I whistled to the chickadees while I walked along the path. Gazed out at the lake, its ice scribed with yesterday's journey. Laced on my skates and set forth in the sunshine as if across the blue heavens I sailed, winged Mercury on holiday without a single message to deliver.

Ninety-three million miles above me, a ball of fire; beneath my feet, Earth's molten core; and precisely positioned between the twain, a sheet of crystallized water on which a man, mostly water himself, may travel miles and miles to no economic or political purpose whatsoever, his goal to sweat away the fat, to purge the bilge water from his brain, and above all, to stretch out his soul to the dimensions of an intricate, elegant, exquisite lake, so that sun and Earth and lake and he are reunited as old friends.

Late that afternoon, I skated toward the russet west; then turned and glided toward the turquoise east; cruised back again toward the purple west; and turned once more and skated toward a rising pearl in a charcoal sky, while the palette of ice, perhaps incrementally curved as the surface of earth is curved, rolled from daytime through dusk into night.

On moonlit ice I made my decision. For years in the classroom I had taught the physical laws of nature, chalking letters and numbers across the blackboard. Tomorrow, when husband spoke, when father spoke, his word too would be law, not to be disobeyed.

SIGNATURES

Between classes on Monday I phoned Helen at the clinic, did not leave a message but phoned three times until I caught her between patients, to tell her when she had no time to argue, "When you get off work, pick up your skates at your mother's or I won't let you into the house. Dinner tonight is a bucket of Kentucky Fried Chicken. PTA phooey. Check your laces. If you need new ones, stop at the hardware store before they close. We roll at six. Six o'clock. Eighteen hundred hours. I love you." Then I hung up.

I found Rebecca, then Ann in the lunchroom. When I told them about our family outing that evening, Rebecca wrinkled her nose, Ann rolled her eyes. Both claimed to have enormous amounts of homework. I did not press the matter in public, merely informed them we would be departing at six o'clock.

At a quarter to six, Helen, much to my astonishment, was ready. Slouched on the couch in the living room, however, no doubt relaxing their minds before that evening's heavy onslaught of academic toil, daughters One and Two sat staring at the fifth member of our family, never mind what the program was, it doesn't matter; what mattered was that Mom and Dad were about to leave the house all evening so the dear girls could use the telephone in secret, a secret suddenly revealed when the egregious bill arrived. They both stared at that clamoring box, pretending they didn't notice me while I, already in my jacket, skates in hand, stared at them.

I could have pushed the off-button. I could have pulled the plug. But the Patriarch set down his skates, went outside to the woodshed, and returned with an ax in one hand, my other arm wrapped around the chopping block.

Helen whispered as I passed her, "Bertram, what on earth?"

I set the chopping block on the floor beside the television, reached for the cord and draped it like a long limp neck over the block. I raised the ax over my head (it scraped our plaster ceiling,) then with a war cry that easily exceeded the televised shrieks which nightly filled our home, I brought the blade down and clove in twain that little black snake. The screen went blank: the link was severed between the robber barons of Hollywood and the inhabitants of my household. I turned to my daughters; they stared at me, stunned, but they realized (for Conan the Conqueror still held his battle axe,) that Dad was serious. They stood, silently left the room to find their skates.

The chicken never tasted better. We even sang in the car as we drove along the highway. But when we turned onto the dirt lane and bumped into the mysterious moonlit forest, everyone fell silent.

Helen held my hand as we followed the path; the girls walked ahead of us, their breath radiant plumes in the moonlight.

On the beach, I scanned the silver-black expanse and listened to trees crack with the cold. Then I pointed at the black feathery tuft in the middle of the lake. "That's Rebecca Island."

My elder daughter looked up at me, her lovely young face filled with curiosity. "It is?"

"Yup," I said. "While we skate around it, I'll tell you why."

As we drew the laces of our skates tight, so that night we tightened too the laces of our family. We skated at first in a wary cluster, the girls gasping each time the ice groaned with the night's cold, but they trusted their Dad, and soon, as I swung my arms and picked up speed, they too found their rhythms. Helen had not lost her girlhood grace, could even skate backwards ahead of us, her feet carving hourglass curves. The girls branched off on their own, not far, but enough to make my heart ache a little, for soon, a few winters more, they would be moving much further away, and from each other as well. But both returned as we neared the island, and listened in rapt silence, the dry gliding strides of our skates woven into a rhythmic whisper, as their mother told them—without mention of the campfire and the sweat and cries in the night, but including in lovingly remembered detail the glow of that summer moon, the hoot of an owl far across the lake, and the joy of skinny-dipping out to the rocks—about Rebecca's conception. Helen pointed out exactly the rock where she and I had sat seventeen years ago, now a long dark shape wreathed with thick tilted shards of moon-translucent ice. At my suggestion, there we sat again: we walked carefully on the uneven ice, reached down with our hands and set our bottoms on the frigid stone, the four of us in a row. Helen pointed toward Polaris. "That night, I saw a shooting star right there." She turned to Rebecca. "And I wished for you."

"What about me?" asked Ann.

I laughed as I answered, "When the frogs are peeping this spring, we'll go sit on your grandmother's dock."

"On Grandma's dock?"

"Yup. I built that dock fifteen years ago, and it wasn't a night old before those frogs gave your mother ideas."

"Bertram!"

"A dock," said Ann with disappointment. "Rebecca has an island, and I have a dock."

"Not just a dock, Sweetheart. A very well-built dock, and thousands of frogs, singing and singing because they were so in love. Oh, your mother was hopping all over the place."

"*Bertram!*"

We skated across the broad belly of the lake. Rebecca wanted to learn from her mother how to skate backwards, and they drifted off on their own. Ann and I explored a bay together, discovered a beaver house capped with a doily of frost: the frozen breath of the beavers sleeping inside.

The light dimmed; looking up, I discovered a blanket of gray wool creeping across the moon. Within fifteen minutes, flakes of snow were drifting down, as if the tiny bright stars had turned to feathers and were falling into our world. Soon, enough snow had dusted the ice that we could see the trails of our skates, and Helen sketched for us a nearly perfect figure-eight.

We crossed to the far end of the lake. More and more hidden from each other by the snow and increasing darkness, we stayed close enough together that we could hear each other's skates. At the far shore, we stood together and stared back into the black abyss we had crossed. We held our breaths and heard December's deepest silence.

Taking a compass from my rucksack, I guided my family toward Rebecca Island and the beach beyond it. I knew that tonight would be our last chance for skating this winter, for the tracks we left behind us would soon be buried beneath a foot, or two or three, of powder. In the spring, all evidence of our passage would melt away completely.

I felt Helen's hands on my hips, and remembered our courting days when we had skated in tandem, our rhythms synchronized. Rebecca held her mother's hips, then Ann held Rebecca's, and like a skating eight-footed caterpillar, left feet, right feet, left feet, right feet, we made our way across the lake. I imagined our trail behind us, a lanyard of tracks. Cold black water, thick translucent ice, and light flakes of snow had formed their layers upon this lake since the last receding glacier, eleven thousand years ago, had left a bowl in the sand. But tonight the ice was traced, like a lithographer's plate, by four interwoven signatures.

FREDERICK ON THE FOURTH OF JULY

I

It must have been the spinach during the tadpole stage, though of course Frederick disagrees. "What, you think only the reptiles were big in the good old days? Why do you insist on short-changing the amphibians?"

I found him, without knowing that I had found anything special, when I was netting tadpoles along the edge of a bog one summer. I caught a bunch of green frog tadpoles, and a few leopards, and one rather large bullfrog tadpole. I was teaching summer school that year, so I put my collection of pollywogs into an aquarium in my classroom with the hope that the students, all of whom had done D and F work in biology during the regular semester, might take a keener interest in the wonders of nature as the tadpoles developed into frogs. Every day during class we fed boiled spinach to the tadpoles, for I had read that spinach was an adequate substitute for the mats of algae on the bottom of a lake. The tadpoles gobbled up the spinach with great delight.

I explained to my students that unlike other tadpoles, a bullfrog tadpole does not become a frog during its first summer. It remains a tadpole through the winter and metamorphoses into the adult stage during its second summer, and sometimes even its third. Thus our lone bullfrog tadpole would be with us throughout the coming academic year. A few of the slouch-shouldered adolescents nodded with faint interest; most stared dead-pan into the busy aquarium with that same coma-like stare with which they watched their weekly twenty hours of televised carnage.

Right on schedule, the greens and leopards grew their hind legs, and then forelegs, and began to absorb their tails. I floated some flat sticks on the surface and covered the top of the aquarium with screen.

I noticed, however, an unusual development in the bullfrog tadpole: though it was already an extraordinary seven inches long when I netted it, it grew another inch during its first week in the aquarium, and three-quarters of an inch during the second. Holding a ruler against the aquarium glass and eyeballing the creature inside, I measured in both inches and centimeters, then logged the data in my notebook. When I stopped feeding it frozen spinach and instead gave it fresh spinach from my wife's garden, the tadpole grew, during the third week, to an astonishing length of eleven inches.

By the end of the summer, when the students and I returned to the lake to release the greens and leopards as full-grown frogs, a tadpole just shy of two feet lay alone on the sand of the three-foot aquarium. We were now ordering organic spinach by the bushel from New Jersey. I wouldn't have said so to anybody, but that giant mud-brown larva with the bulbous head and tapered tail didn't just eat and defecate and thrash with frustration, its nose bumping against the glass while its tail churned up the sand into a murky soup; no, I wouldn't have told anyone, but I was quite sure, after the poor creature settled down exhausted and trapped, that the little round amphibian eye was glaring out of the aquarium at *me*. Of course I considered releasing the tadpole back into the lake where it would have acres to swim and feed. But the students had become mildly interested in this phenomenon, and the local paper had even come to take a picture of it, with me holding a meter stick in front of the tank, my thumb at twenty-three inches. I ascertained that the science department had a small sum remaining in its budget, so I talked with the hardware dealer in town, whose dullard son was one of my pupils, and he agreed to sell, at an end-of-the-summer discount, a backyard swimming pool fifteen feet in diameter and four feet deep, Caribbean blue, with pump and filtration system, but without the ten-pound sack of chlorine. My students and I set up the pool in the school's boiler room, where the heat from the boiler would keep Bob's pond (the students had come up with the eminently imaginative name of Bob) warm through the Adirondack winter. We put in a load of sand, and some nice round stones, and even planted waterlilies. My wife donated a pair of Gro-Lights, which we suspended above Bob's pond. With unwonted excitement, the students assisted me on the Friday before Labor Day when I removed the screen from the aquarium, reached in and gently took hold of soft slippery Bob (he did not thrash, but stared at me as if to say, Well, it's about time), laid him on a wet gunny sack and then ran with him along the corridors, the students running and laughing and shouting along with me, to the stairs down to the boiler room in the basement where we released Bob in his new home.

Bob told me later that it was the most disappointing day in his life.

"Listen," I argued, "would you rather have spent the winter down in the dark cold gloom under a sheet of ice?"

"I didn't *know* about ice. All I knew from my early weeks was basking in sunshine and nibbling on carpets of lovely tanic-flavored algae."

"I'd hardly call what you did 'nibbling.' And really, you didn't like the spinach?"

"Now don't get me wrong. I don't want to sound ungrateful. But nothing can compare with a blanket of succulent spirogyra laid over a fragrant bed of swamp muck."

Wait, I'm getting ahead of our story. When we put Bob into the blue pool, we had no idea that he was feeling down-at-the-mouth, especially since, without a glass wall, I had lost eye contact. I thought he was perfectly happy rooting about the bottom of his oceanic realm.

And of course he grew, which we took to be a sign that he was thriving. When the maples cloaked the mountainsides with a late-September blaze of orange and red, Bob down in the boiler room was three feet long. On Homecoming night, the students in their suits and party dresses descended the steps and turned on the lights, frightening the poor creature so that it thrashed madly around in its pond and, as Bob later told me., badly bruised its nose on a stone. Using a carpenter's tape, the kids measured him at four feet, one and a half inches. He was just short of five feet by Thanksgiving, his head (he hates the comparison) as large as a basketball.

Before Christmas vacation, a team of herpetologists from the University in Albany visited our school and, with an underwater camera and dual-mounted lights, made a forty-five minute documentary of Bob eating spinach. When we viewed the film in class, the students discovered, with great excitement, that Bob was forming the preliminary nubs of hind legs. And I discovered, when Bob's virulent eye appeared on the television screen, that he viewed this intrusion as the last straw; I was reminded of Moby Dick's hateful gaze when the great whale surfaced and glared at Ahab thumping along the deck of the *Pequod*.

Whether it was the warmth in the boiler room, or the genes in this unusual tadpole, or, as Bob now insists, his decision to get all that nonsense over with, the larva did not wait until the following summer to mature into adulthood. No sir. The students, who came faithfully to the boiler room all through their Christmas vacation to feed Bob, to sing carols to him, and take notes, chronicled the rapid development of Bob's hind legs until he had thighs that any tackle on the football team might have envied. By New Year's Day, the forelegs had sprouted, and Bob no longer bounced along the sandy bottom on his belly, but stood, or crouched, or hunkered, or whatever it is a quadrapod tadpole does, on four webbed feet, in a much more dignified manner. He was now absorbing his tail, a process which the students charted with shorter and shorter bars on a graph. Anteriorly, he was becoming less of a blubbery cylinder, and more bony, angular, and distinctly frog-like.

The day of days, the great turning point, occurred in February, shortly after Valentine's Day, when Bob not only rose for a gulp of air, but, raising his head above the surface, cocked his eye on me as if to say, Just you wait.

Any member of the class could now tell you that *Rana catesbiana*, a normal *Rana catesbiana*, has a body of about seven or eight inches long, and hind legs of about ten inches. The average adult bullfrog weighs roughly a pound, some tipping the scales at a pound and a quarter. Well sir, by Easter, our bullfrog sat with its (haughty, there was no doubt about it) nose a good three feet above the water, with an estimated body length of six feet, and an extrapolated hind leg length of seven and a half feet (8"/10" = 6'/x, 8x = 60', x = 60'/8 = 7.5 feet, as anyone in the class could explain to you). With regard to Bob's weight, we could only estimate that he weighed about the same as the Hereford stud bull from Plattsburgh that won a blue ribbon last year at the Syracuse State Fair. Bob was big.

"Of course we can't call him Bob anymore," said Denise, a student who, a year ago, had shown as much life, motivation, and perspicacity in class as some of the specimens pickled in formaldehyde. "Now that he's become a frog, we've got to call him Robert."

We had a time figuring out what to feed Robert. Flies, even if there had been any in April, were too small. I thought about releasing a flock of crows in the boiler room, but how to catch a flock of crows? And would Robert care for a dinner covered with feathers? I bought a pound of tripe at the butcher's, a pound of liver, a sheep kidney, and a beef tongue, then felt like a fool tossing these slimy items into the air in front of Robert as one tosses up and catches a squishy softball, hoping that suddenly, miraculously, that froggy tongue would snap out and grab the kidney mid-flight. But no dice. Robert's vast semicircular bullfrog mouth remained closed in a dour frown, while Robert glowered at my efforts. He began to grow noticeably thinner. The students became worried, for despite Robert's aloofness, they were inordinately fond of him.

His eyes began to glaze over, his temples to sink, until one day Simon O'Reilly—the only student in the history of the school to repeat my class three times, and he probably would have gone on for a world record fourth had not Bob/Robert inspired a few of Simon's hibernating brains cells to stir—descended the cellar steps with a pepperoni and anchovy pizza tucked under his arm. Thwwooooopp! Out came that tongue, twelve feet long (the students measured the distance, in both feet and meters, from Robert to the fourth step from the bottom of the stairs,) grabbed the pizza box from under Simon's arm, and before Simon had time to shout "Hey, that's my pizza!", it was gone. A few seconds later, Robert spat out the mutilated box.

Well I tell you, it didn't take those kids long before they were purchasing twenty-one pizzas a day for Robert, with pepperoni and anchovy, light on the mushrooms, hold the peppers. (They raised the money from bake sales, snow shoveling, and Kisses-for-a-Dollar.) Robert soon learned to be patient, that the students would take the pizzas out of the box for him and thus he could just snap his dinner from their hands. Then Rocko Fayerweather reasoned (yes, actually *reasoned*) that a frog liked his lunch on the wing, so Rocko cocked his arm and sailed a pizza across the boiler room like a Frisbee. Thwwooooopp! No long bomb touchdown pass caught in the end zone the last minute of the game could have thrilled those kids more. Each student developed quite an arm, spinning out those pepperoni pizzas with a hook to the right, a change-up slow drift to the left, a boomeranging sweep and on its way back when Thwwooopp!, Robert snatched it with an unerring tongue. Sometimes they tossed out two at a time, but no double-barreled skeet shooter ever downed his targets with a precision equal to Robert's. The look in his eye became less hostile, even, almost, forgiving. And I may have noticed, though he was a tough character, and he denies it to this day and insists on calling the boiler room "the dungeon," still I may have noticed, at the ends of his vast semicircular mouth, the faint uplifting twitch of a smile.

In May we learned his name was not Robert. The weather

had warmed and the Adirondacks were so fragrant with spring in the air that we pried open the cobwebby boiler room windows that had been shut since the school was built. There's a small swamp beyond the baseball diamond, and in that swamp, toward dusk, peepers began to sing, filling the evening with their lovely high-pitched choir. Robert cocked his big round tympanum toward the window. When a green frog called "Garunk!", Robert stirred in his pond and cocked his opposite tympanum toward the window. Now sure enough, a bullfrog in love began to call to his lady, "Jug o' rum! Jug o' rum!" The students, clustered in the boiler room, held their breaths as they watched Robert and waited like eager parents to hear his first word. He shuffled nervously, like a horse smelling something on the wind. He straightened his shoulders. His yellow throat began to swell. Denise glanced at the clock to record the exact moment. And then Robert announced, (he did not croak, but vehemently announced) "Fre-der-ick!" Enormously pleased with himself, his vast semicircular mouth grinning from tympanum to tympanum, he announced it again, "Fre-der-*ick*!"

So Bob had been Fred, or perhaps Freddy once we had gotten acquainted, and Robert was now Frederick. This happened on the twenty-seventh of May, at 7:32 p.m. If you don't believe me, ask Denise.

II

No vessel ever emerged from a boatworks to be launched on the open sea with more festivity than did Frederick when he emerged from the dungeon on the last day of school. Accompanied by a parade of jubilant students, up the cellar steps he crept, stiff from his cramped quarters; along the corridors he hopped, peering with interest into the classrooms and library along the way; until finally out the school's front door he emerged into the June sunshine, a free frog after a year of academic incarceration.

The plan was to transport him on a flatbed truck to Pickerelweed Lake, where his new home would be on a bog in front of my camp. But Frederick did not hop onto the truck. He jumped over it. While the students whooped and cheered with encouragement, he made several more experimental jumps around the school's front lawn. Then he spotted the football field, a stretch of open space uncluttered by trees. Frederick jumped down the field and back again, frisky as a colt just let out of the barn. The lines every five yards were still visible, though a bit blurry after the winter. The students told Frederick that if he wanted to know exactly how far he could jump, it was just a matter of starting HERE (behind the goal line) and then jumping toward the opposite goal. The students would count the jumps, divide and calculate the average. Frederick readily agreed and the students fanned out on the field with their clipboards and tape measures, prepared to collect the data.

Well, I've seen a forty-yard field goal on that field, and a fifty-two-yard pass once, and a run-back against the much vaunted Saranac team for ninety-nine yards; but I had never seen a sixteen-foot frog (stretched out, toes pointed, he was much longer than we had extrapolated) sail in a handsome green arc from end zone to end zone on his very first jump.

He and the throng of students rode through town on the flatbed truck, drawing gasps of astonishment from people who had heard about a giant bullfrog, had read about it in the newspaper, heard about it on the radio, but still couldn't believe that it was anything other than some joke the kids had cooked up at school. One of the town dogs started to bark and then it chased after the truck, yapping and yelping at the frog to declare that town was *its* territory. Thwwooopp! Out came the tongue. Now you see it, now you don't.

When we reached my camp, Frederick hopped off the truck, waded through ferns and hobblebushes to the shore, then gazed up and down the sun-sparkling lake. He cocked his eye at me, and I knew that at long last, we were friends. The students gathered on my dock to cheer him on. With a great leap, he arched over the water toward the middle of the lake and landed with a splash that looked as if Halley's comet had just hit. He swam and swam and swam, frog-kicking to his heart's content, while the students followed him around the lake in rowboats and canoes. Finally he clambered onto the bog, which shook and half-submerged and bubbled, but held his weight. Frederick appeared supremely satisfied as he made himself comfortable at the bog's edge, the sun warm on his face. His yellow throat swelled up and he announced, "Fre-der-*ick*!" From the far end of the lake answered an echo, "Fre-der-*ick*!" His vast semicircular mouth uplifted into a serene smile.

* * *

That summer was the first in a decade during which I was free from the dismal travails of teaching summer school, for Frederick taught it instead. Though only recently had he been able to vocalize, he nevertheless had absorbed a great deal of English, and thus he quickly advanced beyond the mere utterance of his name to words, phrases and complete sentences. The students were his instructors, teaching him the names of the birds, trees, flowers, and fellow amphibians in his Adirondack world, and the more they taught him, the more they learned. Through the last two weeks of June I lounged on my dock with a cold Utica Club while Frederick, and a flotilla of students in canoes and rowboats, explored the lake from one end to the other, field guides, cameras and binoculars in hand.

They were disturbed one Saturday afternoon by a water ski boat that roared around and around the lake, nearly capsizing the canoes with its wake. Frederick, sitting on his bog, complained that the noise from the engine was "inappropriate to riparian tranquility, incondusive to pastoral contemplation, and spiritually insufferable." (His ten-inch tympanums were extremely sensitive.) Both the driver and the water skier pretended to ignore, as they zoomed past, the students' shouted protests. On the fourth pass, the skier sent a wall of spray over one of the rowboats, dousing two infuriated students and their notebooks. Thus it was that on the fifth pass, as the skier in orange bathing trunks was about to drench Rocko in his guide-boat . . . Thwwoooopp! That skier suddenly found himself with a long muscular tongue wrapped around his neck, a tongue that was not about to let go, though the skier was still being pulled by a 200 horsepower Merc on a boat now dead in the water. No doubt he felt his arms were about to be wrenched from their sockets; yet at the same time he surely anticipated, perhaps with greater apprehension, that if he let go of the ski rope, the anaconda-like tongue would snap him toward the cave-like mouth of a close relative of Tyranosaurus Rex.

Alas, the rope snapped. An instant later, the skier found himself eyeball to spheroid, reddish-bronze, unforgiving eyeball with the giant bullfrog. Frederick suggested, his speech slightly impeded by this lingual encumbrance, "Eat-im-up! Eat-im-up! Eat-im-up!" The skier's eyes bulged nearly spheroid, his mouth gaped ovoid, but his constricted windpipe emitted not a sound. His remonstrations were reduced to madly thrashing arms and flailing legs.

Despite Rocko's thumbs-down, Frederick was merciful. As if he were spitting out a cherry pit, Ptoooooo!, he sent his chastened victim arching in orange shorts toward the motorboat, which fetched him and roared off, the 200 Merc at full throttle. Pastoral tranquility has reigned upon the lake ever since.

* * *

Toward the end of June, Simon O'Reilly mentioned that he would not be attending summer school on Thursday the fourth of July.

"And why not?" asked Frederick sternly, for he brooked no absences without a good reason.

"Because it's a holiday. Besides," explained Simon, "I want to watch the ski jumping at Lake Placid."

"Ski jumping?" asked Frederick.

"Sure. Every summer they bring snow down from a mountain and shovel it onto the ski jump. Jumpers come from as far away as Montreal to compete."

"Ski *jumpers*?" asked Frederick. "Competition?"

The students arranged everything. Denise phoned Lake Placid and registered Frederick R. Catesbiana as the lone contestant from Pickerelweed Lake. She informed Frederick that each competitor would have three jumps, and that the judges would give each jump a combined score based on both distance and form.

The winner would be awarded a silver trophy, and dinner for two at Pizza Palace.

III

Frederick said little as he rode on the flatbed truck, surrounded by his coaches and cheerleaders, along the road that winds through the heart of the Adirondacks toward the Olympic Village. He eyed with interest the lakes and ponds and swamps along the way, but shuffled nervously as we passed through bustling hamlets; random explosions of firecrackers especially set him on edge.

Stuck in slow-moving traffic through downtown Lake Placid, he wanted to jump from car roof to car roof as if they were lily pads, but the students managed to restrain him: he had to save his strength for the Big Jump.

When finally, a short distance outside of town, the truck approached the towering Olympic ski jump, its imposing chute silhouetted against the hills, Frederick sat up and eyed the challenge that beckoned him.

There was a bit of a to-do at the registration table, for never before in the history of the Lake Placid Fourth of July Ski Jumping had the organizing committee been approached by a six-foot, one-ton bullfrog. Perplexed and befuddled, the judge thumbed through his rule book, but found no paragraph which explicitly prohibited bullfrogs from competing. "But where are its skis?" he protested, clearly looking for some infraction of the rules which would disqualify Frederick. Frederick held up a webbed foot, which he then folded into a sleek longitudinal appendage. "Ribbed for stability on the chute," he explained, "and aerodynamic in flight."

Rocko informed the judge, "Rossignol has bid for the patent."

"But . . . I . . . well . . ." stammered the judge.

"Listen, there was no problem at Holmenkollen," said Frederick.

"Wholemacoal?" asked the judge.

Frederick rolled his spheroid eyes with impatience. "Holmenkollen. Oslo. You know, *Norway*. World cup, last January. I placed fifth." He shrugged his green shoulders. "Would've done better but I had troubles with the crosswind."

Well, who could argue with the World Cup in Norway? They gave Frederick starting number twenty-three in the men's open division. As we moved off to where the other competitors were waxing their skis, Denise asked in a whisper, "Where on *earth* did you learn about Holmawhatzit?"

Frederick whispered out of the corner of his vast semicircular mouth, "I've been boning up on this stuff. Books from the school library. See the tips of those skis?"

Denise glanced at the long broad skis laid over the shoulder of one of the other jumpers. "Yeah?"

"I've got to remember to keep my toes curled *up*."

When number twenty-three was called, Denise, Rocko, Simon and I rode with Frederick in the elevator to the top of the jump. The other students were scattered along the hill and around the bowl at the bottom, ready to cheer. Frederick did *not* like the elevator: first the doors closed inches from his nose; then, as we rushed skyward and even I felt a twinge in my stomach, I saw his mouth wrinkle with a grimace and his closing eyes sink completely into his head. When the rocketing box stopped and its door opened, Frederick's eyes re-emerged and he hopped quickly out. "Worse than the dungeon," he muttered.

From the top of the tower, we gazed out at the magnificent vista of meadows and forest and mountains jumbled to the horizon. But when I looked down that chute, freshly covered with snow, I had to grab a railing to steady myself. The drop from the peak of Mount Everest could not have been more precipitous. My stomach wanted to get right back in that elevator and hurry down to pine needles and ferns and bedrock. I turned to Frederick, ready to tell him that if he wanted to chicken out, we would all understand.

But frogs don't chicken out. Frederick moved into position at the top of the chute. He redirected his front toes, normally pointed inward, to forward-pointed positions in the two ski tracks. He folded his webbed hind feet. Curled up his toes. His yellow throat pulsed. Then his spheroid eyes, staring straight down that ghastly chute, focused with a concentration that was absolute.

Frederick nudged forward, locked all four feet into the ski tracks, pointed his aerodynamic nose, raised his hips slightly to allow the wind to pass beneath his belly, gained momentum . . . I could see his knees shaking now with his increasing speed . . . Could he maintain control? . . . Denise clutched my arm. . . . We held our breath as he raced toward the bottom lip . . . Faster, faster! . . . and then he KICKED with his powerful hind legs, but too late! He'd already shot off the end and kicked against nothing but air and so dropped prematurely and belly-flopped high up the hill, higher than where even the worst of the skiers had landed, and so he slid on his belly down the snowy slope and began to spin and was now clearly out of control and a helpless webbed foot reached out and he flipped and tumbled and somersaulted with "CROAK!" after "CROAK!" each time he bounced until at last he slid on his back across the bowl and crashed into the hay bales at the end. The crowd was silent, fearing the worst.

Dusted with snow, Frederick turned himself over. Utterly humiliated, he searched for an exit. The crowd applauded with relief and encouragement. Shovelers on the hill went to work to repair and smooth the potholes he had made. We hurried down in the elevator to give Frederick a pep talk and discuss strategy for the second jump.

Despite his first defeat, his spirits rebounded. "My timing was off," he told us. "My tympanums were vibrating in the rush of wind. Split-second timing is difficult if your tympanums are vibrating."

While waiting for number twenty-three to be called again, the students massaged Frederick's thighs and refurbished his fluids with plenty of Gatorade.

The elevator ride was a snap the second time. No prob. My stomach still sank to my knees, however, when I looked down that chute. But Frederick moved into his starting position, readied his feet, toes up, and then I saw that transformation again in his eyes, from mere stare to a steel-hard focus that encompassed not only the chute but his intended trajectory.

He nudged forward, locked into the tracks, lifted his hips, lowered his nose, and his eyes sank halfway into his head . . . left knee trembling slightly as he cannonballs down the ramp . . . left knee steady now, under control . . . Denise grips my arm . . . I whisper, "Go, Frederick. Go, Frederick! *Go, Frederick*!" . . . He is a green blur approaching the lip . . . and then he KICKED at precisely the right moment and those fabulous ten-foot hind legs stretched out behind him, toes pointed. Whereas the other skiers arched downward to the slope, Frederick arched *upward* into the blue July sky, nose lifted, forelegs tucked against his belly, eyes pulled even deeper into his head. He sailed well beyond the slope (the crowd roaring now at a record clearly in the making) and landed in the bowl with a belly-flop and a "CROAK!" about a foot from the hay bales. He didn't skid an inch, but, stable as an Adirondack boulder, merely lowered his toes and elevated his eyes and, according to the students cheering around the edge of the bowl, grinned with Batrachian satisfaction.

While we waited for number twenty-three to be called a third and final time, we had to fend off a television crew that wanted an interview. "Tell them," whispered Frederick out of the corner of his mouth, "to set up their camera in that meadow down on the other side of the highway."

"Which meadow?" I asked, puzzled.

"Didn't you see it from the top of the tower? There's a nice green meadow way out there on the other side of the highway. Load the students onto the flatbed truck and tell them to get their cameras ready."

"But Frederick, that meadow must be a mile away."

"Right," he said with a knowing look. "I hope there aren't any thistles."

The television crew wouldn't budge. They pooh-poohed any thought of leaving the Olympic site. But the students, remembering Frederick's great jump on the football field, hopped aboard the flatbed truck, which I drove out of the parking lot and down to the highway and then along an obscure lane to a meadow which lay directly in line with the chute. The students quickly ascertained that the meadow contained no thistles, only timothy grass and vetch, clover and buttercups, and a sprinkling of black-eyed susans. We turned our eyes toward the ski jump towering against the sky.

Even from a mile away, we could see a large green lump at the top of the jump. We watched it descend . . . gaining in speed . . . Denise squeezed my arm . . . then we saw those two hind legs stretch out like a pair of telephone poles and we knew at once that he'd not only mastered the timing, but, as he launched into the blue heavens, that Frederick had caught the Olympic spirit.

His rear feet were not pointed, but spread so that he gained loft on webs of tiny posterior wings.

And then (I could hardly believe it, still can hardly believe it to this day, but Simon's color photographs serve as irrefutable proof,) Frederick tucked his nose and rolled into a full airborne somersault as if Mars-made-of-green-cheese were hurtling across the sky. He stabilized with a little webbed foot action, eyeballed the landing site (we stepped back to give him plenty of room,) plummeted earthward and belly-flopped with a gargantuan "CROAK!"

Rocko determined, by triangulation and trigonometry and a tricky cosine or two, calculated with the given height of the ski jump tower, that Frederick had traveled a baseline distance of 5281 feet, a hypotenuse of 6427 feet, and, as the frog flies, a parabolic trajectory of well over seven thousand feet.

"Might've done better," said Frederick, "but there was a pretty tough crosswind up there."

He frog-kicked around Lake Placid that evening, fêted by the crowd along the shore. People Frisbeed pizzas across the water to him until Pizza Palace ran out of pepperoni. The fireworks made him nervous at first, especially the cannon blasters that rattled his tympanums. But, as he told me later, "I liked those red and gold powder puffs reflected on the black water. We'll have to come back next year."

When school started in September, Frederick refused to step foot in the dungeon, and requested that we move his pond to the library. The librarian was skeptical, but Frederick promised not to drop any of her books into the drink. He complains, however, that though dog stories are abundant, as are horse stories, and there's even a fat book about a whale, good frog stories are appallingly few.

He keeps the kids in line: any whispering or giggling in the library elicits an immediate Thwwooopp! of a sticky wet tongue on the student's ear.

Frederick trains every afternoon: lies on his back with a round Adirondack boulder cradled in each webbed hind foot, then he pumps his legs bicycle-style, building up those thighs. My wife is knitting him a winter outfit, jade green, with magic number twenty-three on the chest. Hibernation is out of the question. He dreams of that perfect, clear, windless day in January, when the World Championships come to Lake Placid, so he can look down from the top of the tower at the judges with their tapes, waiting for him at the far end of the meadow, where the students have already prepared a nice soft bed of snow.

THE POTATO

I often marvel that I am the means by which a potato can become a poem. This potato on my plate, russet red, steaming hot, as yet uncut and unbuttered, contains within it the makings of a sonnet, an ode, an elegy. I slice it open, inhale the fragrant steam, insert deep into the hot crevasse a fat dollop of butter, then wait until the butter has melted, and begins to drip out from both ends of the longitudinal slice. Now I cut crosswise, and spread symmetrically on my plate two rows of buttered chunks of potato. If I am eating with company, I cut the chunks into smaller pieces; if alone, I wolf them down whole.

This combination of tuber grubbed up from the earth, and milk sucked from the udder of a cow, now proceeds down my gullet to my belly. The belly, a necessary appurtenance in every poet, welcomes the potato with all the warmth and cordiality that one naturally bestows upon an old friend.

Already, while I continue to eat my potato, chunk by splendid chunk, the magic begins. Down in that happy, acid-filled sac, the potato is reduced to molecules of starch. Not with a surgeon's knife could I slice up a potato into pieces the size of molecules. Not even a well-aimed sledgehammer could do the job. These molecules, tiny packages of sustenance and energy, pass through the stomach's wall, and then, one door leading to another, pass through the wall of a capillary, whence they are whisked away in the bloodstream.

Some of the starch flows downward, where it is burned and warms your feet. Some of it travels up to your shoulder, then journeys beyond elbow and wrist to your fingertips, which tap on your desk, waiting for something to do. Some of that starch is freighted through the Grand Central Station of your heart, then surges upward via the trunk line of your aorta, and lesser lines of artery and arteriole, to your eardrum, where the starch is consumed by hungry cells that vibrate whenever your girlfriend sings your name. The potato feeds your optic nerve as you gaze upon your beloved's lovely face. That smile which lifts your lips is powered by potato.

But the poem, the poem! Did we not begin this treatise by stating that within a potato dwells a poem?

A portion of that wondrous potato voyages from the belly to the bloodstream to the brain, where it nourishes a variety of cells as potentially harmonious as the members of a symphony orchestra. Some cells of the brain specialize in memory; plied with potato, they recall that moonlit night when the two of you first met. Another group of cells, now gobbling and gorging and gourmandizing upon molecules of starch, specialize in the articulation of concepts into words; these are the language cells, and flush with their feast of potato, they send forth via synapse and dendrite a series of words in iambic pentameter, extolling the soul of your sweetheart. And yet another cluster of cells, their vacuoles bloated with potato, assist with a timely ringing of chimes; each musical cell emits on its network of nerves a pair of words that serve as rhymes. Perhaps, but only perhaps, a cell or two exists within your brain with the capability and training to perform that penultimate but oft-neglected function: aglow with a banquet of potato, it checks your spelling.

Together, these various categories of cerebral cells, assembled in concerted effort like the string section and woodwinds and percussion and horns beneath the sweep and stab of a conductor's baton, muse and mull and deliberate and cogitate until verse after verse, strophe upon strophe, with rhymes intertwined to the final consummate couplet, a poem is written. By you, so you say. So you exult, and boast. The love in your heart now crowded and elbowed by your sense of triumph, you present your sonnet to the girl of your dreams.

Don't be fooled. You are but the middleman between potato and poem. That mute tuber on your plate waited a geologic epoch or two for someone to discover it, and take a bite. The next genius to come along roasted it in a campfire, or at least dragged it out of the coals into which it had fallen, and took a bite. With the invention of the cooking pot, someone boiled a potato, then sliced it up into chunks. Or mashed it, and served it with a garnish of parsley. All of which was in the potato's patient plan. I sometimes think that at the potato's request was man created, not as a man, but as an amanuensis with an insatiable belly, and an eardrum, and an eye. For the potato has no hands, yet when tiny portions of the potato reach my fingertips, tapping absently on my desk, they rise to the typewriter keys and know exactly what to do.

Kite Tale

If you only glance, and hardly look at all, you will see two girls walking along the sidewalk, one tall and thin, the other short and plump.

If you watch more closely, you will see that the tall girl glides along with one step to a sidewalk square, while the short girl hurries with four steps to a sidewalk square.

If you watch even more closely, you will notice that the tall girl is looking up, watching the world above her, while the short girl is looking down, searching for things that lie on the ground, like a piece of string.

And if you were to watch them on a windy morning in May, this is what you would see:

As Amanda leaned into a gust of wind, she wondered, "Clothilde, what's the perfect plan for such a windy day?" She discovered an old shoelace on the sidewalk. She picked it up and put it into her pocket.

Clothilde looked up at a robin repairing its nest. All winter long, a fluffy white chicken had roosted there.

"Shall we put on roller skates," wondered Amanda, "then open two umbrellas and sail all the way to Zanzibar?" She bent over to pick up a bit of yellow birthday ribbon. She put it into her pocket.

Clothilde watched a weathervane wagging its rooster tail in the wind, as if it tried with all its might to take off and join a flock of crows.

Amanda wondered, "Shall we open the windows at both ends of my attic, then we'll trek through a Sahara dust storm?"

Clothilde watched a smokestack that was puffing a family of dragons.

While Amanda was pondering her plans and expanding her plots, she spotted a cat's cradle left in tangles on a park bench. She straightened the string, then coiled it neatly and put it into her pocket.

Amanda wondered, "Shall we cling to a tree with an eye pealed for flying coconuts, while we survive Havana's most horrible hurricane?"

Clothilde held out her long thin arms and sailed like a graceful swan high above the worst of the hurricane, just high enough to bounce above the clouds from billow to billow.

Then short plump Amanda jumped a quarter-inch off the ground. "I've got it!" She looked up at her friend Clothilde. "Today, on this windy morning in May," she queried, "would you be willing to be a kite?"

Lithely flapping her long and elegant wings, Clothilde looked down at Amanda and winked that the plan was a good one.

So they hurried to Clothilde's house and took her big orange bedspread from her bed. Then they walked beyond the last street in town, to a meadow where the wind was somersaulting through the new spring grass.

Standing behind Clothilde, Amanda took pieces of string from her pockets and tied the bedspread to Clothilde's hands and feet. Amanda warned Clothilde to keep her wings tightly folded, or she would sail away in the wind before Amanda was ready.

With her feet together and her arms pressed against her sides, Clothilde stared up at a hawk that circled high overhead.

Standing now in front of Clothilde, Amanda tied a red ponytail ribbon to Clothilde's belt. Then she tied a skate key string to the ponytail ribbon. And then she tied a length of fishing line to the skate key string. Reaching into the pockets of her jacket, the pockets of her shirt, and the pockets of her jeans, she walked backward across the meadow as the kite string of many knots and many colors got longer and longer.

When finally she reached the far end of the great green sweep of grass, she called with the wind, "All right, Clothilde. Open your arms and jump!"

Clothilde sprang into the air and opened her wings. She felt a sudden gust that scooped her up as if the wind that day had been waiting.

Amanda felt a great tug on the string as the big orange kite rose into the windy blue sky. She reached into her jeans pockets and shirt pockets and jacket pockets for more balloon string and yo-yo string and newspaper loops. She tied them on as quickly as she could.

Clothilde looked up at puffy white clouds that were becoming her neighbors. She wiggled her right hand: the kite swooped to the right. She waggled her left hand: the kite cruised to the left.

Amanda tied on more and more pieces of string. The long bowed line of many knots and many colors led up to a small orange square in the huge blue sky.

Clothilde swooped a loop-the-loop through a little cloud. She felt its mist cool on her face.

Then she discovered that the hawk had come a-calling. Flapping her wings, she showed the hawk how to swoop a loop-the-loop. The hawk, who had gone around and around in flat circles all its life, now angled its tail as up and over and down it flew. Soon the two were looping twin hoops in the blue. With each hoop that she looped, swooping Clothilde whooped a cheer, "Yahooo!"

Amanda reached into the innermost pocket of her innermost T-shirt for more string. She tied on a piece of twine so quickly that too late she discovered there was no twine . . . her pockets were empty, and what she had tied on and now held was nothing but air!

Amanda jumped to catch the end of the kite string. But short plump Amanda could jump no higher than a quarter-inch.

The string floated across the meadow like a long wagging tail. Clothilde was sailing away!

Amanda ran across the meadow, trying to catch the string. She raced around a lilypad pond. She jumped from stone to stone across a creek. She climbed a fence that kept the cow in. She ran past the cow. She climbed a fence that kept the cow out. But the wind was strong on that morning in May, and the long bowed string of many knots and many colors rose higher and higher. The kite was no longer a small orange square in the huge blue sky, but now a tiny orange spot.

Clothilde was no longer looping: she was zooming, for she had been freed from her last bond to earth. She raced the hawk across the sky, until the poor hawk, exhausted, had to call, "Good-bye!"

Clothilde spotted a rainbow in a shower beneath a cloud. Angling her wings, she zoomed through the band of indigo. She almost hollered, "Yahooo!", but she sneezed instead, "Hachooo!"

Amanda, meanwhile, was about to collapse in the grass. She staggered and she stumbled, she huffed and she puffed, but she knew that she would never catch the long bowed string of many knots and many colors. Poor Clothilde! Her friend might land on a frozen mountaintop in Nepal! Or she might come down in a Russian forest where the wolves hadn't eaten in weeks!

Rising and diving across the sky, Clothilde wrote her name in loopy orange letters. But she was going too fast to cross the t and dot the i.

Just as she was about to flop flat in the grass, a hummingbird hummed past Amanda's ear. It hummed on one side of her, hummed on the other side of her, hummed just ahead of her, then it hummed up and landed on the string.

A finch came zipping and bobbing over the meadow. It fluttered past Amanda, then landed on the string beside the hummingbird.

A sparrow flew so near Amanda's ear that she felt the whirr of its wings. The sparrow landed beside the finch. Further along the string perched a chickadee, a nuthatch, and a flycatcher. Beside them landed fourteen warblers, warbling fourteen different springtime songs.

Amanda kept running ("huff huff") after the long bowed string ("puff puff") of many knots ("huff") and many colors ("puff!"). She wished she were a bird herself.

A chimney swift whished overhead on its long slender wings. It rode up the wind, glided down again, then it landed on the string. Beside it perched a kingfisher, a meadowlark, and a spotted thrush. An oriole and a cuckoo flew up too, and a dove that quietly cooed.

Along came a grouse and a goose and a grebe.

They were joined along the string by a brown pelican and a pink flamingo, a partridge and a swan, a white-crested egret and a bald-headed vulture.

A pigeon. A wigeon. And an owl.

Down swooped the hawk. It loop-the-looped the floating row of birds, then beside the flock it perched.

A shadow circled the ground around Amanda. She looked up and saw an eagle spiraling down from the sun. It flapped its great wings and settled on the string.

With the weight of all these birds, the end of the string drooped closer to Amanda. But Amanda was pooped. Even if she were as tall as Clothilde, she would never catch the long bowed string of many knots and many colors.

So the birds clutched the string tightly in their claws, and together they flew down toward the little girl on the ground.

The hummingbird hummed as hard as it could.

The finch fluttafluttafluttafluttered.

The flamingo flapflapflapped.

And the eagle's great wings went Hoosh! Hoosh! Hoosh!

Amanda watched with growing hope as the birds pulled the string closer . . . and closer . . . and a bit closer still. She reached up, and with a mighty three-quarter-inch jump, she grabbed the end! She gripped in her fist a yellow birthday ribbon. "Hooray!" she gasped. "Clothilde is saved!"

Amanda began to wind the string into a ball. The birds sailed down to the grass and watched. The tiny orange spot became a small orange square. As the square grew larger, so did the ball of string, until the ball of many knots and many colors was as tall as Amanda.

Clothilde watched two orange butterflies flutter by on an updraft. She flapped after them, but the string pulled her down, down, down toward Amanda.

Clothilde swooped a final loop-the-loop over the meadow, then she tucked her wings and settled into the fluffy tufts of grass. She winked at her friend as she untied the big orange bedspread. "Thank you, Amanda."

"But it was the birds who saved you," said Amanda.

Clothilde looked at the birds gathered around her in the meadow. She whistled, "Thank you."

The birds twittered and chirped, warbled and peeped and honked, cheeped and squawked and hooted and cooed, "You're welcome."

Then short plump Amanda jumped a quarter-inch off the ground. "I have a plan!" she said. She pointed at the finch who sat atop the ball of many knots and many colors. "What do the birds do in spring?" she asked.

"They build nests," said Clothilde.

"Yes. And what do they build them with?"

"String!" said Clothilde.

So Amanda and Clothilde untied the many knots of many colors. They gave old sneaker laces and bright bits of ribbon to ravens and robins and pipits and pigeons and plovers. Late in the afternoon, they untied the last piece of red ponytail ribbon for the last little peewee.

Then they folded the big orange bedspread, and leaned into the wind as they walked across the meadow toward home.

The Seed That Could

A man and a woman carried a shovel and a hoe into their backyard. Together they dug a patch for a garden. The man dug deep and turned the soil over; the woman hoed the soil until it was fine and smooth. They planted seeds, then they sifted the earth through their fingers to cover the seeds.

Near the new garden stood an apple tree covered with pink blossoms. The tree filled the backyard with its sweet perfume.

Every evening after dinner, the newlyweds watered their garden. The pink apple blossoms fell and made a fluffy circle on the lawn. The woman laughed as she shuffled barefoot through the petals.

One of the seeds they had planted swelled with water until it split its shell open. A white root pushed down, nudging grains of dirt. A green shoot shouldered upward.

But then the man and the woman no longer came out of their house after dinner to tend their garden. Weeds grew, tall and thick. One of the weeds wrapped its roots around the seed like a snake around a mouse. The roots found the crack where the seed had split open, and reached inside for the meat of the seed.

The green shoot poked above the soil, its tiny fiddlehead surrounded by a forest of weeds. Only a little light trickled down and touched the fiddlehead as the sun passed overhead.

One evening the man rolled a wheelbarrow to the edge of the garden. He shoveled gravel onto the weeds until they were bent and broken and covered. His wife watched from the window. They did not have time to pull weeds.

The weeds were crushed and buried. The roots of the weed

which had clung like a claw to the seed now withered and died.

The green fiddlehead had been bent and buried beneath the gravel. But it was not broken; it continued to grow, looking for a hole up between the stones.

When the sprout finally emerged, it was pale green, almost white. Sunlight touched the stem and bud and folded leaves, and slowly they turned green again. The leaves opened, pointed and finely toothed.

The roots of the seedling began to branch into the earth.

The apples on the tree were now small and green.

One afternoon the woman came out on the back steps of her house and threw a box toward the garage. It landed on the gravel and overturned and spilled out papers and bottles and old clothes. The plant was bent sideways under a bottle. When the man came home, he threw more trash on the heap: books and records and a broken lamp.

The plant grew around the bottle. It pushed beneath the papers. It twisted through the books and clothing. It lifted an envelope. And then once again, the plant emerged into the sunshine and grew and stood up straight beneath the blue sky.

The man came home in a new car and honked its horn in the driveway. The woman looked from the window at the shiny red car. He kept honking until she came out and stumbled over the trash and got into the car. They drove away. The next day a truck came and movers took the furniture out of the house. But they did not take away the trash.

The plant grew, spreading its leaves above a rotting newspaper. The sun shone down on the pointed, finely-toothed leaves, turning them deep green. The roots sent up cool water. The long, white, twisted stem carried the water to the tall bushy plant, and the plant carried the water up to a bud swelling at its top.

The apples were now red.

A wind began to blow. It bobbed the branches of the apple

tree. The bushy plant trembled in the gusts. Clouds tumbled over the sky; rain lashed down. The storm thrashed the apple tree through a day and a night. The plant bent nearly to the ground as rain beat against it. The leaves of the apple tree and the leaves of the plant were twisted and torn.

When the sun rose in the morning, the air was quiet and fresh. The apples lay shining and red on the gravel.

The apples rotted.

The bud at the tip of the plant swelled.

But no one was there to see the bud unfold into a flower as red as a flame lifted up to the sun.

GEORGIA AND THE SPOTLIGHT MAN

Georgia went with her mother to the circus at the city amphitheater. Her mother did not have much money, so they had to sit in the highest balcony, looking down through ropes and pillars and people who never sat still.

But Georgia didn't mind that they sat in the very last row, because their seats were near the spotlight man. His blue beam followed the baby elephant as it paraded with the bigger elephants around the ring far below.

The spotlight man's blue wand swung back and forth as it followed an acrobat who hung by his knees from a swinging trapeze.

Georgia watched the man as he pointed his blue beam. He reminded her of an old elephant, for his eyes were tired and droopy. On the lapel of his baggy gray uniform, he wore a white rose.

Georgia leaned forward in her seat and peered down at a clown pushing a baby buggy into the ring. In the buggy was a giant egg. The clown held up a huge sledge hammer to show the audience, then he swung the hammer down on the egg, cracking open the shell. Out flew a dozen white doves. Blue and red spotlights shone together on the rising flock, turning the doves purple as they sailed high above the clapping crowd.

Georgia and her mother watched a white horse as it pranced around the ring. When the horse jumped over a fence, it turned blue in the spotlight man's blue beam. Then as it jumped through a flaming hoop, the horse turned orange. Georgia looked across the amphitheater at the orange spotlight pointing down above dark rows of people. While the horse was dancing to the music of the orchestra, other beams shown down, so the horse with a long sweeping tail became red, then yellow, and now green. When the horse reared up on its hind legs, it became blue again and shook its flowing blue mane.

Georgia wondered what it would be like to put her head inside the blue beam.

She wanted to stare down the tunnel of blue at the blue horse. Did the spotlight man ever put his head inside his blue beam, then look down at the circus far below? Georgia watched him. His eyes were half-closed in the curling gray smoke of his cigarette.

Georgia had read on a circus poster that fifteen elephants would stand up together in a circle, each elephant leaning on the elephant in front of him. She asked her mother if they could go down to the ground floor of the amphitheater so they could stand where the elephants would parade into the ring. Her mother thought for a moment, then she nodded, "Perhaps we could." Georgia and her mother stood up. They said "Excuse me . . . Excuse me" as they walked in front of people along the row of seats.

Before she left the balcony, Georgia looked back at the spotlight man. He was staring right at her. His eyes were old and sad. Georgia waved good-bye to him. Lifting his hand slowly, the spotlight man waved back.

Her mother led her down many flights of concrete steps, then they walked halfway around the ground floor (buying popcorn along the way) until they stood in sawdust at the opening of a big tunnel. Acrobats and jugglers and clowns in bright uniforms talked to each other in the tunnel while they waited for their turn in the ring.

Further back in the tunnel, an enormous brown bear paced in its red and gold cage. Georgia had never been so close to such a big bear.

A family of acrobats ran past Georgia and somersaulted into the spotlights. Each tumbler lit two torches, then he bounced higher and higher on the trampoline until he spun through the air onto another tumbler's shoulders. When the family stood five high, (a boy Georgia's age stood on top,) they juggled their torches and made a tower of spinning flames.

Suddenly a loud growl near Georgia made her jump with fright and grab her mother's hand. The bear, out of its cage, sat ten feet behind her, wearing a blue collar around its neck. As the tumblers came cartwheeling back toward the tunnel, the bear, lit by the blue spotlight, stood up on its hind legs and walked with its trainer toward the ring. The towering shaggy bear walked very close to Georgia. As she squeezed her mother's hand, she was lit for a moment by the blue beam.

The bear climbed on top of a big silver ball and rolled it around the ring. The ball glittered with flashes of blue. When the trainer clapped his hands, the bear stood up on its hind legs atop the ball and clapped its paws. And when the man roared, the bear roared five times as loudly.

Then the blue beam disappeared. The bear was in the dark. After a long moment, a red beam shone down on the bear, and the green beam, and now the yellow, so that a jumble of colors followed the bear while it climbed a set of steps and walked across a narrow bridge toward a giant playground slide.

The red beam swung upwards. Georgia looked up and discovered the blue spotlight: it shone across the top of the circus. She searched from one end to the other of the horizontal blue beam, but she couldn't see any acrobats. Nor any clowns. The blue beam didn't seem to shine on anything. It just made a big blue spot on the concrete wall near the ceiling.

At first the red beam crossed the blue beam, making an X with a spot of purple where they touched. Then the red beam lifted slightly and shone just across the top of the blue beam. Someone was standing up there! Georgia could see a dark figure in the red beam, standing on top of the blue.

The yellow beam swung upwards, and now the green beam as well, leaving the bear once again in the dark. The three spotlights, red, yellow and green, crisscrossed each other just above the blue beam.

Several white beams swept back and forth across the top of the circus, until they all converged on a man who stood higher than the highwire, higher than even the trapeze. The dozen spotlights crisscrossed like the spokes of an enormous cartwheel. At the hub, someone was walking on top of the horizontal blue beam as if it were a tightrope. Georgia saw now that he was the spotlight man in his baggy gray uniform. His rose became red, then yellow, and for a moment it was gold as all the spotlights followed him.

Georgia stared up with excitement. "Look, Mama!"

The spotlight man walked along the top of his blue beam with slow, tired steps. He was stooped over, and he walked like an old, old man who carried a heavy load on his back.

Then he stopped walking and slowly unbuttoned the front of his baggy gray uniform. He pulled one arm out from a gray sleeve, and then the other arm. Underneath his uniform he wore a suit of diamonds that sparkled in the spotlights with a thousand shots of color. Bending down even lower, he slowly pushed his uniform down from his legs, then he stepped out of it. Standing straight up now, as if his tired back no longer hurt him, he laid the limp gray uniform over his arm and unpinned his rose from the lapel. Then he dropped the uniform down through the blue beam. It disappeared into the dark. Standing tall in his suit of glittering diamonds, the man sniffed his rose.

A parade of elephants shuffled out from the tunnel and into the ring. Georgia glanced at them as they walked past her. Then she looked up again at the spotlight man. Holding his arms out for balance, he slowly bent his knees, then he stood up again. He lifted one foot, then set it down on the blue beam. He lifted his other foot, then set it down. Now he bent forward as if to roll into a somersault . . . but he only hunched over, his hands resting on his knees. When he stood again and held his hand up for applause, Georgia clapped.

A dove flapped down and perched on the man's finger. The spotlight man slowly shuffled along his blue beam, which grew wider as it crossed the top of the circus. The dove walked up the man's arm until it stood on his glittering shoulder.

Now the spotlight man looked up into the darkness above him. Then he reached up—one of the white spotlights followed his sparkling arm—and he took something down from the steel girders under the ceiling. Georgia saw when he opened it, that it was a silver umbrella covered with diamonds. He laid it on his shoulder and spun the umbrella above him, so that it cupped and reflected a half-dozen spotlights into one single beam of glittering rainbow sparkles.

And this new beam he pointed down at Georgia. Looking down the middle of his beam, the spotlight man smiled at her. Then he tossed down his white rose. It fell down, down, down through the dazzling rainbow beam . . . and landed in the sawdust at her feet. Georgia knelt down and picked it up. Thrilled with his gift, she looked up at him and waved. "Thank you!" she called up to him. The spotlight man waved back.

Holding the umbrella's handle with both hands, the spotlight man took a step and floated down into the blue beam. The dove flapped its wings as the man gently descended. He landed on the bottom of the blue wand; his suit glittered with a thousand blue sparks.

One by one, the other spotlights swung down to the circus ring. Now only the blue beam shone across the top of the amphitheater, with the spotlight man standing inside it.

He folded his umbrella and hooked it over the bar of a trapeze. He walked along the inside of the blue beam to a unicycle that hung from a tightrope pole. He set the wheel of the unicycle on the bottom of the blue beam, then he sat on the seat. Holding out his arms like glittering blue wings, he pedaled forward, and then backward, and now forward again along the blue beam. The dove sailed back and forth on blue wings above him.

The spotlight man zigzagged on his unicycle up and down the curved blue walls. With a burst of speed, he circled all the way around the beam! He circled again and again, spiraling along the blue beam across the top of the circus. Georgia heard drums roll and a cymbal crash with each loop.

Then he balanced in one spot on the bottom of his blue beam. With his arms outstretched, his wheel moving slightly back and forth, he dipped his head with a bow toward Georgia. As she clapped, she heard a roar of applause.

Suddenly an angry man shouted beside her, "Where's the blue spotlight? The Stupendous Circle of Pachyderms is our climax! The blue beam is supposed to shine on the littlest elephant. Somebody go wake him up. Tell him he's fired!"

Pedaling gracefully forward, the spotlight man rode inside his blue beam across the top of the circus, until he rode through the big blue spot on the concrete wall. As he rode along the widening blue tunnel, the blue dove flew ahead of him. The man became smaller and smaller as he rode further and further away, until Georgia could no longer see him.

She turned to her mother. "Mama, where did he go?"

"Who, Honey?"

"The man riding the unicycle in the blue light."

"Georgia, weren't you watching the elephants?"

"He smiled at me, and he threw down his rose."

"A rose? Sweetheart, who were you watching?"

Georgia held up for her mother to see: a fresh, fragrant white rose.

The Lark and the Apple Tree

Once upon a time there was an apple tree with apples so sour, the farmer fed them to his pigs. He said that one day he would take his ax and cut the tree down.

A lark landed on a branch of the apple tree. She began to sing. The leaves of the tree stirred as if a breeze blew through them.

The lark liked the apple tree, though the tree never knew why. He knew only that when the lark sat in a spruce tree, her song was beautiful, but not as beautiful as when she sat on one of his branches. When she sat in a maple tree, her song was lovely, but not as lovely as when she sat among his red apples. When she sat in a willow tree, her song was lively, but not as lively as when she sat in the crest of the apple tree.

Her song was so beautiful that a crow came to sit beside her. "Cawww!" said the crow, his way of saying hello. The apple tree shook as if the gust of a storm blew through his branches. The crow nearly fell off, and so with a "Cawww!" of complaint, he flew away.

The lark flew away as well. But when she came back, the apple tree did not shake his branches. He stood strong and sturdy, and she sang to him with her most beautiful song.

The apples on the apple tree became red and ripe, and the farmer came to pick them. The farmer held an ax in one hand as he took a bite from an apple. If he puckered again this year, he would cut the tree down.

But the apple was not sour. It was the biggest, reddest, sweetest apple he had ever eaten. The apples were so sweet, he filled a basket for his wife so she could bake a pie.

As the days grew cold, the leaves on the apple tree began to fall. The lark became restless. She sang only part of a song, then she stopped and seemed to think of something else.

The branches of the apple tree began to droop.

In the middle of her song, she flapped her wings and flew across the orchard. And she was gone.

The apple tree tried to remember her song. But winter came, freezing his branches, freezing his trunk, freezing him down to his roots.

Come cut me down, he thought. Come with your ax and chop me into pieces for your stove.

* * *

The snow lay deep around the tree that winter. The apple tree did not see how beautiful he was with snow on his branches. He thought, Next summer I will make no apples, then the farmer will surely cut me down.

One night in the middle of the winter, the moon shown down on the apple tree. The tree was so beautiful, glowing white in the moonlight, that once again he remembered the song of the lark. He felt how much he loved her. He let the love in his heart reach down deep into his roots, and he let the love in his heart reach up into his branches. He let the love in his heart reach into the tiny buds that would become apples. Filled with love, covered with snow, glowing in the moonlight, the tree slept through the winter in a deep peaceful dream.

When spring came, the snow melted and the bare branches of the apple tree were black. But as the days grew warm, the apple tree took all of his love and turned it into fluffy white apple blossoms. He was so beautiful that when the lark returned to the orchard, she did not sit in the spruce, she did not sit in the maple, she did not sit in the willow. She sat in the fluffy white apple tree and breathed the sweetest perfume she knew. Gripping with her feet a branch of the apple tree, she sang to him her most beautiful song.

As the days passed, the white petals began to fall. In a nearby forest, another lark was calling. The lark in the apple tree stopped in the middle of her song to listen.

The apple tree called to the wind. "Please, please, please," said the tree to the wind, "gather up my love and give it to her as my gift."

The wind swirled into a little cyclone sweeping around the tree. It picked up all the white petals and lifted them in a whirling cloud into the sky. The wind spun the white petals so fast that when suddenly the roar of the wind stopped, the apple tree heard the flutter of wings.

A lark flew down from the sky and landed on a branch of the apple tree. He sang his song of love, a song so beautiful that the lady lark flew to sit on the branch beside him.

They collected sticks and built a nest. In the nest they laid their eggs.

The apple tree made apples so sweet that year, the farmer sold his pigs. If you would like a piece of the best apple pie you've ever eaten, just down the road is a little café called The Song of the Lark.

THE NEST AND THE GRAVE

from the novel "CHILDREN OF THE SUN"

Angelique parked the jeep behind the beach, then turned to Ulysses curled on the passenger seat, his freshly brushed fur lit by the full moon through the windshield. With forced cheerfulness, she asked, "Ulysses, yo' want to go to the *beach*?" He lifted himself with his forelegs to look out the window. She tousled his soft, twitching ears. "The beach, Ulysses." He nudged her arm with his nose: he wanted to get out.

When she opened her door, stepped out and walked around the front of the jeep, she felt her movements were not real; she was following the script of some insane play. As she opened the passenger door, she sang, as much to calm herself as to comfort her dog, "Uuuuulyyyyyseeeees." With one arm slung beneath his strong chest, one under his atrophied hindquarters, she lifted him from the seat, then carried him to the beach. Under the coconut palms, the sand was dark with ragged shadows. She felt like Death, bringing the unsuspecting victim to the chopping block.

She carried him beyond the palms, to where the sand was radiant with moonlight.

A wave lifted a gleaming stripe along its crest, then splashed milk-white foam on the shore.

Clouds drifted in stately solemnity over the sea, their flat bottoms dark, their billows blue-white, their bulbous crowns luminous beneath the moon.

She grew increasingly angry, because the night was so soft, so beautiful, so perfect, and so all the more absurd. She and Ulysses should be running along the shore, chasing the turnstones. They should be swimming in the shimmering water.

They should be—

But she did not want anger to clutter a time that ought to be pure and peaceful. With an abrupt decision, she banished her rage. And in its place, she felt a sudden gratitude. Yes, the night was perfect, honoring Ulysses with a final magnificent evening. As she carried him, she squeezed him against her heart. "Ulysses, we gon' build a beeyoooootiful campfire."

She put him down beside a stack of driftwood she had collected that afternoon. The sticks looked now like a pile of bones. Ulysses sat with his ears perked toward the sea. She asked with a whisper full of suspense, "What yo' see out there? Sea monsters lurkin' in the bay? Yo' keep guard!"

Down the shore stood a cluster of Australian pines, tall and shaggy against the stars. "Ah be right back. Yo' stay. Yo' *stay.*" As she walked toward the pines, she often glanced back, for even these last days when his legs quickly collapsed, he would try to follow her, dragging his hindquarters. But tonight he was more interested in watching for birds.

Crouching beneath the boughs, she gathered handfuls of fallen needles. Then she returned to Ulysses and shaped the needles into a hollow mound on the sand. Over this tinder she built a teepee of twigs. When she lit a match, the needles sparked and popped. The orange flame flickered up into the twigs. The smoke smelled sweet. She added larger sticks, one by one, until the campfire blazed, warming her face. Despite Act Two, she was determined that Act One was going to be a celebration.

Sitting with her legs crossed, she straightened his salty, tattered bandana, Karl's gift, and wondered if she should have washed it for tonight. No, Ah want this night to be as normal as possible.

While she tended the fire, and he sat facing the water, she told him stories. About the time when they camped together on the sandbar and she had forgot to pack his dog food in the sloop. "And yo'," she giggled, "yo' had to eat tuna-noodle casserole for dinner. Yo' looked at me like Ah must be crazy to eat such stuff. Ha! "

She recalled their hike through the mahogany forest with Nick, when a downpour soaked them, but afterward rays of sunshine beamed through holes in the jungle canopy, spotlighting the green dripping trees with patches of gold. "Ah ain' never forget that day."

She scratched his chest and told him about the summer they snuck through mangrove trees toward the mud flats at Great Salt Pond. Hundreds of egrets and stilts, herons and avocets were wading in the shallows. "Yo' stayed right by meh side, silent as a tiger. But oooooh yo' saw them birds! Ah whispered, 'Okay,' and yo' took off like yo' been shot from a cannon. Yo' galloped, blacker and blacker with mud, until yo' filled the whole sky with them big beautiful birds, sweepin' back and forth in crisscrossin' flocks. Oooooh, yo' been in heaven then!" She blew on his ears, tickling him. He gave her a quick kiss, then continued his sharp-eyed survey of the shoreline. "When there ain' been a single bird left on the ground, yo' come runnin' back to me with yo' tongue hangin' out. But yo' wasn't any dog Ah knew. Meh dog been brown, but yo', meh friend, been the blackest creature Ah ever seen! Drippin' with muck. We had to swim in the bay for an hour before yo' come clean. But even then," she brushed her cheek against his soft fur, "it been weeks before yo' stopped stinkin' like that ol' mud flat."

The fire collapsed with a dry crunch; a fountain of sparks joined the stars. Just above the palm thatch, Orion leaned forward as he sprinted across the sky. At his heels leaped his hound with the bright eye. But the constellation was not Orion any more; there was herself running along the shore, and the hunter's sword a stick she was about to throw. Yo' ain' need a marker, Ulysses. Yo' got one already, gon' last me all meh life.

She raked the coals into a circle, placed four conch shells around the periphery and set a wire grill on top of them. Then from her picnic basket she took out the steak, and laid it over the coals. Ulysses stretched his nose toward the sizzling meat. She asked with an excited voice, "Yo' hungry, Bear. Yo' want yo' *dinner*?" He stared at the feast with eager eyes.

When the sirloin was cooked on both sides, she laid it on a driftwood board and cut it into ten pieces. With the tip of her knife, she slit a pocket in each juicy morsel. Then, her fingers trembling, she reached into the basket, took out a small envelope, and inserted a tranquilizer inside each chunk of warm meat.

Ulysses took the chunks gently from her fingers and gobbled them down. But he spat out two of the pills. Feeling like a traitor, she picked the capsules out of the sand, rinsed them with water from a thermos, then held his lower jaw, placed the pills on the back of his tongue, held his muzzle closed and stroked his throat until he swallowed them.

She filled his bowl with water. He drank thirstily.

A breeze quickened over the beach. The circle of coals glowed brightly. Stroking her dog from his head to his bony hips, she sang his name, "Uuuuuulyyyyyyseeeeeeeeeeeeees." She wanted him to fall asleep in a peaceful world where everything was the way it was supposed to be. "Uuuuulyyyyyyysseeeeees."

His head wobbled unsteadily as he gazed with half-closed eyes at the coals.

Karl's dark form emerged from the shadows.

No! she thought desperately. She stopped singing, dug her fingers into Ulysses' fur. She wanted to reach up and grab the swinging pendulum of the moon and cast it into the sea; but she knew the Second Act had begun.

He sat beside her. "How are you?"

She leaned against him. "Not so good."

He scratched Ulysses behind the ears. "Hi, ol' pal. How's our Pirate?"

The dog stared blearily at him and lifted the tip of his tail in greeting.

Karl asked her, "Do you want to take a walk for a little while?"

She would clutch at the stars to keep the sky from turning.

She would cap her hands over the rising sun. "Not yet."

Ulysses laid his muzzle on his paws and closed his eyes.

Her body rocked back and forth with a slow rhythm as she petted him and sang his name, her voice as faint as the glow of the coals, as soft as the breeze through the palm fronds, as pure as the moonlight on the beach, "Uuuuuulyyyyyyyysseeeeeees."

"Thud," came a sound from the water's edge.

Startled, she peered toward the sea, but saw nothing unusual. She wondered if a log had washed up and were bumping the shore.

"Thud."

Ulysses lifted his unsteady head and stared toward the water.

"Thud."

He barked, his voice the high thin cough of an old dog. Then he pushed himself up on his front legs and twisted toward the water, growling.

Cautiously, Angelique stood up. Something black and dome-shaped, like a giant beetle, was emerging from the sea onto the bright sand. It reached forward with two long pointed flippers and dropped them—"thud"—on the beach. With a thrill, she whispered to Karl, "It's a turtle!"

He marveled in a hushed voice, "She must be six feet long."

"She's a leatherback."

Ulysses barked again. Angelique knelt and hushed him, "Shshshsh. She won't hurt us. We ain' want to scare her away." Silent, ears cocked, he stared at the strange creature.

The turtle gasped as she dragged her enormous bulk up the slope. Her flippers, ten feet wide from wingtip to wingtip, left a rippled trail.

Forty feet from the water, she rested.

Then with her rear flippers, she began to dig.

Ulysses pulled against Angelique's arms. He wanted a closer look. She knew that once the nesting process had begun, the turtle would no longer retreat. She braced Ulysses' hips as he staggered forward. He peered warily at the turtle's head, twice the size of his own. The leatherback ignored him. Ulysses led Angelique in a half-circle around the silent, ponderous sea monster, until he stood behind it and stared at the movement of the rear legs. He stretched his nose low to the ground, sniffing.

One flipper, and then the other, scooped up the damp sand and pushed it into piles beside the hole. The flippers moved like giant black hands working in slow motion. When the leatherback had formed a nest a foot wide and three feet deep, she spread her flippers like fans over the top.

She let out a breath as if wind were rushing from a deep cave. Her head slowly bobbed. A clear mucus, rinsing sand from her eyes, trailed like heavy tears down her cheeks. From her jaws burst another enormous breath.

Ulysses stared with keen attention. Angelique lowered his hips so he sat.

Then she and Karl stepped closer. Peering down between the two protective flippers, they glimpsed her treasure: a cluster of white eggs as big as tennis balls. Karl put his arm around Angelique.

Entranced, she studied the five knobby ridges running down the turtle's back. She admired the carapace jutting protectively over the tiny tail: like the ridges and armor of a dinosaur. She watched the turtle do what turtles had done on this beach beneath a million bright moons. She heard the great breaths bursting into the night, and remembered the gasps of her patients, laboring mothers pushing their child closer and closer to life.

Now one flipper reached to the side and dragged a load of sand back into the nest. The flipper reached into the hole and pressed the sand down. Then it fanned once more over the top.

The opposite flipper scraped a second load of sand into the nest and carefully pressed it down.

Ulysses lay down to watch; his eyelids began to droop.

Angelique sat beside him, his last sleepy minutes filled with fascination. She gazed at the turtle, then up at the bone-white moon. Though she had no drum to send her prayer, she thought, T'ank yo'. T'ank yo'.

The leatherback filled her nest with sand, then swept her rear flippers back and forth like two brooms, obscuring the site. She reached her front flippers forward—"thud"—and tossed two great loads of sand into the air. Suddenly covered with grit, Angelique blinked, and laughed out loud. She brushed off Ulysses' face, then lifted him away from the spray the turtle kept throwing behind her.

Dragging herself in a U-shaped path, up the beach, along it, then back toward the water, the turtle cast sand over a large area until her nest was completely hidden.

As she hauled herself toward the sea, Ulysses tried to follow. Angelique walked behind him, bracing his hips.

At the water's edge, a mat of foam washed over the turtle's face. She paused, her head rinsed clean, her back still spattered with sand.

The next wave wrapped around her with bright bubbles. She reached forward—"splash"—and nudged a few inches as the water swept away.

The third wave carried her several feet, swiveled her slightly, then set her down again. She pushed against the soft wet sand.

The trio huddled behind her, watching her departure.

A surge of water carried her out to sea. She swept her long wings and sailed weightlessly, her head etching a silver wake across the black surface.

Ulysses waded after her until he was chest deep. Angelique supported him against the slap and pull of the waves. She wanted to dive in herself, to swim close behind the leatherback. But she held her feeble dog.

The turtle ducked her head and disappeared beneath the shimmering surface. Though Angelique stared for a long minute, scanning back and forth over the bay, the turtle was gone.

Ulysses tried to turn toward shore, but he floundered. Angelique slung her arms beneath him and carried him, his fur dripping, back to the circle of coals and ash. His drugged eyes half-closed, he watched as she added twigs and blew on the coals until she had built up a small flame. He lowered his muzzle to his paws and closed his eyes. Within a minute, he lay unconscious, his head turned slightly on its side.

Karl walked to the jeep and returned with her black bag in one hand, a folded bed sheet and a spade in the other.

Following the relentless script, she opened the bag and took out the hypodermic needle, then a glass vial with a skull and crossbones on it. Not daring to pause in the role she was playing, she stuck the needle into the vial's rubber cap and drew back the plunger, drawing the clear moonlit fluid into the hypo's calibrated tube. Struggling to maintain her professional calm, she turned to Karl and asked, "Do you still want to do it?"

He took the hypodermic from her. "Why don't you go down to the water."

She buried her face in Ulysses' soft fur. "Good-bye, my wonderful friend. Thank you for five and a half precious years." She could no longer hold back the tears. She dug her fingers into his coat. "Ulysses, we . . . "

She looked up at Karl's anguished face in the firelight. "I want to hold him," she said. "I want to be here."

She watched as he pushed the needle into Ulysses' shoulder. His thumb pressed the plunger.

Ulysses' eyes opened wide. Awakened by a surge of feeling, he raised his head and stared hard at the light of the flames.

Then his head slowly lowered, and lay beside his paws on the sand.

Karl drew out the needle. Angelique pulled the limp dog into her lap and hugged him while she cried with blind, wrenching shrieks.

When she looked up, Karl was gone. Her black bag was gone, and the picnic basket was gone. She gazed numbly across the dark bay. Zosia's round window, filled with fragments of color, shone in the night. Zosia and Karl would be waiting for her.

But the script was not finished. She looked down at Ulysses:

his head drooped from her lap. His tongue hung out of his mouth. She tucked it back inside his teeth. Then she laid his body beside the circle of ashes.

She stood, opened the sheet and spread it on the sand. Picked up Ulysses, his forelegs dangling now as his rear legs had dangled before. Placed him on the radiant white cloth. Folded one corner up, one corner down. Tied the other two corners together, lifted the loop over her head and stood with Ulysses slung in a hammock across her chest. She reached for the spade.

As she walked along the water's edge toward the far end of the beach, she hugged his warmth against her.

Fringing the last thirty yards of beach was a flat bank covered with grass, well above the reach of storm waves. She stumbled with her burden up the bluff, then waded through knee-deep grass. Lifted the heavy loop over her head and set Ulysses down. Opened the sheet so the moon could shine on him.

Stepping on the spade with her bare feet, she shoved its blade through thick roots, outlining the grave. Lifted out chunks of sod and tossed them aside. Dug down several feet; piled the loose damp sand beside the hole.

When the job was done, she crouched beside Ulysses and ruffled his ears. Tried to sing, "Uuuuuulyy--" But her voice cracked. She forced out the hoarse words, "Ah come visit yo'."

She straightened his wet bandana. Patted his strong shoulder. Folded one corner of the sheet up, one corner neatly down. Straddled her legs over the grave and lowered him to the bottom. She turned her eyes away as she shoveled in the first load of sand. Only when he was covered could she watch her work.

She did not replace the chunks of sod, but returned to the beach several times for shovelfuls of dry white sand. On the last trip, she stuck the spade into the beach, scooped up two handfuls of sand, walked back through the parted grass and let the sand sift through her fingers like fine white sugar.

She knelt, and imagined Ulysses' shoulder as she patted the grave. The imprint of her hand showed clearly in the moonlight.

TONY THE TORSO

from the novel "CHILDREN OF THE SUN"

Today's the day we remember. And there's a certain vet who deserves remembering. If you don't mind, I'd like to tell you about Tony.

After Joe's funeral, I heard that another guy from DeKalb, a guy named Tony Montadori, was in Great Lakes Naval Hospital recovering from wounds he'd received in Vietnam. I knew Tony vaguely—he had played shortstop with Joe on the Little League Team—so I thought I'd go visit him. To cheer him up, y'know. I knew that Joe would've made the trip. So I called Tony's home and spoke with his father. Mr. Montadori sounded grateful, and he gave me directions to the Navy base. It was north of Chicago, about two hours' drive from DeKalb. I was seventeen and I had my driver's license, and Pop said I could take the Chevy. This was just before Christmas, you see, the first Christmas without Joe, and I was trying to do something positive, because I was feeling pretty rotten.

I found the Navy base all right. I can remember that as I walked from the parking lot toward the hospital, the elms were covered with ice because there'd been a storm off Lake Michigan the night before. The branches were click-clacking against each other in the wind.

Inside the hospital, up on the third floor, I was directed through a pair of swinging doors. I entered an enormous room with two aisles and at least a hundred beds. The aisle in front of me stretched all the way across the ward. It was lined on both sides with small American flags, like a street decorated for a parade. Each flag stood on a stick taped to the foot of the bed, so every sailor knew what he had been fighting for and why he had ended up in that bed.

I was stunned by the pandemonium. The ward was filled with the noise of televisions and shouting men. I asked an orderly—I had to holler to make myself heard—if he knew where I could find Tony Montadori. He pointed down the aisle. "Two-thirds the way down, on the left." Feeling pretty self-conscious, because I was healthy, I could walk, and I hadn't done a darn thing for my country, I started down the aisle.

Televisions hung from the ceiling over every bed. Most of them were on and they were cranked up loud, though there weren't three in a row tuned to the same channel. I glanced at one guy whose face was scar tissue. He was staring up at his television. I couldn't see the screen. I could see only his dead-looking blue eyes—utterly blank—staring at that television. And I could hear the buzzer and clanging bell of a quiz show, and some woman cheering and clapping because she'd just won a trip for two to Hawaii.

Over the racket of the televisions, the guys were shouting to each other from bed to bed. Hollering back and forth, one man louder than the next. It was such a madhouse in there, that all of a sudden I wanted to get out. I nearly turned around and bolted toward the door. But I didn't, because I'd come to visit Joe's friend, and I knew that Joe would've stayed and said hello. Joe would never have bolted. So I kept on walking down that aisle.

I found Tony, having a bath. Two orderlies were sponge-bathing him. He needed help, you see, because Tony had no arms or legs. He was only a torso covered with lumpy yellow-white scar tissue. The one part of Tony that hadn't been burnt was his face. He had a handsome Italian face, and lots of curly black hair. I didn't introduce myself just then, of course. I stood near his bed, waiting until he was done with his bath.

The orderlies scrubbed his bumpy chest. They rolled him over and scrubbed his back. Then they turned him over again and washed his hair. They did a good job, those two. They gave him a nice vigorous massage, and rinsed his hair well, and dried it with a towel and then with a hair blower. But they didn't say much, and Tony never said anything. He just let them do their job.

When he was clean and dry, one orderly lifted him in his arms while the other changed the sheets. Then they laid him down and put a fresh jock strap on him, for as badly hurt as he was, he still had . . . well, there was part of him still there.

The orderlies pulled the sheet up to his chin and moved on to the next bed. I thought that now I would introduce myself. But I hesitated. Because Tony just lay there, staring up at the ceiling. I didn't know if he wanted to be disturbed. I stared at his pale, handsome face gazing up from those bushy black curls. He was so detached from the wild uproar around him, I suddenly wondered if he was deaf.

Suddenly a voice called from the end of the ward, "Gentlemen!" I saw a seaman in a white uniform standing by the swinging doors. He cupped his hands and shouted, "Could we turn down those televisions, please?"

No one paid the slightest bit of attention to him.

"Gentlemen, this concerns the visitation today by a number of young ladies."

Then, *then*, the place went totally nuts. The TVs were drowned out by hoots and catcalls. Sailors pumped their fists in the air. The seaman in his white uniform raised his arms to quiet the ward, then he reached for a microphone on the wall. Across the ceiling, speakers boomed with his voice, "Gentle—", but a piercing electronic squeal filled the room, so loud I couldn't even hear the men. The seaman adjusted a dial on the wall. "Gentlemen. Coming your way today are twenty-seven young ladies from the major stores in downtown Chicago." The men in their beds bellowed and roared. "These salesgirls bring Christmas gifts donated by Marshall Fields, Carson Pirie Scott, Montgomery Wards, Sears, and let's see . . . "He checked his clipboard.

A sailor in the bed beside Tony's sang out, "I know what I want! Roll me over, in the clooooover!" Well, I'd best not get too graphic. Anyway, the seaman at the microphone admonished his troops, "Gentlemen, as members of the U.S. Armed Forces, you will conduct yourselves with all proper accord."

About a minute later, the women came in through the swinging doors. They were nicely dressed, each of them carrying a box wrapped with Christmas paper. But they huddled by the doors. Some whispered, most were silent, as they stared nervously at the room filled with wild men shouting at them.

Slowly, the noise subsided. One by one the televisions were turned down, until the ward became almost silent, filled with expectation. One of the women, a brave one, walked out from the cluster to a nearby bed. She was a redhead with big gold rings on her ears. She said to the delighted sailor, "Hi. I'm Anne."

The other women began to disperse through the room. There were only twenty-seven of them, and there must have been a hundred men. It seemed like poor planning, but the guys didn't mind. Five or six would call for one girl's attention while she stood in the middle of an aisle, and she would try to talk with all of them at once. Some of the men didn't say anything. They seemed glad just to stare at a pretty woman.

I looked at Tony. He had rolled his head on his pillow so he could watch one of the women walking down the aisle in his direction. She had long blonde hair with perfectly cut bangs, and a nice pink sweater. Her face was frozen as she glanced from side to side, her shoulders lifted with fright. Several men called to her, but she walked past them. When Tony saw she was going to walk past him too, he lifted his head and even his chest with surprisingly strong stomach muscles. The sheet fell to his waist. "Hello," he called to her. "I'm Tony."

She stared at his armless torso and put her hand over her mouth. She dropped her gift on the floor—it was a long narrow box with ribbons, maybe a fishing rod—then she turned and shoved through the women behind her and ran up the aisle between all those flags toward the door. Tony stared at her. She cried out something, words I couldn't understand. But Tony understood. His eyes were dark points that saw into the whole rest of his life.

She threw open those swinging doors and disappeared.

Tony lay back down. Then with a snapping motion, he jerked his shoulders so hard that he rose right up on the stubs of his thighs, and there he balanced in his jock strap. He looked like a Roman torso carved in marble, rough-hewn. He stared toward that door with an anguish I'll never forget.

Then he threw his head to one side, toppling himself out of bed so that he crashed on the floor. Someone shouted, "Medic!" Tony arched his back and smashed his forehead against the floor as hard as he could. He arched and banged his head again, and again. Blood splattered across the tiles. An orderly came dashing up the aisle. He wrapped his arms around the writhing torso, lifted Tony onto the bed and buckled the straps. Tony's face was covered with blood. He was shrieking incoherently. A second orderly stuck a needle into his shoulder. Tony convulsed under the straps for another half-minute, his handsome Italian face turning red as he screamed like someone burning at the stake.

Finally he lost consciousness. The orderly pulled the bed on its wheels into the aisle, then he pushed it, American flag flapping, up the aisle away from the women. At the far end of the ward, he pushed Tony out through another set of swinging doors.

The entire ward was dead silent. I could feel my heart pounding. Then a sailor near me said, "Aw, never mind, Mary Beth. This place gets a little crazy. Where ya from, Mary Beth?"

Conversations began again. I'd been in that room for maybe fifteen minutes. I hadn't said a word to anyone. No one had noticed me. I hurried down the aisle and pushed out through the swinging doors. The blonde woman was in the lobby, sobbing in a chair. A couple of other women were kneeling in front of her, trying to talk with her. I dashed down the flights of stairs and bolted out the front door and took a huge breath of the cold December air.

FLYPAPER PHIL

In a small town on the Maryland-Virginia border, half of the town in Maryland, half in Virginia, stands a bronze statue of a man who holds a strip of bronze flypaper. He extends his arm as if he held a sword or a Bible. But no, he holds flypaper. Bronze flies are stuck along the length of the spiral strip. A plaque on the pedestal to this monument reads, "Dedicated to the Spirit of Flypaper Phil." Flypaper Phil, as anyone in the town will tell you, did not invent flypaper. He didn't even own the Flypaper Factory at the edge of town. He was just a worker there.

Nobody knows in which state the town was first settled. It simply grew, generation after generation, on both sides of the border. Neighbors tipped their hats and said "Good morning!" to neighbors. They brought picnic baskets to the town park every Fourth of July. No one thought it really mattered what state the town belonged to. Until the troubles of 1861. Then, hearing the call of two different bugles, townfolk seemed to lose their minds. Fistfights in the schoolyard ended with bloody noses. Families gathered for Sunday dinner abruptly stood up from the table half way through the meal and shouted curses at each other. And the men at the Flypaper Factory argued with an anger never before known in that peaceful little town.

This calamity was witnessed by Flypaper Phil, known then simply as Phil, a quiet fellow who stirred the glue in the vats at the Flypaper Factory to be sure it had just the right stickiness. Phil stirred the glue and listened to the quarreling among his friends. He stirred the glue and watched the two sides eat their lunches at opposite ends of the factory. On the day that War was officially declared, he came to work and found the factory empty. Some of the men had joined the Confederate Army, and the rest had joined the Union Army. Phil went home and told his wife about the empty Flypaper Factory. She asked him what he was going to do. He said he didn't know.

The men were gone for several months with their armies, bombing the North, burning the South. Now they returned to conquer their town. Men who once had been master glue mixers now marched as sharpshooters and cannoneers. The Gray made their camp in a woods. No invader from the open plain could overwhelm the Gray soldiers ranged behind the trunks of oak. The forest was their fortress. The Blue made their camp on a hilltop, with sentries behind every rock. Between the woods and the hill lay a broad grassy meadow. At the western edge of the meadow stood the Flypaper Factory. On its loading dock, where wagons once had pulled up for shipments of flypaper, stood Phil. He looked at the smoke rising from dinner fires in the woods. He saw flames flicker from dinner fires on the hilltop. Tomorrow at dawn the bugles would sound, and his friends would meet their death in that meadow.

Phil worked all night. He drove a wagon, pulled by the four strongest horses in town, through the darkness to a valley in Virginia which a week ago had been a battleground. The valley was covered now with fresh graves and empty brass shells from rifles and artillery. The shells glittered in the flickering light of Phil's pineknot torch, and he had no trouble finding every empty casing on both sides of the creek. He loaded them into his wagon.

The clock on the church steeple in town read five minutes after midnight when Phil drove the wagon to the loading dock of the Flypaper Factory. The clock read ten minutes after three when he drove away. He headed straight toward the woods.

Only an hour remained before dawn when he drove his empty wagon out of the woods and trotted his horses back to the Flypaper Factory. Half an hour later, he drove up the hillside.

Down the hill he drove his empty wagon in the first light of day. Phil was standing on the loading dock when the sun rose over the meadow, blood red.

The soldiers in both camps prepared bayonets. Every man rechecked his rifle. Every cannoneer made double sure his charge and fuse were ready. The bugles sounded their challenge. Cannons appeared at the edge of the hilltop. Cannons appeared between the trees at the edge of the woods. The great guns aimed down from the rocky castle, and pointed up from the wooded fortress.

Now down the hillside marched the infantry, rifles readied as their drums beat a tattoo. And out from the trees marched the infantry, rifles readied as their drums beat a tattoo. Behind them on the hillside pranced the cavalry, ready to gallop toward the enemy's flank. And behind them on the plain pranced the cavalry, ready to gallop toward the enemy's flank. The flapping proud banner of the Blue advanced toward the flapping proud banner of the Gray.

No one knows who fired the first shot. With a Rebel yell and a Yankee howl, the march became a charge. Cannons roared, rifles cracked, and the two armies surged toward each other beneath twin blasts of what they thought were grapeshot and bullets. Phil stood on the loading dock and grinned.

Through the air flew two thousand uncoiling flypapers, glopped with glue. Staring with astonishment and horror, the Yanks and Rebs watched the familiar curlicues come soaring toward them. The air was so thick with those twin volleys of flypaper that no bird, bat or bee between them could have hoped to escape. Had someone actually fired a bullet from the hill's craggy top, the slug of lead would, midflight, have oozed to a stop.

The night before, Phil had driven his wagon into the Gray camp with fresh shells for the battle. "Just shipped in," he told the camp commander, "from the armament works in Richmond. Use these shells first. They're guaranteed." The riflemen took the old shells out of their rifles and loaded up with these new ones. The cannoneers hefted the new shells into the breeches of their cannons. Everyone trusted Phil. He said that he had finally made up his mind.

Less than an hour later, Phil had driven his wagon into the Blue camp with fresh shells for the battle. "Just shipped in," he told the camp commander, "from the armament works in Baltimore. Use these shells first. They're guaranteed." Everyone trusted Phil. He had been their friend for years. He had finally made up his mind.

The flypaper struck its targets with a slap and a whap of curlicued glue. Soldiers snared by long sticky strips kicked and struggled, for the guck was stuck to their pistols and wound around their bayonets and firmly affixed to their shiny brass buttons. Captains discovered their swords adorned with stuff that proved impossible to remove. Cannoneers still holding lighted matches found flypaper draped over their smoking muzzles, and their mustaches.

Horses whinneyed and reared, smeared with glue, and soon they adhered two by two in a coagulate that grew until the whole herd cohered, (the same as true for the Gray as the Blue).

These great armies, though grievously impeded, struggled forward, undeterred by what had occurred, until finally they surged upon each other in hand-to-hand combat. They wrestled and they lunged and they punched, until they had become one adhesive mass of soldiers stuck together in the green meadow grass.

Amid the curses and the snarls and the gasps, a soldier started to laugh. No one knew to which army he belonged, the Gray or the Blue. Impossible to tell, in all that glue. But every warrior there will swear it's true: somebody guffawed with glee at the fool in front of him, who flailed and flounced and floundered in a filigree of flypaper.

One by one, the Rebs and the Yanks began to chuckle, laugh and howl at the fix they were in.

On the loading dock stood Phil with a satisfied grin.

* * *

Today in the town square stands a bronze statue of Flypaper Phil. Not a shot was fired in or near that town for the remainder of the War. Brother worked beside brother in the Flypaper Factory, father beside son. Demand for flypaper elsewhere in the nation was at an ebb, but that did not deter townfolk. They hung flypaper in every room in the house, down in the cellar, up in the attic, and a dozen strips at least out on the front porch. It was the worst town for a fly to pass through anywhere in America.

Even now, more than a century later, there's not a bedroom nor a barber shop in town without at least one spiral coil of flypaper dangling in it. And once a month, volunteers polish the statue in the park until it gleams. Young boys are brought on their birthdays with a brand-new handkerchief to shine the curlicue of bronze flypaper with bronze flies stuck to it.

Because people never want to forget the spirit of Flypaper Phil.

Men of Stone

Only with great reluctance did She decide that one creature would eat another. She had bestowed life upon the fishes of the sea, and the beasts of the earth, and the birds of the sky, and she was not pleased when one of her treasures abruptly ended its life in the gullet of another.

Her plants did not eat each other, but fed from the sun. Rooted to the earth, they opened their leaves to the light in the sky. Her animals, however, free from bondage to the earth, had paid for their freedom by forfeiting their bond with the sun. They could roam the land, swim the seas, and soar across the sky, but they fed upon her plants, or upon each other. Life must feed upon life, thereby bringing death into her world.

With compassion in her heart, She ordained that the spirit of her animals might escape death. While the great fishes ate the smaller fishes, and while the wolves devoured the calves, and the eagle swooped down to catch the hare, a multitude of spirits rose up to her. She cupped them with her hands, and bent her face over them, and she breathed her breath upon them, filling each spirit with renewed life. Then she blew upon them, and sent these spirits on the river of wind from her lips back down to the earth, where they brought new life to the sea and to the land and to the sky.

So beautiful were the treasures of her world, and so great was her love for them, that She conceived a great desire to share her world with others. New creatures would She create, with eyes that could see beauty, and with hearts, like her own, that could love. Man She created, and woman She created, with eyes that beheld the beauty of the rolling sea, and in the fertile green land, and in the ever-changing sky. And man and woman had eyes to behold as well the beauty in each other.

Man She created, and woman She created, and She gave them hearts that could love the creatures of the sea, and the creatures of the land, and the creatures of the sky. And man could love woman, and woman could love man.

Even as She loved all She had created, so She cupped in her hands the spirit of a man, and the spirit of a woman, and She warmed them with her breath, and blew them on the river of wind from her lips down to the earth, where they and their children and their children's children could behold and love the treasures of the world, and could behold and love each other.

Among the multitude of spirits rising into her cupped hands, now rose the spirits of old women, who at the end of their years had lain upon the earth in peace. And the spirits of old men rose unto her, men who at the end of their years had lain upon the earth in peace. Into her hands as well came the spirits of children, who had lain upon the earth in sickness. And of young women, who had lain upon the earth in the pains of childbirth. And of young men, caught by the claws and teeth of the bears they hunted. For such were the ways of the world She had created. She bent her face over the spirits of children and young women and young men, and over the spirits of old women and old men, and She comforted them in her hands. She blew her warm breath over them, and She sent them down on the river of wind from her lips back to the earth. Like wheat planted in the furrowed soil, these spirits, replenished with life, were planted in the loins of women, and in the loins of men, that man and woman together might make a new life.

* * *

Now it came to pass, that spirits rose from the earth which were unlike any spirits that She had cradled in her hands. These now were wounded and torn, and they did not rise to her in peace, but with cries of anguish. She cupped them in her hands, and She saw that her hands were stained with red.

Looking down upon her world, She stared with disbelief as soldiers plundered a town, then butchered with their swords and axes all who had lived within.

Though her anger against the soldiers was great, her anger against herself was greater, for She had failed. She had failed to give her people a heart that could love as strongly as her own heart could love. Their hearts were weak, and so they fought, counting as nothing the precious life She had given them.

They will learn, She thought. Surely they will learn from their suffering never to fight each other again. She did not reach down to stop the battle, as She did not stop the fish from swimming, or the birds from flying, or the great herds from roaming the earth, but let all creatures live according to their nature.

She bent her face over the spirits of children who had been slain, and women who had been slain, and warriors who had butchered until they too had been slain. She did not blow these spirits on the river of wind back down to the earth. She opened her lips, and She inhaled all who had died from a plague of man's own making. She who had created these spirits took them once again inside her, and She kept them in her heart. In her heart, where they might be comforted, and where they might learn.

* * *

But the peoples dwelling below in the world, they did not learn. Into her hands She gathered torn and battered and broken spirits, and these She took into her heart. Centuries passed, and She gathered spirits by the thousandfold, no longer bludgeoned by axes and pierced by swords, but brought to earth by a tiny stone of lead. She witnessed man's ability to learn, for he forged weapons ever more ferocious.

The carnage spread across the land, and over the sea and into the sky. Her garden had become a battlefield, where prayers imploring victory came from nearly every quarter, while prayers of gratitude for sunshine and birdsong came from nearly none. Before, She had smiled between each breath of life. Now She frowned with deepening anger as She blew down life, and inhaled death, and blew down life, and inhaled death.

Until the day came when her heart was full, and She could bear the agony of no more children who had been shot and bombed and poisoned and burned, or buried alive in the rubble of their homes.

Stepping down in the darkness of night, over the ravaged land She walked, from country to country, from town to town.

When the people awakened on the following morning, they found in their towns and in their cities and on the lawns in front of their palaces and parliaments a multitude of stone slabs, standing upright. Upon them was written:

> He who raises his weapon against another,
> He who bears a weapon in his hands,
> He who builds the arms of war,
> He who sells the arms of war,
> Shall become men of stone.

For several days, men discussed among each other, and in their newspapers and on television, who it might have been who could have stood a million stones around the world in one night. Many conjectured, many were adamant, but no one really knew. So the discussions took a new direction, as people debated the rightness or wrongness of each of the four categories addressed in the cryptic message.

The prohibition against raising weapons against each other: yes, that was clear enough. Of course the ancient habits of war were barbaric, and any right-thinking person preferred peace. How often had people shaken their heads at the wars that seemed to smolder and blaze up endlessly in Africa, in central Europe, in southern Asia, in Latin America. Those folks just never seemed to get tired of killing each other.

But this caution against bearing arms? Surely a man had the

right to stand at the ready, prepared to defend his country, his family, his beliefs.

Those who manufactured the weapons of war: were they not patriots who provided their nation with the means with which to warn all other nations to beware? The modern blacksmiths, forging their electronic weapons, were surely the keepers of peace.

And the merchants? Those who strengthened the armies of their allies, and thereby filled their own nation's coffers: were they not patriots too?

Clearly, whoever had inscribed those slabs did not understand the unfortunate reality of today's world. It's dog-eat-dog out there, and top dog wins. If he's a well-behaved dog, as certainly we try to be, he'll merely growl, and upon occasion, snap if he must. Dog fights we don't really want anymore, but that certainly does not mean that we are willing to give up our teeth.

The stones were bulldozed, or covered with tarps, or ignored. And day after day, decade after decade, the hands of the creator were stained with red.

Whereas in the old days She had held in her hands more soldiers than children, She now held more children than soldiers. For less and less did soldiers battle with each other, and more and more did they turn their weapons upon each other's peoples. Soldiers no longer fought to conquer, but to eliminate.

Her anger became so great that She wished these people to live no more. She would send down her breath of life to the wildflowers. She would send down her breath of life to the birds, and to the fishes, and to the dwindling herds. So She had done and so She would continue to do. But no longer would She send down the breath of life to these people who had eyes that could not see beauty, and hearts that could not love. She would let them butcher themselves unto extinction, according to their nature.

Thus in her anger was She determined to let her people die.

But her heart told her otherwise.

No, She could not bring to an end that which She had once

created. She would begin anew. If their hearts of stone would not learn, then shall they themselves become men of stone.

Reaching down toward a country where neighbor fought neighbor, She held her hand in front of the sun, so the country lay in the shadow of her hand. When She took her hand away, and the sun once more shone upon the land, She heard a great stillness. Children peered out from the wreckage of their homes. Women stepped into the rubble-cluttered streets. Old people looked up at the sun and felt its warmth on their faces.

But the soldiers who had aimed their artillery down from the surrounding hills at apartment buildings and factories and hospitals and schools . . . had become a ring of stone statues. Their cannons and their rifles, now with barrels made of stone, were silent.

She passed her hand over country after country, darkening the sun, darkening the sun, darkening the sun. Wherever the shadow of her hand passed, warriors became statues, hurling stone grenades, aiming stone rifles with stone bayonets, smoking stone cigarettes, their laughter and their curses as silent as their guns.

Generals in their tanks, ministers in their palaces and parliaments, presidents in their offices—all who issued the orders of war—were turned to stone. The speechmaker standing in front of a battery of microphones, shaking his fist in the air as he encouraged his countrymen to conquer their foe, became an open-mouthed statue of stone.

The great warships at sea, She turned to stone and watched them sink. The great warplanes in the sky, She turned to stone and watched them plummet. The missiles in their silos, She turned to great stones within the earth.

Until in all her round garden, every gun was stilled.

In her mercy, She smote not the standing armies, nor the governments who believed in strength as the key to peace. But their arsenals, their rifles and mines and jeeps and trucks and tanks, She turned to stone.

In her Mercy, She smote not the builders of weapons, for

they too believed they had labored for peace. But their computers, their scale models, their testing facilities, She turned to stone. Their research and development laboratories became palaces of stone.

Woe to the profiteers who sold the tools of death. In their offices, while placing orders on a telephone; in secret hotel rooms, today meeting with generals from the north, tomorrow with generals from the south; on their yachts, in their swimming pools, on the seventeenth green, She turned them into stone. Weapons merchants, weapons brokers, weapons expediters, hawkers and clients and financial advisors at international arms bazaars, all became, as the sun above them darkened, stone.

Her hand passed over the troubled cities, where a kind of warfare seethed among the people. On street corners and in alleys, in the stairwells and on the subway, in the hands and in the homes of people who knew not their purpose in the world, switchblades and pistols and semi-automatic rifles became sandstone that crumbled into pebbles.

Now She drew back her hand, and once again the sun shone upon her world. The sea glittered, the mountains rose exultant into the blue sky, and to her ears came the songs of birds, the whisper of the wind, the laughter of falling water.

And now to her ears came as well, from inside the ring of stone soldiers, from the streets of a hundred cities, from the crossroads of a thousand thatched hamlets, from the dungeons beneath the palaces and parliaments, a multitude of prayers. Thanking her for sunshine. Thanking her for birdsong. Thanking her for peace.

She cupped her hands, and into them She blew a thousand spirits whom she had kept and comforted in her heart. Spirits fresh from learning the lessons of her heart, She blew into her cupped hands. She breathed her warm breath over them, filling each with the breath of life. Then She blew them on the river of wind from her lips down to the earth, into the loins of women, into the loins of men, that together men and women might bring forth children who understood the beauty of a butterfly that alights atop the stone grenade in the stone hand of the stone soldier who once, long ago, was hurling death at his enemy.

NOAH AND THE BEGINNING

Noah was an old man, an ancient wise man, who plowed with his sons in the fertile earth, and cared well for his cattle, and obeyed the word of the Lord every day of his life. He was careful in what he said and in all he did, and he thought deeply day and night of the work he should rightly do, so never to transgress the law of God, and never to transgress himself.

Since the beginning years of the world, the people of Noah's country had gathered every seventh day to sacrifice a lamb on the altar, and to kneel and pray according to the law of God. For many years had Noah knelt and prayed with the people of his country. On the Sabbath afternoons, he invited his neighbors to his house, so he could share with them his food and wine. Even in the barren years without rain, he brought them home and fed them well, for he knew that next spring, or perhaps the spring thereafter, the rains would return and the earth would again be green. If he but prayed and waited, the rain always fell, and the people of his country said that Noah was wise in the goodness of the Lord.

But today, only Noah and his wife and his sons and his sons' wives had knelt before the altar to send up their prayers to God. They alone had knelt and prayed, as they had knelt and prayed alone for over a year. Noah thought of the people of his country, thought of his neighbors, one by one, and he shook his old head that they had not been with him to speak the ancient words. Noah knew that God was watching His people, that God had seen the temple nearly empty. And Noah ached in his heart.

Noah and his wife and his sons and his sons' wives walked

home alone from the temple. Shem, the oldest son of Noah, walked at the side of his father and looked in the direction of his father's house. He looked to see if people were waiting at the gate, for though they no longer knelt at the altar, they came still to Noah's house, and with him ate the Sabbath feast. Noah asked his countrymen, speaking quietly with each man, why they made no sacrifice, why they sent up no prayers, but he always fed them well. Then fewer of his people had come to his house, and though Noah no longer asked them questions, even fewer came. Shem, as he walked, looked in the direction of his father's house.

Shem was a shepherd who kept the sheep of Noah, for Noah had a great herd. Shem slept during the warm nights and during the cold nights in distant fields, but he returned every Sabbath to the house of Noah, that he could walk with his family to the temple of the Lord. With his father's blessing he had married a girl from the village, and he walked with her now beside his wise and righteous father in the direction of his father's house. And Shem was silent.

Ham, the second son of Noah, walked with Noah, his eyes lifted up to the mountains. Ham had wanted when still a boy to take a tent up into the mountain wilderness, there to dwell with God. But Noah said No, stay with your people. A man, said Noah, should live with men to help them in the bad years and to enjoy with them the good. So Ham stayed, and when he was grown, he married the daughter of a neighboring farmer. But today, though his wife walked beside him, her father and her mother and her brothers and her sisters had not knelt at the altar, and Ham was silent.

Japheth, the third son of Noah, was a giant man, and a carpenter. Japheth went to the forests with an ox and cart, gone for days in the places he knew, and when he returned the cart was laden with logs for lumber. Once he brought to his father an empty cart and a girl from a distant village, and he married her with his father's blessing. Japheth had built the altar, and as he walked today, he was silent.

Noah's wife spoke to Noah, but he was distant in thought and did not hear. She often spoke more loudly than Noah thought a woman should, but she worked with Noah all the years of her womanhood, mothered his sons well, and obeyed him always. Noah's wife loved Noah, and after she spoke she fell silent.

Shem turned to Noah and said that at the house, there was no one. Noah looked across the fields and saw his gate, where no one waited. Then he stared down at the dust of the dry earth on which he walked. Noah and his wife and his sons and his sons' wives walked together from the altar where no one else had been, to the house where no one was, walked in the dust of the dry earth, and in their hearts they grieved.

God looked down upon the world in all its places. The Lord listened on this Sabbath for the ancient words, and in all the world He found only Noah and the family of Noah who spoke them. He listened to their prayers and He was pleased, but their prayers could not fill the silence that covered the earth. God looked in every place and found men asleep, men plowing their fields, men drinking wine and eating of the fattened calf. And He found men ranged by the thousandfold on the border of another people's land, arming for war, and from these warriors rose a noise which was not according to the law of God. Yea, God found Noah and his wife and his sons and his sons' wives, these alone who came to him with obedience and peace in their hearts, only eight of all the peoples of the world.

* * *

On the evening of the Sabbath, Noah went outside to his well to draw water. As he brought up the bucket on its rope, he heard a great thunderclap, though the sky was filled with stars. Then a voice spoke down to Noah, and Noah fell to his knees, spilling the water, for he was sore afraid. From the firmament spoke the voice of the Lord unto Noah, saying, "Thee have I seen righteous before me in this generation. The earth is filled with violence, but with thee will I establish my covenant." Noah trembled, his hands upon the dust of the dry earth, as the voice of the Lord spoke unto him, "Make thee an ark of gopher wood. For I will cause it to rain upon the earth for forty days and forty nights; and every living substance that I have made will I destroy from off the face of the earth."

Noah lifted his face to the firmament and asked about his countrymen, if they too would build ships. But God said there would be one ark, and the rest of the world would be flooded.

Noah lowered the bucket again into the well, and drew up water, and walked with the water to his house and gave the water to his wife. He told her of the Lord's commandment, and of His covenant, for she had heard nothing. All night he was not able to sleep, and he was awake when the sun rose. Through the night Noah had thought of the people of his country, but in the morning he went out with his sons and began to build the ark.

Noah made the ark three hundred cubits long, and the breadth of it was fifty cubits, and the height of it thirty cubits, as the Lord had told him, of gopher wood pitched inside and out. Japheth, the carpenter, fashioned three decks with his great axe. These decks he built open in the middle, so Noah could see up or down, forward or aft, to every place inside the ark. Japheth built hutches and dovecotes and stalls, and troughs for water and bins for grain. With his great axe labored Japheth, according to the Lord's commandment to his father.

The wives gathered the grains of the field into baskets, then stored these baskets in the holds of the ship. They piled sheaves of grass against the ribs of the ship. They filled lamps with oil and put them in every corner, for the ark would be sealed from the light of the sky outside.

Now the people of Noah's country came to see Noah once more. But Noah hid inside the ship he was building. The people shouted questions to him, but Noah told his family to answer nothing. More people came, and one called him friend again. Noah saw no clouds in the sky, and heard not the voice of God, but he listened to the voices of his people. Each night he made himself measure board lengths in his mind, and he hammered as loudly as he could each day.

Noah and the family of Noah were at their labors inside the ark when they heard a tapping on its roof. They looked up. The tapping, the knocking and the banging spread across the roof. And now from the walls of the hull, they heard a thumping that was not the sound of a hail storm. Noah climbed the ladder which Japheth had built from the bottom deck to a hatch in the roof. Carefully lifting the hatch, Noah looked out. Thirty cubits below were the people of his country, many hundreds of them, throwing rocks at the ark and now at him as they cursed his name. These, his people, stayed for three days, and then they began to throw rocks at each other. Noah saw them fall into groups and move slowly away, stoning each other and leaving a scattered path of the crawling and the dead. From the open hatch watched Noah, and in his heart he grieved.

When Noah and the sons of Noah had finished the ark, Japheth drove his great axe into a beam to show that they were done. The day was not a Sabbath, but Noah said that his family could rest. They slept through the afternoon, until Noah heard in a dream—but it was not a dream, for when he awoke, he continued to hear—the trumpeting of an elephant from outside the ark. With Japheth's help he lowered the ramp by its ropes, and he discovered, lined two by two and waiting quietly, every animal from all parts of the earth. The animals marched up the ramp and into the ark, and birds flew down through the hatch. Noah and the family of Noah watched with reverence as the covenant of the Lord began to be fulfilled.

After seven days, a pair of oxen clattered with their heavy hooves up the ramp, the last of the animals to enter the ship. Turning his face to the rising wind, Noah beheld a bank of black clouds about to swallow the afternoon sun. He and Japheth drew up the ramp. They knotted the ropes, and with pitch they sealed the hull tight.

Noah climbed the ladder to the hatch. He looked down at

the land, empty save for his farmhouse and his barn, his deserted crops, the stumps of trees which Japheth had felled for lumber, and the flock of bleating sheep he had left behind. Noah's wife lit the lamps in every corner of the ark, and then Noah drew shut and sealed the hatch. He climbed down the ladder and stood beside his wife, and the faith of Noah was great against the thunder that rumbled in the west.

Rain pattered on the roof, and Noah could no longer hear the flapping of the birds inside the ark. The rain hammered in sheets across the roof, and Noah could no longer hear the lowing of the cattle in the ark. Now the inside of the hull roared with the blast of a tempest driven against the ship. Noah and Noah's wife and his sons and his sons' wives stood in pairs, and they listened as the storm raged with the full fury of God's anger against the wicked of the earth. Noah's wife turned to Noah, and Noah said unto her, and unto all his family, his voice loud above the roar of the storm, "It is good." For Noah had a covenant with God, a covenant to keep the animals and to preserve their breath of life, until the day when he would lead his family down the ramp and set his foot upon the earth of a new world. Yea, he had a covenant to make a new beginning upon the earth.

After twelve days, Noah and the family of Noah began to hear, along with the sound of the rain and the wind sweeping across the ark, the sound of water streaming over the ground beneath the keel. The water deepened, washing higher and higher in waves against the planks, until the lower deck became quiet, protected from the lashing winds. The slap of the waves had risen above Noah's head when, with a heave that shook every creature in the ark, and then threw them to the decks, the great ship moved in the water and began to float.

* * *

The storm dulled in Noah's ears to an endless drumming. The cattle feasted from the troughs of grain and began to show a chubbiness around their bellies. Noah slaughtered newborn lambs and calves for the meat-eaters. Japheth had built a spigot into the hull of the ark, so there was water to last forever.

Noah and the family of Noah worked hard, ate well, and slept quietly.

After forty days and forty nights of rain, the drumming on the roof diminished, and the rumble of thunder slowly faded, until the sky became silent. Noah could hear the cooing of the doves, the lowing of his cattle, and the beating of his heart. He climbed the ladder, past the watchful eyes of all the animals, and he opened the hatch and filled the ark with light. His sons shouted up with joy at the light from the gray sky, and his wife both laughed and cried, praising God through her tears. Noah climbed out and stood upon the wet deck, and he looked across the gray water as far as he could see. The ship turned slowly in the wind, leaving a swirl of water where it moved, and there was nothing on the surface of all the water but the ark.

Noah thought of the earth below the waters, when it would be dry. As he stood upon the deck, he dreamed of the day when he would leave the ship and measure a field again with his footsteps. And his heart, his ancient, wise and righteous heart, was exceedingly glad.

But after the family had prayed and broken bread together, and had cared for the animals, and were preparing for bed, Shem and Ham argued over a blanket, each claiming it to be his own. Noah scolded them, and both were silent with shame. Noah took the blanket, but he did not lie in his bed beside his wife. He climbed the ladder and stood on the deck and wrapped himself in the blanket against the cold night, and he searched the stars that covered the firmament, and the stars that shimmered on the dark water. For Noah was troubled in his heart.

How are we different? he wondered. How are we different from the other people of my country?

Long had it been since Noah had thought of the people of his country. But he thought of them now, for they were drowned, and there would be for them no songs at the planting, or songs at the harvest. They would never see their children grown. Nor would they one day think, I shall go again to the temple, for so I was taught, and long has it been since I knelt to ask forgiveness.

Noah found in his heart a great love for the people of his country. He watched the moon arch white and swollen across the sky, watched it all night, and saw it drown in the water before dawn. Noah thought of the people of his country, thought of his neighbors, one by one, the moon down and the sun not yet up. He listened to the heavy waves that rolled against the hull of the ark, and to the spray that fell back into the sea. And Noah cried out a great cry that was not words, and the sound flew across the waters and lifted up to the firmament. The voice of Noah travelled upon the waters and lifted unto the heavens, for he was alone, and in all the world there was only the water and the cry of Noah. And then he fell silent, for the man was too alone to make any sound.

"Noah," called his wife. "Noah, dost thou need me?"

Noah looked down into the ark and saw the face of his wife lifted toward him, lit by the wavering flame of a lamp. And his heart was soothed. He heard the voice of his wife, and the flapping of a bird, and his faith came back unto him. He knew that his God was a just God, that He had punished the wicked, and that He would begin again. Surely God would teach his sons, and the sons of his sons, how to live without wickedness.

"Sleep, wife," he called down. "I am well. I come to be with thee now."

Noah unwrapped the blanket from his shoulders and cast it into the sea. Then he climbed down the ladder into his ark, and he lay with his arm wrapped around his wife, and his heart was at peace.

* * *

The ark drifted for the eighth month since the rains had stopped, and the ninth month, and in the tenth month Japheth died from sickness. Noah tied a rope around Japheth's chest, then with the other end of the rope he and his sons climbed the ladder to the deck, where they laid the rope over their shoulders and struggled to walk, hoisting the body of Japheth up to the hatch. Noah could hear his wife wailing with grief deep inside the ark, and he could hear the wailing of the wife of Japheth. Noah lowered Japheth on the rope into the water, then he watched his son wash limp in the waves, until the ark turned in the wind and passed over Japheth, who sank back to the earth of the old world.

Noah sought the wife of Japheth to comfort her, but he could not find her, until he heard her cry the name of Japheth. She was hidden in a stall behind two donkeys, and she tore her hair and would not be comforted. Noah did the work of Japheth, and the wife of Japheth, as well as his own, and he tried to comfort the wife of Japheth, but she spat upon his face, and he did not go near her anymore. In the evening of the Sabbath, she fell from the ladder, and he lowered her too into the water.

In the eleventh month, the floors of the grain bins began to show, and the hay rotted. Shem and the wife of Shem, and Ham and the wife of Ham, became sick and could not work. They lay in their beds and begged for food, but there was none, for the sheep had stopped lambing, and the rice had been eaten by a multitude of rats. Noah's wife begged him to slaughter a sheep, but God had commanded Noah to keep two of every beast, male and female, that their seed would remain alive upon the face of the earth, and Noah would not go against the commandment of the Lord. His sons and his sons' wives died of sickness, and of starvation.

Noah's wife had helped Noah to build the ark. She had filled the bins with grain, and labored with the cattle to keep them well. She had kept Noah warm during the nights, and had comforted him when Japheth died. She had wept because her son would not see the beginning.

But now she pleaded without exhaustion for food, would not sleep but begged until Noah covered his ears. She shrieked his name and shook her hair, but he looked at the blood-eyed cattle and at a lizard creeping across the filthy floor, and he said No. He caught her one night crouched with a chicken, grabbing at its feathers before it was even dead, and he beat her.

In the morning she was gone.

The animals which had gathered two by two into the ark now began to perish. The ship was filled with their groans of hunger, and with the kicking of an ox that could no longer stand, and the thump of birds that collapsed from the rafters. Noah could throw only the small overboard. The rest stayed below and the living were buried in the stench of the dead. Noah became sick, his body covered with sores, and he lay in his cold bed and listened to the waves that rolled unceasingly against the hull of the ark.

The gray sky of day and the black sky of night, and the gray sky of day and the black sky of night passed above the open hatch.

Noah struggled up the ladder, holding it against him with his weak arms wrapped around it. He crawled through the hatch and onto the deck. Lifting his face to the stars, he called, "God, I am a man. Give me something with which to live. "

From the firmament spoke the voice of the Lord, "Thou shalt live until the time thou diest. Thou shalt obey the commandments of the Lord thy God. All this thou hast."

Upon his knees, Noah held up his hands and pleaded, "Then give me other men. If a man must live in misery, then give him other men to share his curse. That, I know, is the least measure of justice a man should have."

God said nothing. Noah waited, but God said nothing. Noah climbed down the ladder into the ark. He held himself upright, and he waited.

Then Noah took Japheth's great axe from the beam and he raised it over the belly of the ship.

"No!" thundered the voice of the Lord, and the ark shook with the force of His cry. "Thou shalt have men."

* * *

In the morning, when Noah climbed up to the deck, he saw a ship sailing toward the ark, a ship with tall white sails spread against the gray sky. He waved and he laughed and he began to weep with his joy. As the ship sailed closer to the ark, he searched the faces of the people to see if perhaps they were from his country.

And then a man threw a rock. Another threw an iron spear that arched across the water and struck the deck of the ark. Now the horde on the ship raised their voices in a clamor, and rocks beat against the ark and a stone struck Noah to his knees.

He crawled to the hatch. He climbed down the ladder, leaving blood on the rungs. Then he lifted the great axe and he vowed, Never before have I killed, but now I will slaughter until I myself am slain.

But Noah had no strength to kill. He slumped to the floor and leaned against the ladder, and he laid the axe beside him. Noah sat, and he made neither sound nor movement.

Near his boots lay a dove, its head lifted, for the dove was watching Noah. Noah reached and took the bird in his hand. He tore a strip of cloth from his shirt, and he wrote upon it with a bit of charred wood, "Send to me a man who would live in peace." He tied the cloth around the foot of the dove, then he tossed the bird into the air, toward the blue sky above the hatch.

HERBERT'S MOUNTAIN

Herbert dug holes. Operating his steam shovel and his backhoe, he could dig a perfect basement hole, with straight walls, right-angled corners, and flat floors. In the countryside, he dug basements for new houses. In the city, he dug basements for skyscrapers. Herbert also dug long straight trenches for buried pipelines, and small deep holes for septic tanks. When Herbert had been working his way through college, he dug graves in a cemetery: neat, straight-walled holes exactly six feet deep. Perhaps digging all those graves had made Herbert sad. Whatever the reason, while he dug his basement holes today, Herbert never smiled.

Herbert lived in the city, in an apartment on the sixth floor. His wife Harriet sometimes dreamed of having a garden, but there was no place for a garden in the city. So Harriet knitted. She had learned to knit from her Norwegian grandmother, long ago. Once she had knitted sweaters for her sons and her daughter, but they had all grown up and left home. Now she knitted an occasional sweater for Herbert, with Norwegian reindeer parading across the chest, to keep him warm while he operated his backhoe in the winter. Herbert, however, had more than enough sweaters, and a new sweater no longer made him smile.

When Herbert came home from work, he had little to say during dinner. What could a man say who had done nothing all day but dig a hole? After dinner in the summertime, he might stand at the window and look down at a large vacant lot beside his apartment building, a vacant lot covered with old bricks and rubble, where several years ago some old office buildings had been torn down. If anybody ever bought that vacant lot, with plans to build a skyscraper, Herbert would apply for the job of digging the basement hole. It would be a big hole, the biggest hole he had ever dug. First he would have to scoop up all that rubble and dump it into a truck, to be taken away. Then he would scoop up countless bucketfulls of dirt and dump them into a truck, to be taken away. He never asked where they took the truckloads of dirt. His job was just to dig the hole.

But nobody seemed to be interested in buying the vacant lot and building a skyscraper. Investors today were building shopping malls on the north side of the city, and out in the western suburbs. The real estate market downtown was in a slump. So every time Herbert looked out his sixth-floor window, he saw the same old bricks and rubble in the vacant lot below.

After dinner in the wintertime, the evenings were dark. He could not see much outside his window, except the lights of the other apartment buildings around the black vacant lot. So he washed the dishes, without a word, then sat in front of the television, without a word, while Harriet knitted.

One Friday morning in late April, Herbert drove west out of the city to the site of a new housing development. His boss showed him the plans. Herbert was to dig sixteen basement holes in a row on one side of a street, then sixteen holes on the other side of the street. There would be three parallel streets, ninety-six holes altogether, of four basic types: a square half-basement, a rectangular full basement, an L-shaped prestige basement, and a U-shaped deluxe basement. Herbert's boss pointed in various directions across the flat, spring-green land, indicating the layout of the streets. The land had once been a corn field. Fresh green blades of grass were sprouting between long rows of brown corn stubble. His boss pointed at an old white farmhouse in the far corner of the field. The building was to be torn down. When it was gone, Herbert was to dig a hole on the site, an L-shaped prestige basement. Behind the farmhouse stood a grove of oaks. Most of the trees were to be removed to make room for a square half-basement. These two additional houses brought the total of basement holes to ninety-eight.

Herbert nodded. Ninety-eight holes. Already the surveyors were pounding their stakes into the green field, each stake with an orange ribbon tied to it, marking the corners of the holes Herbert would dig.

Already he could hear a buzz saw biting into one of the oaks.

Herbert spent all day Friday digging the first rectangular hole. He scooped up the moist black earth and dumped bucketful after bucketful into the waiting trucks. As each loaded truck drove away, an empty truck arrived to take its place. With his steam shovel and backhoe, Herbert dug the walls straight down, then he formed the right-angled corners, then he scraped the floor until it was perfectly flat.

He finished the first basement hole at ten minutes to five. The dump truck drove away, puffing a plume of black smoke as it labored with its heavy load across the green field toward the highway.

By five o'clock, the surveyors were gone. Their hundreds of orange ribbons flapped in the spring breeze.

The roar of the chain saw stopped at exactly five. Herbert sat in the cab of his backhoe and looked across the field at the now much smaller grove of oaks. There, where the trees had stood, he would dig hole number ninety-eight.

He climbed down from the cab and walked across the green field, his boots sinking slightly into the soft earth, until he stood and gazed at a dozen fallen oaks, their branches already sheered off and heaped nearby. Interspersed among the massive trunks were a dozen stumps, most of them two feet in diameter, some of them three. Few showed signs of rot; the wood in nearly every stump appeared to be healthy, all the way to the core.

First, the trunks would be cut into pieces, and the pieces hauled away as trash. Then he would bulldoze the stumps, and dig any remaining roots out of the ground. Once the site was cleared, he would dig a square half-basement.

No, he thought sadly, it will not be a basement that I dig.

That ninety-eighth hole will be like digging a grave.

As he turned toward his car, parked near the old white farmhouse, he heard a strange gruff voice that called, "What is it that happens here?"

Herbert looked toward the voice. It seemed to have come from the half-dozen oaks that were still standing. He searched among the trees, but saw no one. He might have called "Hello?", but years had passed since he had called "Hello" to anyone, so he again turned toward his car.

"Please, I ask you, what is it that happens here?" The gruff voice carried a note of anger, as if it did not merely ask a question, but demanded an answer.

Curious, Herbert walked in a winding path among the stumps and fallen trunks and so approached the grove of huge oaks. Then he spotted, peering out from behind one of the trees, a short shaggy man who wore a shirt and trousers that seemed to have been sewn from the skin of a goat. The man's beard had not been trimmed for ages, if ever. His nose was exceedingly large. He stared back at Herbert with unconcealed fear in his eyes, and seemed ready to bolt for cover somewhere deeper in the trees. But there were few trees left, leaving him with little place to hide. So he stood his ground, his fear balanced with anger.

Herbert, perplexed, had the feeling that he had met the burly old man somewhere before. "Hello," he called with a gentle voice. "Do you live here?"

"Yes, we live here," snapped the man, his eyes flashing with fury beneath his shaggy mop of hair. "We have lived here for a century and a half. Until this!" He waved his arm at the stumps, in the midst of which Herbert now stood. Then he glared at Herbert. "Why have you done this? We never bothered *you*!"

Now Herbert remembered the pictures in Harriet's book, an old book her grandmother had given her when Harriet was a girl, and he realized that the man who seemed so strange and yet so familiar was a Norwegian troll. Harriet often read the stories in her book aloud, for she liked to practice the Norwegian she had learned from her grandmother. Herbert of course did not understand a word of it, but he did enjoy looking at the pictures of trolls with ferns and briars and small trees in their hair. According to Harriet, her grandmother had insisted that trolls were real. They lived in the mountains of the Old Country, where every farmer had better watch his step with them, and never say a cross word about them, or they would steal his goats, and then his cows, and even his horse, until the trolls drove the poor farmer off his land. Many a Norwegian had been forced to sail for America because the trolls would give him no peace. Though a man's family might have farmed a patch of upland meadow for ten generations, still they were looked upon by the trolls as mere intruders, to be tolerated as long as the trolls might steal an occasional chicken. But woe to the farmer who set his dogs after the thief! The dogs never returned, and thereafter the goats and cows disappeared one by one.

Whenever Harriet had told him these tales with a solemn voice, Herbert had shaken his head, scoffing silently. But now here he stood, face to face with a troll, a troll outraged at the loss of the woods in which he had lived.

Herbert rarely spoke, but when he did, he spoke the truth. "Houses are to be built here." He swept his arm across the field behind him. "Ninety-eight houses in a neighborhood called Whispering Oaks. Houses on Whippoorwill Lane, and Meadowlark Lane, and Blue Jay Lane."

"There?" exclaimed the troll, aghast. He stepped out now from the trees into the light of the late-afternoon sun. Herbert saw that ferns and briars and an oak sapling grew in the troll's shaggy hair. "They will build houses *there*? And how shall we watch the sunset?"

Looking behind him, Herbert saw that indeed the new neighborhood would block the view of the sun setting over the flat farmland to the west.

"And you, *you* dig the potato cellars!" The troll's voice shook with rage. "Go away!" He marched defiantly past Herbert, yanked one of the stakes out of the ground and snapped it over his knee. "Tell the others never to come back. This land is our home."

Herbert shook his head sadly. "Me tell the others? I don't own this land. Some big shot in Chicago owns this land. He talks to his broker, his broker talks to a contractor, the contractor talks to my boss, and my boss tells me to dig a hole. I'm sorry, but—"

The troll pulled up another stake and snapped it over his knee. "We have lived here since Ole Jenssen plowed the first furrow with an ox. We never had any problem with Ole. Nor," he glanced at the vacant farmhouse, "with any of his kin. But now *you* want to force us out."

"Not me. Not me." Herbert shrugged his shoulders, helpless.

He noticed now another wizened face, peering at him from behind one of the oaks. Scanning the woods, he saw that at least a half-dozen trolls were watching him, some of them women, all of them ancient, shaggy, and frightened.

Herbert knew that at eight o'clock on Monday morning, the surveyors would be back, cursing the kids who had pulled up and broken their stakes. The chain saw would snarl and bite. His boss would march back and forth with his clipboard, shouting orders. And Herbert would dig hole number two.

"You will make them stop," insisted the troll, standing now in front of him, about as tall as Herbert's belt, a broken stake in each hand.

"But I can't," murmured Herbert, ashamed to let the other trolls hear.

"Then who can?"

Herbert pondered. A troll might steal a farmer's goat and drive the farmer from his land in the Old Country, but never could these trolls succeed in driving away ninety-eight families with mortgages and deeds. And dogs. Were poodles and spaniels and Dalmatians to disappear, surely the homeowners would call the police. And the police would comb the woods with bloodhounds.

Perhaps Harriet's grandmother would know what to do with a group of dispossessed trolls. But she had returned to the Old Country, and a year later had been buried in the mountains she had loved.

Well, perhaps he could ask Harriet. He could bring her out here tomorrow morning, and she herself could talk with the trolls.

He suggested, "I think you should talk with my wife. Tomorrow is Saturday, and she—"

"Your wife?" The troll glanced around. Seeing no one else, he narrowed his eyes at Herbert, suspicious that he was in some way about to be fooled. "Where is this wife?"

"We live in Chicago. We could drive out here tomorrow morning, and be here by ten o'clock. I can't promise that she'll—"

"The owner of this land lives in Chicago?"

"Yes, but I don't know him. I'm just—"

"Then we come with you."

"Come with me?" Herbert laughed at the impossibility of such an idea.

The troll turned to the woods and whistled. Herbert watched as one by one, the other trolls cautiously emerged from behind the oaks. Forming a muttering cluster of seven, each of them dressed in the skins of a goat or a cow, or perhaps a horse, they followed the lead troll as he marched with determination through the stumps and around the farmhouse to Herbert's blue pickup truck. Chattering in their strange language, the seven climbed into the back of the truck. Their leader swung the cab door open, stepped up and settled himself on the passenger seat, ready to roll.

Well, thought Herbert, I guess Harriet will be glad for a little company.

* * *

In the evening twilight, Herbert parked his pickup truck at the curb in front of the vacant lot. When they had entered the city, the chief troll, who introduced himself as Olaf, had stared up in awed silence at the skyscrapers. Only when the truck stopped at the curb did Olaf speak. He turned to Herbert with a glint of excitement in his eyes. "This is like going into the mountains. Something tall around us. How good, after a century and a half on that flat land, to finally look *up*."

The other trolls too seemed pleased. As they climbed out of the back of the truck, they stared up at the multitude of buildings that towered around them. Though Herbert could not understand what they were saying, he detected a tone of approval in their gruff voices.

Olaf stood alone for several moments as he surveyed the vacant lot. Then he followed Herbert and the other trolls along the sidewalk toward Herbert's apartment building.

The trolls became silent when Herbert, holding the door open for them, invited them into the great building. Their curiosity turned to apprehension, however, when they peered into the elevator, a small box with no windows. Only Olaf's courage as he followed Herbert into the box enabled the others to enter too. As the box shot upward, the trolls grabbed their stomachs and gasped with horror. "It's all right," Herbert reassured them. "Perfectly normal." When the box stopped and the steel doors opened, the trolls with ferns and briars and oak saplings in their hair scrambled out with great relief.

Herbert's apprehension was focused on Harriet. What would she say when she learned that he had brought eight guests to dinner? Especially eight such unusual guests. He decided not to open the door with his key, but to ring the bell. Better that she opened the door and—hopefully—invited them in herself.

When the door swung open, Harriet's welcoming smile turned to a look of astonishment as she stared at the short, shaggy people wearing goat-hide coats and leather boots. Clustered behind Herbert, the strange creatures stared back at her with shy embarrassment.

Herbert tried to explain, "These are trolls from out near

Rockford. They lived in the woods where those new houses are going up. I thought that maybe you—"

"Trolls?" she asked. With a smile of surprise and delight, she looked at them again and said something in Norwegian.

The trolls immediately repeated her greeting. The men trolls bowed and the women trolls nodded politely.

Speaking again in Norwegian, Harriet stepped back from the door and swept her hand in invitation. The trolls, greatly cheered by someone who spoke their language, paraded into the apartment. One by one they paused to slip off their boots. They placed the boots neatly in pairs along the wall, then, wearing wool socks that seemed to have been darned a good many times over the decades, they accompanied Harriet into the living room. Herbert, following their example, took off his boots, twice as large as theirs, and placed them at the end of the row.

Harriet quickly learned the names of all the trolls, then she repeated their names to Herbert, saying "Ørnulf Ørnulfsen" slowly and clearly, for she had some trouble with these strange names and even stranger vowels from the Old Country. Then she excused herself, and began to set the dining room table with her grandmother's plates and coffee cups. The four troll women insisted on helping her in the kitchen, and soon they were chattering happily with Harriet while they peeled potatoes.

Herbert did his best to make the troll men feel comfortable. He asked Olaf to tell the others to make themselves at home. Would anyone like a beer? Yes, they murmured with shy smiles, they *would* like a beer. Herbert busied himself with pouring five Old Milwaukee's into five beer mugs, then he served his guests, each of whom nodded and said, "Tock." He would have liked to have struck up some sort of conversation, but Olaf now stood at the window, ignoring the others as he sipped his beer and stared down at the dark vacant lot.

When Harriet entered the living room and asked Herbert if he would run down to the A & P to buy five tins of herring, a package of crackers, six pounds of fresh codfish, and a dozen turnips, Herbert was glad to have something to do. He nodded cordially to the troll men, called to Olaf, "I'll be right back," then he put on his boots and hurried out the door.

When he returned with the groceries, he saw that the trolls were gathered around the coffee table, looking with great interest at Harriet's book. They laughed and slapped their knees at an engraving of a troll with three heads. They hushed with reverence as Olaf read an old poem. But their faces filled with sadness and longing as they gazed at picture after picture of Norwegian mountains. They became so silent, they might have entered a church.

During dinner, a feast which earned Harriet an abundance of compliments, Herbert occasionally glanced across the table at Olaf. The old troll sat deep in thought as he ate potato after potato, consuming at least two dozen before he looked up at Herbert and asked, "What are you going to do with all that dirt?"

"All that dirt?"

"Today you told me you would dig ninety-eight holes. What will you do with all that dirt?"

Herbert shrugged. "They take it away in trucks. I don't know what they do with it."

Olaf pointed toward the window, hooking his gnarled old finger in a downward motion so that he indicated the vacant lot below. "They could put it down there."

"Down there? But they'll have more than enough dirt to cover that lot."

Beneath his shaggy patch of briars and ferns, Olaf's eyes sparkled. "Exactly. What you need is a mountain."

The other trolls looked for a moment at Olaf, then one by one their wrinkled faces lit with the idea, the possibility, the hope, that all that dirt could be turned into a mountain. Now, one by one, the trolls turned toward Herbert, the man who scooped up the dirt and dumped it into the trucks. Harriet too was watching him, waiting to hear what he would say.

For the first time in years, Herbert thought not of making a hole, an empty space that someone else would fill, but of making something solid, something with shape and size. His mind raced, quickly calculating the total number of truckloads of earth that would be hauled away from the holes he would dig through the summer. He envisioned himself at the controls of a bulldozer, scooping and shoveling and piling that dirt higher and even higher in the middle of the vacant lot. Building a mountain, with a cave inside for the trolls, and trails up the slopes for city people to climb during the summer, and for children to ski down during the winter.

Then Herbert's thoughts came to a halt, for he was a practical man. "We don't own the land," he said. "Only a millionaire could afford to buy such a piece of property."

Olaf asked, "Is it for sale?"

"There's a FOR SALE sign down there on a post. The kids keep throwing rocks at it. The owner keeps standing it up again."

"How much?" asked Olaf, setting down his fork.

"Oh, I couldn't say. There's no price on the sign, just the dimensions of the lot, and a phone number."

"Then I suggest that after coffee, we go down and take a look at that sign."

So they did, Harriet along with them. Walking awkwardly over the loose bricks, the ten of them gathered with a flashlight in front of the sign. Herbert shone the beam on the white rectangle. "300 feet by 210," he read aloud, and then Olaf translated. "755-32446," read Herbert. Olaf translated. Then the chief troll asked, "May we phone on a Friday night?"

"Well," said Herbert doubtfully, "let's be realistic. Do we have the necessary funds for such a purchase?"

Olaf conferred with the other trolls; he seemed to gather information from each of them. Then he turned to Herbert. "Perhaps we do. I suggest that we phone the owner to obtain a preliminary figure, and then we barter on the basis of full payment in cash."

Once again Herbert's mind leapt forward. He switched off the flashlight and surveyed the dark lot, surrounded on three sides by apartment buildings, bordered on the fourth by 43rd Street. Plenty of room, really, for a good-sized hill, though certainly not a real Norwegian mountain. Room for a meadow at the base, planted with oak trees. Room for a gradual slope on the north side, for sledding. And for a steeper slope to the south, for skiing. He could grade a spiral trail that wound up the mountain, so that one and all could reach the summit. And he would make little flat spots along the way, where he would put a green park bench for the old folks to sit on. Yes, and the summit would not be a peak, but would be fairly flat, a perfect place for picnics. A park, that was it. He would build a park for the city, with oak trees in the meadow, and spruce trees on the mountain. He slipped his arm through Harriet's arm. A park with bright beautiful wildflowers from the bottom to the top. Harriet would finally have her garden.

If . . . Herbert looked down at the trolls, who were talking excitedly among themselves as they pointed up into the empty air where their mountain would be. If this group of investors had the cash . . .

Back to the elevator they marched, and up they rode—the trolls held their bellies with grins and faint giggles—to the apartment, and the telephone.

A pad of paper on the desk, a pen ready in his hand, Herbert dialed the number. With a dignified voice, he said, "Good evening." Then he inquired into the particulars concerning the property on 43rd Street. He raised his eyebrows when he heard the price, then laid his hand over the phone and repeated the figure to Olaf, who translated to the others. The trolls scowled and shook their heads with utter refusal. After a brief consultation, Olaf turned to Herbert and suggested that he offer sixty percent of the figure, in gold coins, cash on the table, tomorrow afternoon, Saturday, at two o'clock, in the owner's office.

Herbert again raised his eyebrows. "Gold coins?"

Olaf pointed his gnarled finger at the telephone. "Ask him."

With the voice of a man who daily dealt with enormous sums of money at the Chicago Merchandise Mart, Herbert repeated the offer to the man on the other end of the telephone. The man on the other end of the telephone said absolutely nothing for a long moment, then he guffawed. "Gold coins? Listen, pal, don't waste my time."

"Our offer is entirely sincere," asserted Herbert. "Can you afford not to meet us tomorrow at two o'clock?" He added, "We suggest that you invite your banker, so that he may attest to the authenticity of our specie, and confirm its present market value. Gold, may I remind you, is the preferred currency in all international transactions."

While Herbert listened to another long silence on the phone, Harriet kissed his cheek.

"All right, pal. Tomorrow at two. Three twenty-one Wacker Drive, suite twenty-three oh five. My banker will be with me, and my attorney. Don't be late."

Herbert hung up the phone and turned to Olaf. "Where on earth do you have such a sum of money?"

"Not 'on'," said Olaf, "'in' the earth. Under those oak trees. We'd have to move it anyway, before you dig your half-basement."

"But . . . Where did it come from?"

"From the Old Country, of course. We brought it with us when we emigrated with Ole Jenssen. We thought we might need it to buy land, but Ole let us stay on his place for free, as long as we didn't steal his cows."

"But where, if I may ask, did you get so much money in the first place?"

"Ah." Reluctant to reveal the origin of his funds, Olaf conferred with his shaggy colleagues. They seemed to assent, for he then admitted with some pride to Herbert, "We stole the money one night off a Viking ship anchored in the fjord. They had just returned from Byzantium and were drinking mead on the beach. We rowed out very quietly, climbed the anchor line, found the sacks camouflaged as ballast under the deck, and dropped them one by one over the gunnel to Ivar." Olaf nodded at one of the other trolls, who nodded back with a sly grin. "Ivar sat in our rowboat and caught the sacks as silently as if he were catching a dozen cannonballs. He rowed the booty further up the fjord and set it on shore, then came back to fetch us. We counted the coins in our cave deep in the mountain," a low rumbled chuckle of satisfaction arose from the trolls, "and we were very pleased. "

"Gold coins from Byzantium! How long ago was this?"

Olaf closed his eyes as he calculated. "Nine hundred and ninety-six years ago." He opened his blue eyes; they sparkled with anticipation. "And now we know how we're going to spend it!"

* * *

The trolls slept on the sofa and on the floor, wrapped in all the blankets that Harriet could find. The next morning, after a hearty breakfast of herring and cucumbers on thick slices of bread, Herbert and Harriet and the eight trolls drove in Herbert's blue pickup truck to the deserted cornfield near Rockford, where a crop of stakes with orange flags covered the land. Harriet winced at the sight of the fallen oak trees. The trolls led Herbert and Harriet into the grove of trees that were still standing, then showed them, between the roots of one of the oaks, a hole slightly larger than a groundhog hole. The hole was hidden by tufts of last summer's brown grass, though when Herbert, at Olaf's invitation, knelt and peered down into it, he was able to discern earthen steps leading to a tunnel that extended beyond the light of day. Olaf then pointed at something near the edge of the grove of oaks. Herbert saw nothing at first except a heap of rocks. Then he discovered a black stove pipe sticking up above the stones. Below, in the earth, the trolls had their stove!

"Back in a minute," said Olaf, and then he led the other trolls down the stairs to their cave beneath the roots.

While she waited, Harried stared sadly at the fallen trees, at the orange ribbons, and then at the old white farmhouse, its front porch sagging slightly, its red brick chimney still pointing proudly into the blue sky. "Who will live there now?" she asked.

"They're gonna tear it down," Herbert told her. "Where it stands, I'll dig a prestige L-shaped basement for a new house."

Just then, as it had last night, Herbert's mind raced forward and embraced a new idea. Perhaps, if there were coins enough . . . perhaps, if the trolls would loan him a bit of their capital . . . perhaps he might ask his boss if that old white farmhouse, and all the furniture in it, might not be moved on a flatbed truck to the foot of the mountain.

Those fallen oak trees, to be chainsawed into pieces and hauled away as trash: certainly there was firewood enough to feed the troll's stove inside the mountain for many a winter. A pile of rocks on the slope would keep skiers from colliding with the pipe. And who would even know that inside the mountain lived eight trolls in their cave? Nobody would know, unless the trolls wanted them to know.

Now up from the hole appeared Olaf, struggling as he tried to squeeze both his belly and a heavy round sack through the door at the same time. He disappeared back down the hole, then with a great groan of effort, he lifted the sack above his head and pushed it out of the hole ahead of him. The other trolls emerged behind him, each with a heavy bulging leather sack. Olaf untied the rope around the neck of his sack and took out one golden coin that shone in the morning sun. He bit it, looked with satisfaction at his teeth marks that now stippled the face of some ancient emperor, then he offered the coin to Herbert. "Bite it and see for yourself."

Herbert did not have to bite the heavy coin to know it was real. The strange lettering, the imperfect roundness, and the weight, especially the weight, told his hand that what he held was pure gold. He offered the coin to Harriet so she could hold it too. She smiled mischievously. "Those poor Vikings."

"Don't feel sorry for them," said Olaf as he counted the fourteen sacks that now stood in a row beneath the oaks. "They had each stolen a nice fat young Byzantine woman and brought her back to Norway. We took their gold, but," he glanced warily at one of the troll women, who glared at him with a stern eye, "we let them keep their girls."

With the sacks of gold under a tarp in the rear of the pickup, the ten would-be landowners drove back to the apartment building. They arrived at five minutes past noon. Ignoring the stares of neighbors on the sidewalk and in the lobby, the trolls carried their heavy sacks to the elevator. Most of the trolls made two trips, until all fourteen sacks stood on the floor of the little box. Herbert and the trolls squeezed in. Herbert pushed button number six, the doors slid shut. Then a buzzer blared and a red light blinked. "We're too heavy," said Herbert. "We'll have to go up in shifts."

While they took up five sacks, and then five, and then four, Harriet walked to a shop at the corner and bought a copy of the *Chicago Tribune*. Returning to the apartment, she found all fourteen sacks safely stowed in the living room. She put on a pot of coffee, then turned to the financial section and showed Olaf and the other trolls the market value of an ounce of gold. Herbert brought out the bathroom scales while Harriet calculated the price of the vacant log in terms of pounds of gold. While the trolls watched attentively, Herbert weighed a sack of gold and Harriet wrote down its weight. He weighed a second sack, and then a third. With nine sacks, they were close to the price they would offer. Olaf untied the neck of his sack and placed a stack of coins on the scale. He added another coin, then another, until the weight in gold equaled the price of the vacant lot. He added one coin more, for good measure. Then he asked Herbert, "Have you a sack for this loose change?"

Harriet found a pink pillow case.

The ten financiers now sat down to a lunch of waffles topped with goat cheese. Then everyone had a cup of strong coffee, strong enough to carry them through their negotiations at two o'clock.

Herbert and the eight trolls carried the nine sacks of gold; Harriet carried the lumpy pink pillowcase, the financial section and the bathroom scales. They rode down in the elevator in three shifts, and again ignored the stares of their neighbors as they climbed into the pickup truck.

They arrived at 321 Wacker Drive at five minutes to two. In a large, gleaming elevator, they rose swiftly, with a far worse tingling in their stomachs, to the twenty-third floor. Walking in a solemn procession, Herbert in the lead, followed by Olaf and the seven trolls, Harriet guarding the rear with a wary eye, they found suite number twenty-three oh five. Holding a heavy sack of gold in one arm, Herbert took a deep breath and knocked on the door.

"Come in," growled a voice inside, the voice of a man not to be fooled with.

Herbert swung the door open and saw a large oval table in a conference room. At the far end stood a man smoking a black cigar. To his right stood a portly gentleman in a pin-stripe suit. To his left stood a thin, bald gentleman in a dark gray suit. The three men glowered at Herbert, clearly ready to do business on their own terms.

Their glowers dissolved as one by one the shaggy trolls wearing goat-skin jackets marched into the conference room. The trolls placed their heavy round sacks on the table, then stood behind the chairs and glowered back, clearly ready to do business on their own terms.

Herbert introduced himself and his wife, then Harriet introduced each of the trolls, for only she could properly pronounce their names. The land owner, chewing his cigar, introduced himself, his portly banker, and his bald attorney. Though disconcerted by the fact that never before had he negotiated at this table with people with ferns and briars and oak saplings in their hair, nor with noses quite so large, George Thompson, entrepreneur par excellence, nevertheless bid them all to be seated.

Harriet commenced the discussion by citing the current market value of gold per ounce. George Thompson turned to his banker, who affirmed that the price quoted was accurate. Herbert then presented his calculations, equating a certain weight in gold with the price of the land.

At this point, George Thompson began to dicker. He had

not agreed to that price, he said. He had merely agreed to meet with prospective buyers to discuss the price. "Now, the going market value for commercial property in downtown Chicago is . ." and he began to reel off prices from recent property sales, with the intention of determining, as he said, "a fair ballpark figure."

While George Thompson stabbed his cigar at the air to emphasize each price, Herbert glanced at Harriet, for they had no way of knowing whether or not these prices were accurate, or grossly inflated.

Meanwhile, Olaf untied the rope around the neck of his sack and began to take out his coins, one by one, and to pile them in front of him on the oak table. Perhaps he nodded to the other trolls, for although Herbert perceived no noticeable signal, they too opened their sacks and began to stack on the table growing piles of golden coins. The trolls did not merely place the coins atop the stacks, but let them fall flat from their gnarled fingers onto the stacks with a steady musical jingling.

George Thompson, citing a figure recently paid by Marshall Field for a three-level parking garage inside the Loop, fell silent, mesmerized as his eyes went around and around the oval table.

Herbert once again quoted the price offered, and its equivalent weight in gold. Harriet placed the bathroom scales on the table.

"Ah, but how do we know your scales are accurate?" queried George Thompson with professional suspicion.

"Perhaps you would like to weigh yourself?" offered Harriet. She set the scales on the floor of the conference room, beside a potted plastic palm tree.

George Thompson weighed himself, and nodded that indeed the scales were accurate. Just to be sure, he bid his banker to weigh himself. The portly gentleman stepped upon the scales. Looking down past his prosperous girth, he affirmed the accuracy of the figure. Just to be absolutely sure, George Thompson bid his attorney to weigh himself. The lanky attorney stepped onto the scales. Peering down with his weasel eyes, he averred that the scales read exactly what his scales at home had read that morning, not a pound more, not a pound less.

"So," said Harriet, placing the scales once again on the oaken table, "I suggest that we ascertain the accuracy of the amount herewith offered."

The coins were returned, with a merry tinkling, to their sacks, and then the nine sacks and one lumpy pink pillowcase were placed in succession upon the scales. George Thompson, his banker and his attorney each peered at the weight registered by the scales' arrow, and each of the three kept a separate tally of the figures. When all the coins had been weighed, the three added up their ten weights. Each came to the same figure, exactly one dollar and forty-six cents more than the price of the land.

"And that," stated Olaf with a gruff voice, "is our final offer. Yours isn't the only heap of rubble in town."

George Thompson met Olaf Olafsen eye to eye, but though George Thompson had dealt with the steel-fisted magnates of Chicago, Olaf Olafsen had snatched the prize from a cutthroat band of Vikings who wielded broadsword and battle-axe.

Herbert looked at his watch. "Gentlemen, if no business is to be concluded here today, we have an appointment elsewhere at three o'clock."

"Done," declared George Thompson. Sticking his cigar back in his mouth, he reached across the table and shook hands with Herbert, then with Harriet, and then with each of the eight strangers who had come from he knew not where, but who would leave behind, when they left, nine sacks and one pink pillowcase filled with enough gold to make him feel like Bluebeard the Pirate.

The attorney opened his briefcase and placed the deed of property on the table. Herbert, Harriet and Olaf read through it, asking questions whenever a point needed clarification. Despite various delineated conditions, nowhere in the deed was it stated that the land could not be used as a park.

Olaf explained the deed in general terms to the other trolls.

They asked about conditions regarding forms of residential dwellings on the land. Assured that the deed contained neither prohibitions nor restrictions concerning their particular type of dwelling, they assented to the terms.

Herbert signed, George Thompson signed, Harriet signed, the banker signed, Olaf Olafsen signed, the attorney signed, and then one by one, passing the pen from gnarled hand to gnarled hand, the seven trolls signed the document, taking immediate possession of said property.

* * *

Herbert spoke with his boss, who spoke with the contractor, who was glad to have somewhere to dump all that dirt. Herbert also spoke with the appropriate authorities at City Hall, who listened to his proposal, examined the deed, and, despite their initial surprise, approved the plan for a park which contained a rather large hill to be used for public recreation. They commended Herbert for his civic generosity, agreed that he might place one old farmhouse on the southwest corner of the lot as the "caretakers' residence", and offered to provide him, at city expense, with a bulldozer.

A bulldozer! thought Herbert. Not a backhoe to scoop out a hole, but a bulldozer, to build a mountain.

Herbert began to work harder than he had ever worked in his life. During the days, Monday to Friday, he dug holes. But he did not think of the work as digging holes; he thought of it as loading trucks with dirt.

During the lengthening spring evenings, Monday to Friday, he bulldozed the bricks and rubble into a heap in the middle of the lot, thus creating a foundation for his mountain. He then bulldozed the fresh black earth, which the trucks dumped along the 43rd Street edge of the lot, across the outer rectangle, until the flat layer of earth around the heap of bricks and rubble was two feet deep, deep enough, certainly, for young oaks to take root in.

Herbert's neighbors in the apartment buildings that towered around the lot did not mind that his bulldozer roared every evening until nine o'clock. They watched him from their windows, they watched him from the sidewalk, and often they waved to him, wishing him well, for they knew he was building them a park.

At night, while everyone else was sleeping, the trolls dug deep into the heap of bricks and rubble. Experts at subterranean architecture, they excavated a comfortably large cavern. They mortared the bricks into massive walls, and built a sturdy ceiling with beams made from branches of oak. The more they worked, the more pleased they became, for never beneath the roots of the trees by the cornfield had they been able to fashion such a spacious and elegant cave.

As soon as the trolls informed Herbert that they had completed their new home, he began to cover the heap of bricks and rubble with dirt. He dumped and shoveled the black earth higher and higher, until he had built a mound which completely covered the bricks. But that mound was just the beginning.

On Saturdays, when he had the full day to work, Herbert began to sculpt the perfect mountain. With his bulldozer's big blade, he heaped and graded the slopes of the growing hill of earth. His bulldozer pushed steeply upwards, then tilted to the left, and now tilted to the right, as his curved steel blade lifted and shoved and packed the earth with the confidence and care of a sculptor's great hand.

Every Saturday through the month of May, he worked a little higher. And higher still in June. And even higher in July. His bulldozer rumbled and roared as it rose to the level of the third floor, and the fifth, and eighth, and now the eleventh floor of the apartment buildings around him. Harriet noticed that the higher Herbert worked, the more he smiled. When she called up to him at noon on Saturday that it was time to stop for lunch, he would look down from his tilted bulldozer with a grin she had not seen in years.

The summit: how high would the summit be? That depended on how much dirt came out of the holes. Digging a hole a day, square half-basement holes, and rectangular full-basement holes, and prestige L-shaped basement holes, and deluxe U-shaped basement holes, Herbert dug twenty-one holes in the month of May, twenty-two holes in June, twenty-two holes in July, twenty-two holes in August, and eleven holes in the first half of September.

Before Herbert dug hole number ninety-seven, the old white farmhouse was moved onto a flatbed truck. The house was brought to the southwest corner of the park during the night while Harriet was sleeping. In the morning, Herbert called her to the apartment window and asked her if she saw anything new out there. She gazed down at the lovely old farmhouse with its sagging porch and tall brick chimney. She surveyed all the black dirt around it where she could grow her gardens. Then she looked at Herbert with a smile he had not seen in years.

Herbert had problems with hole number ninety-eight. Before he could dig it, he had to pull out the stumps of the oak trees. But the roots of those oaks had held the earth, and once he had pulled out the stumps, the ground collapsed into the cave beneath them. (The trolls had already moved their stove and table and eight beds, which Herbert had transported to town in his pickup. The stove and table and eight beds were now deep inside the mountain.) Herbert could not dig a proper hole, with vertical walls and right-angled corners and a flat level floor, because every time he tried to scoop up the earth, the earth collapsed down into the cave. He called his boss over to discuss the problem. His boss was surprised at the existence of an underground cavern, and speculated that the glaciers had played some trick there, ten thousand years ago. The surveyors were called over, and after some discussion, Herbert was instructed to dig a new hole a hundred feet to the north, where Ole Jenssen had once tilled his potato patch. The surveyors measured the new site and pounded into the ground four stakes with orange ribbons. Then Herbert went to work, and filled five trucks from hole number ninety-eight.

With those last five truckloads of earth, Herbert built a beautiful summit. He brought the spiral trail up to a broad, slightly domed oval meadow, or what would become a meadow, once it was planted with grass and wildflowers and scattered spruce. After he had graded and banked and smoothed the last patch of black earth, he throttled his bulldozer to idle. He looked over its steel blade at the apartment building where he had once lived. He counted floors, and smiled with satisfaction that his mountain was eighteen stories high.

Then he looked to the west on that sunny Saturday afternoon in September, and he saw, with even greater satisfaction, that his mountain was taller than the twelve story building across 43rd Street. His mountain was tall enough that he was able to see over the rooftops of all the buildings to the west. From his summit, he could wander his eye over the great flat Illinois plain. And that pleased him, for now the trolls could watch their sunsets.

Herbert looked down and waved to Harriet, who stood in her sunbonnet on the porch of their new home. She smiled up at him and waved. Now that he was done with his mountain, he could help her give the old farmhouse a fresh coat of white paint.

He began to drive his bulldozer down the trail that spiraled around the mountain. As he descended, he heard something, something that came to his ears through the chugging and puffing of his engine, and through the cranking and creaking of his caterpillar treads. He looked up, and then he looked all around, and he saw that in most of the windows of the apartment buildings that towered around his mountain, people were applauding. Waving handkerchiefs. Calling through cupped hands, "Bravo!"

Herbert raised his curved steel blade and wagged it, as a wave of the sculptor's hand, to the people who would soon be invited to climb his mountain.

* * *

The snow was deep that winter. The trolls carved their skis from the boughs of the fallen oaks, and carved two pairs as well for Harriet and Herbert. The children of the neighborhood were delighted to ski in the company of eight Norwegian trolls, who howled with great gruff belly-laughs whenever anyone tumbled face-first into the snow.

Harriet and Herbert invited the trolls to a Christmas dinner in their new home, where Harriet cooked a turkey in Ole Jenssen's big, black, oak-burning stove, and served the dinner on her grandmother's Norwegian china. The trolls invited Harriet and Herbert to a New Year's Eve feast in their cave deep inside the mountain, where the troll women boiled a pot of codfish atop their oak-burning potbellied stove, and the troll men served tankards of mead. Olaf Olafsen raised his silver tankard with a toast, to the westernmost mountain in Norway.

In the springtime, people poured out of the apartment buildings to help plant grass, and to sow wildflowers, and to dig small holes in the rich black earth for oak saplings on the flat apron around the mountain, and for spruce saplings up on the slopes. Neighbors for ten and twenty and thirty years met each other for the first time, as they dug and planted and patted the earth.

And Herbert? He stopped digging holes. He and Harriet were hired by the City of Chicago as caretakers of the park, and so their days are spent in tending the largest garden in Illinois. As well as the tallest garden in Illinois. They finish each day with a picnic on the summit, where they and the eight trolls eat herring on crackers and watch the red sun slowly disappear beneath the flat, flat horizon. Then they lie in the grass and look up at the stars that appear one by one in the lavender sky.

And neither Herbert nor Harriet were ever so happy as they are now atop Herbert's Mountain.

POTATO PATCH

I

Ambrose had mounted the two-wheeled contraption half an hour ago, but still he hadn't caught his balance. He wrenched the handlebars through sweep and veer as if he wrestled the horns of a wild bull. When he had purchased the Wright Brothers' bicycle, he felt he had joined the Modern World—and now he meant to master the vehicle that promised both grace and speed.

His mule trotted beside him, pulling a wagon laden with the tin peddler's wares. Tea pots clanked and tin cups clinked as the wagon jolted along the rutted road. The mule, its ears twitching with wary skepticism, stayed well to the side of the lane, affording plenty of room to the two-wheeled beast that gee-ed and hawed as if pursued by an invisible swarm of horseflies.

An hour ago, the tin peddler had sold Orville and Wilbur a new copper coffee pot. But his profit was peanuts, compared with the opportunity they had offered him. The bicycle builders had fashioned a motorized kite which they called an "airplane", a vehicle not of the Modern Age, but of the Future! They told him that tomorrow, there would happen a thing so extraordinary, no man could believe it unless he looked up with his own eyes and saw it for himself. And they invited *him* to be there! Ambrose pedaled his bicycle as fast as he could—his progress a composite of wobbling curves, swerving near-misses at the verge of a ditch, and sinuous negotiations snaking betwixt pothole and rut—for he was determined to share this once-in-a-lifetime miracle with his old friend, the potato farmer.

Now he spotted Ben's cabin, set back twenty yards from the road. The roof sagged like a hammock in which sat the humble stump of a chimney. A few bricks more were missing from the chimney than had been missing the year before. The log walls were a bit more moss-covered, the cabin now more green than brown.

A dozen hogs in Ben's front yard, nestled ear-deep in mud, grunted with curiosity when the approaching wagon disturbed their euphorial afternoon. They swung their bristly chins through the cool ooze as they watched mule and wagon turn up the driveway.

But when a gleaming demon, a legless creature composed of bones without flesh, jerked and lurched toward their wallow, the hogs lifted their snouts and squealed appeals of protest and panic.

In the middle of the pig sty grew an apple tree. On its bottom branch sat the farmer's son. The boy bit off and molared chunks of an apple as he watched the Modern Age pass by. His eyelids drooped as he chewed. One finger the color of Ohio's finest humus bored into his ear in pursuit of an itch deep within. When the lad dropped his smudgy apple core, the hogs' squeals of alarm abruptly stopped, and became a volley of competitive snorts, followed by one satisfied grunt.

Ambrose had been so interested in the "go" of things that he had left unconsidered the "stop". Undaunted, he circled once around the hog wallow, then rode head-on into a handy haystack.

The hogs now watched as an ordinary pedestrian brushed off his coat. The skeletal Thing grazed with its head buried in the hay. The hogs snuggled their snouts into the ooze with renewed complacency.

Ambrose stepped to the edge of the odiferous muck and greeted the boy, "Howdy, Brewster." He remembered the boy's filthy shirt as once the father's, its shoulders now stretched, both sleeves torn open at the mud-caked elbows.

Brewster picked the ripest Ida Red within reach and tossed

it down to his father's friend. "Hi-dee, Mister Smith!"

Ambrose caught the apple with one hand, touched the brim of his tall black top hat with the other. "I thank ye, Brewster." Taking out a white handkerchief, he polished the hefty apple until it gleamed, then he savored its harmony of sweetness and tart.

When he turned toward the cabin, the tin peddler saw the gray-haired Missus in the doorway, beaming at him with surprise and joy. He swung down his top hat and bowed with ambassadorial cordiality. "Good day, Sarah, good day. My, if you're not looking a year younger!"

Though sweating from her toil at the stove, Sarah stood tall and proud that such fine company as this world traveller should come to *her* house. She shivered with anticipation of the news he would bring. And she sighed with relief that her old tin tea kettle, a dented and blistered antiquity with a drip that nearly doused the fire, would at last be fixed. Wiping hog grease from her hands into her patchwork apron, she called over her shoulder, "Emlie-Lou! Look who's come to visit. It's Mister Ambrose Smith!"

Wearing an apron of burlap sacking, the girl appeared beside her mother. Ripe with the faintest brief bloom she would ever achieve, she smiled shyly at Ambrose, then stared down at the toes of her clodhopper boots.

Ambrose whistled with admiration. "Why, Emlie-Lou," he declared, "you're the likeliest blossom in these parts."

The corners of the girl's lips fluttered with a faint smile. She glanced up, her blue eyes lit less with happiness than hope.

"Ambrose," said the Missus, "we'd be proud to have you to supper."

The peddler bowed a second time, sweeping his hat like a man just nominated for governor. "No more pleased would I be anywhere in all Ohio to accept such a well-qualified invitation." Then he spoke to the Missus in a hushed voice, as if the pleasure were so great it was almost a sin, "Since the very crack of dawn, I've had nothing on my mind but your skillet-fried pork chops."

"But!" barked the Missus, her eye suddenly as stern as a schoolmarm's. She pointed a chapped red finger at the bicycle. "What is *that*?"

Though outwardly stalwart, Ambrose inwardly quivered before her glowering countenance. Should she ever suspect his plan to provide Ben with one morning of freedom, he'd likely find his head in her soup pot.

Then he realized that the bicycle could serve as a decoy: her attention focused on one threat to the household regimen, she would never suspect another. A salesman to the core, Ambrose strode to the shiny vehicle, patted its seat and announced, "This here is a great stride forward. For with it, a man ain't got to stride at all."

The Missus snapped, "Don't give me your city talk polished like a shoeshine. What's it fer?"

The peddler never flinched. "Tis a modern means of personal conveyance. I thought that perhaps Ben—"

"No! " The Missus clomped her hobnails down the log steps and glared at Ambrose with an eye like the burning burl of an oak. "Ben's got taters t'dig."

Striking a reasonable tone, Ambrose suggested, "I thought perhaps tonight after supper, he might take just a short ride down the road."

"No! " She poked her calloused finger at his retreating nose. "He'll finish diggin' them taters t'night by lanternlight."

The peddler pondered a moment, then patiently proposed, "Maybe tomorrow morning—"

"No!" She jerked her thumb toward a dilapidated shack behind the cabin. "Tomorrow he's diggin' a new privy pit." She frowned at the bicycle's wire spokes. "Ain't got time for tomfoolery."

Ambrose sighed with resignation. "Well then, perhaps we'd best hide the bicycle in the barn."

"In the *back* stall, where he won't see it when he milks the cow."

Bowed with defeat, Ambrose tugged the handlebars from

the haystack, then wheeled the intruder into the barn. He laid it down in the last stall and covered it with forkfulls of hay, until the beckoning pedal was completely buried.

Emlie-Lou watched the concealment with wistful curiosity.

The Missus watched with a dour frown, then warned both daughter and guest, "Not a word to Ben."

Ambrose promised abjectly, "Not a word." He scuffed his feet toward the barn door.

However, back out in the sunshine, he sniffed the wind. His spirits lifting, he inquired, "Do I detect the fragrance of a fresh apple pie in the neighborhood?"

The Missus beamed at her daughter. "Emlie-Lou here made it."

The girl blushed apple red.

Ambrose extended one arm to the Missus, one arm to Emlie-Lou, then with the grace and aplomb of a gentleman, he escorted these two fine ladies toward the door of their ramshackle cabin.

II

That evening after supper, Ben's pipe was a mere inch from his lips when Sarah's voice like a lash nearly snatched it from his hand. "Them taters want diggin!"

Ben's burly chest was broader than the bib of his overalls. His shoulders were tanned from the labors of May, June, July, August and September. He jutted his stubbled jaw forward, ready for battle. "I'll dig 'em up tomorrow."

"Tomorrow?" She thumped her fist and five plates jumped. "Tomorrow there wants diggin' a new privy pit."

Ben looked to Ambrose for support. "By tradition, we ought to have us a mornin' of fishin'."

"No!" thundered the Missus. Her gray head tilted back with dignity. "I'll not sit over that old privy pit one more time. There ain't but a two-inch drop."

The somber truth stilled all further argument.

Ambrose offered, "Ben, I'll give you a hand tonight in the potato patch." Then he turned to the Missus with a nod of complete agreement. "And best be on my way early tomorrow morn."

Clamping his teeth on the cold pipe, Ben growled at his son, "Brewster, you can help dig them dang taters."

Brewster uttered a porcine snort of protest. He continued picking his teeth, his chin propped on his hand, his elbow in his gravy.

His father warned, "Ifn you don't lend a proper hand, I'll send you to *school*."

Brewster's mouth snapped shut like a rat trap on whatever further protest might have sprung out. He hurried from the table to fetch a tater trowel.

Ben grumpily gulped his tea, glared with silent grievance at his wife, then stomped gruffly out the door.

Ambrose lingered over his tea, his business with the Missus unfinished. Certain that she would accept no payment for the dinner, he recompensed her with a feast of news, exclusive of his visit to the Wrights'. And he paid for a second slice of Emlie-Lou's apple pie with compliments exclaimed, purred and moaned with every bite.

From the smoking stove, the Missus lifted her dull tin kettle, then poured with poise into Ambrose's tarnished tin cup. He eyed the blackened, battered kettle, with its ill-fitting lid. Fine merchandise it had been, a decade ago. But now the patient was so patched that further surgery upon the pit from which it dripped seemed impractical. He knew she would not tolerate a penny less than the full price of a new pot, so strict was her pride. And the full price could she never afford. So he pondered his plan to provide for Sarah as fairly as he would for Ben.

"Excuse me please." He stepped outside to his wagon and fetched his finest copper kettle, with a swan-necked spout. Returning to the cabin, he held the vessel in the candlelight as if it were a jeweled crown. "Top quality copper, walnut handle, sold 'em to fine people all over the state. Why, the governor's wife in Columbus purchased this very model for the annual state ball. And the price, folks tell me, can't be beat. Going for a dollar, that's all. Folks are glad for the chance to spend a dollar on this top-of-the-line aristocratic tea kettle."

He offered the burnished beauty to the Missus for her appraisal. And never mentioned that at five-ninety-five, the governor's wife had provided him a dollar's profit.

Sarah received the golden-red kettle into her hands with a shiver of joy. Every time she lifted the elegant vessel from her second-hand stove, she could imagine herself in a satin gown, a ribbon in her hair, as fancy and fine as the governor's wife in Columbus.

She was proud to count her dollar, an assortment of pennies and nickels, nothing larger than a dime, onto the rough plank table.

Ambrose declared, "Paid in full!" His motive in selling this kettle was not mercantile profit. Yea, he was compelled by more than friendship and kindness. For in truth, he hoped to save his hide. The transaction constituted an insurance policy, or so he hoped: an indemnity that tomorrow she would remember that he was one and the same man who had sold her the kettle. Though really there was no guarantee of its civilizing effect. But he hoped, O how he hoped, that she would at least fire a warning shot before she drew her bead.

III

Fireflies blinked over the potato patch. Ambrose walked toward a lantern that cast a circle of amber light on the ground: half of the circle was dark with clods of upturned earth, and half was green with potato bushes. The son held the lantern while the father crawled on his knees, digging with a trowel. The lantern cast the boy's shadow over his father as if a giant tree had fallen across the man's back. Heedless of Ben's exertions, Brewster gazed across the dark landscape toward the fishing hole.

Ben troweled with one hand, then reached into the loosened soil with the other. Working by touch alone, he lifted the coal-black tubers out of the ground and dropped them into a basket. Abruptly he hollered, "Bring up that light!"

Brewster shuffled a few steps toward his father, then stood like a statue, grubby, slouch-shouldered, as if half way through the creation from clay to man, the process had stopped.

Ben complained, "Here! Can't you see? *Here* is where I need the light."

Brewster snuffled, then shuffled forward. "We goin' fishin', Pa?"

His father worked a potato loose.

"Huh Pa? We goin' fishin'?"

Ambrose entered the circle of light. He could smell scorched cotton, for the lantern dangled against Brewster's pantleg. Ambrose took the handle from the boy, then held the lamp so its light poured onto Ben's dirt-covered hands as the farmer rubbed another russet potato clean. Ambrose chided, "Brewster, your Pa's got work tomorrow. He's got no time for fishing."

Ben grumbled as he grubbed at the ground.

"He's got a privy to dig. A proper privy hole is at least shoulder deep. That's a sight of work."

Growling, Ben flung a potato into the basket.

"Then there's moving the outhouse from the old hole to the new. But that shack is so rickety, the Missis'll likely want a new one. And Brewster, to build a new outhouse, well, *that's* a sight of work."

Ben pounded the earth with his fist.

Ambrose added casually, "And this time she'll probably want a two-holer."

"No!" roared Ben. He leaped to his feet and glared at the heavens with anguished eyes. Shaking his trowel at the firmament, he demanded to know, "Why must a man labor so?"

Ambrose mentioned, "Then, of course, there's still the old hole, filled plumb to the top and staring at you, and what does a man do about that?"

Ben's revolt collapsed. His shoulders slumped. He sank to his knees and jabbed the earth with his trowel.

The lightning bugs danced.

Brewster's voice whined from the edge of the lantern light, "We goin' fishin', Pa? "

(Now the angler cast his lure, a skillfully tied trout fly, which he placed lightly upon the surface precisely over the hole where the lunker lurked.) Ambrose announced breezily, "We're going to do something much better, Brewster. Tomorrow, we're going to watch a man sail up from the earth on wings."

Ben peered up, in no mood for such frivolity. "Ambrose, I'll thank ye not to talk nonsense."

The peddler stated with confidence, "Yessir, this man's going to fly higher than you can toss your hat."

Ben scoffed, "Only thing goin' to fly tomorrow is dirt comin' out from that privy pit."

Ambrose shrugged. "Privy can wait. Ain't often you'll have a chance to watch a man circle on wings around his pasture."

"Privy kin wait?" snorted Ben. "Ambrose, a man flappin' around on wings may be tall talk, but crossin' the Missus is plain unthinkable." Perplexed, Ben studied his friend. "You tryin' to stir up trouble?"

Ambrose explained, "Tomorrow morning, a man is going to fly the first circle in all history. No little Kitty Hawk hop across the sand dunes. They've been fiddling with the controls, learning how to turn. Wilbur told me he's going to pilot the first flight that circles back to where he came from."

"Wilbur?" Ben shook his head that he knew no Wilbur.

"He and his brother Orville. Them bicycle boys. Two wheels instead of four. I told 'em a bicycle would fall over like a two-legged horse. But it didn't!"

This was puzzlement upon perplexity. Ben pondered, "What call's a man got for a two-legged horse?"

Ambrose pointed southwest. "The Wrights are your neighbors, two farms over. They're using a pasture called Huffman Prairie, belongs to the president of a bank in Dayton. He's letting them fly their airplane there."

Ben stared southwest into the night. "Airplane?"

(The angler twitched his Royal Coachman; the lure danced upon the water.) "And tomorrow morning at seven a.m., we can watch Wilbur fly." Ambrose smiled smugly. "At least, *I* can."

Ben raised himself upright on his knees. "You goin' to be there, huh?"

"Wouldn't miss it for the world."

"Two farms over?"

"A mere fifteen-minute stroll."

Fireflies blinked across the dark distance to the southwest as Ben considered. Should he dig that privy hole? Or go see this thing, no matter what it was, just to see it?

A privy with pink curtains had been Sarah's dream once. The shack he'd banged together years ago was about to collapse—on its fifteenth hole. He'd never had a dime to spare for pink curtains. And now, was he about to run off on a lark . . . while she toiled with her red hands in the washbucket?

But if a man *was* going to fly tomorrow, hadn't she earned the right to be there too? Ben scratched his bristly jaw with fingernails caked in dirt as he wondered aloud, "Might the Missus come watch?"

Ambrose suggested, "We could leave her an invitation on the table, then scoot. By the time she finds it, we'll be halfway to Huffman Prairie. And by the time she catches up, she can thank us for the favor of inviting her."

Ben asked warily, "You think she'll thank us?" His brow knotted with apprehension at what she might do if she found nothing for which to thank them; if, for example, she found no man flapping around in circles above the pasture.

(The angler reeled his line a short, teasing distance; he readied his rod for the strike.) "Ben, perhaps I've overestimated you." Ambrose sighed with disappointment. "Thought you'd be keen for a little adventure. Thought you'd be man enough to know who's head of the household. But," he shrugged, "I see I've misjudged."

Ben climbed up from his knees. His eyes firm, his jaw squared, he stated, "I'll be there too."

Ambrose shook his head with doubt. "No sir, not you. Why, I'll bet ten dollars that tomorrow morning, you'll be doing none other than digging that privy pit."

Ben blinked. The sum was enormous. If he lost, he could not pay it in his lifetime. But if he won . . . He cocked his head with the pride of his manhood and held out his hand to shake on the deal. "Ten dollars says I'll watch that airyplane fly."

(The angler yanked his line taut.) In the amber glow of the lantern, the two men shook hands. "It's a bet," declared Ambrose. "A firm wager. No getting out of it." (Hooked!)

Beaming with confidence, Ben turned to his son, a shadowy stump silhouetted against the stars. "Brewster, you want to come? Man's goin' to fly tomorrow!"

"We goin' fishin', Pa?"

"Yer Ma's a-comin'. And Emlie-Lou too."

"Ifn we ain't goin' fishin' . . ." The plaintive whine trailed off. As did Brewster, into the dark.

In silence, Ben watched his son disappear.

Ambrose noted something deeper than disappointment in his friend's eyes.

Fireflies blinked and drifted.

The two men were still working when the moon rose. Each of them confident of the fortune soon in his pocket, they chatted and laughed as they gathered the harvest. Ben held every potato like a precious nugget, savoring its weight and russet color in the lanternlight. Surely the work would have gone faster if he had simply dug and dropped the spuds into the baskets. But there was a pause with each potato, a cradling in the hand for a moment, a satisfaction and a thanking, that slowed the job.

Ben washed the last potato in a stream at the end of the potato patch. Wrapping his hands around each half, he broke the huge potato in two. He and Ambrose chewed the raw sweet fruit of their labor while they surveyed the splendor of an accomplished field, sprinkled with brimming baskets, in the warm, soft, heaven-lit, cricket-filled, firefly-festooned peacefulness of late night.

IV

At 6:40 a.m., Ambrose stood up from the breakfast table. "Well, I'd best hitch the mule and get ready to go."

"Aye," agreed the Missus, leaning over a washtub as she scoured the griddle. "We've all got a job to do, and best get to it." She scowled at Ben, hunched gloomily at the table, then returned to her work with a vehemence she would soon apply to her husband were he to dally a minute more.

Emlie-Lou, leaning over the same tub while she scrubbed the oatmeal pot, peered at Ambrose with shy and silent longing.

Ambrose slid a folded sheet of paper beneath his plate, then hurried out the door. No one in the house could read his invitation. However, the very presence of that cowardly missive would inform the Missus that something was up, and it wouldn't be long before she was on their trail to find out what.

Ben growled to his wife, "Where ye want it?"

She growled back, "Behind the buckeye tree. We ain't dug there yit."

With a disgruntled "dag nab", he stomped out the door, his hand clapped over his mouth to stifle a giant guffaw. He ran across the farmyard and rounded the corner of the barn at full tilt.

Ambrose gripped the brim of his top hat as the two fugitives sprinted across the potato patch, its dirt turned from one end to the other, not a spud undug. Like a workhorse unstrapped from the harness, Ben gamboled and sprang and galloped. He bounded across that potato patch as if his nocturnal toil, bared beneath heaven's blue eye, had earned him, in all fairness, the morning off.

BOOM!! blasted a musket behind them. As the escapees dove for the dirt, they heard rocksalt whistle but inches overhead. The two men glanced back and saw the Missus reloading her ancient firearm. The outhouse, shaken by the thunderclap of her ordnance, collapsed in a heap.

The men sprang up and dashed toward a meadow of goldenrod. "Emlie-Lou a-comin'?" queried Ben, high-stepping into the waist-deep flowers.

"She's invited, in the note," answered Ambrose across the butter-yellow fuzz between them.

"I shore hope so. Maybe it'll settle her. She's wantin' to go to school. But we cain't spare her."

"A hard worker, is she?"

"Keeps up with her Ma to the bone-weary end of the day."

Ambrose pondered this new revelation. "School, huh?"

BOOM!! roared the musket. The derelicts dove deep into the ragweed. Yellow tufts beheaded from their stems fluttered down on top of them. While the Missus reloaded, the men jumped up and raced toward a rail fence.

"Emlie-Lou stands every mornin' at that washtub, scrubbin' the oatmeal pot while she watches them other kids walkin' down the road. They're dressed up nice, each with a pair of school shoes. She ain't got but them clodhoppers. So she won't go herself nohow."

Farmer and peddler vaulted the fence, then ran stride matching stride across a field of clover. Ahead of them, a boy with a bridle walked toward a butterscotch horse.

"Mornin'!" called Ben to the lad, a neighbor he had never met. "Some fine horse ye got!" he called, but he kept on running.

Ambrose recognized the trees ahead: a row of elms twice as tall as the phone poles beneath them. "That's . . . the place," he puffed. "Huffman . . . Prairie."

BOOM!! crashed the musket. The two truants belly-flopped into a thicket of thistles.

"Dang her mean streak," complained Ben. "What that woman won't do fer pink curtains."

Ambrose lifted his head to search for any sign of an airplane. BOOM!! His top hat spun through the air. It landed in the grass, looking like a birdhouse with an entrance and an exit.

"Got both her barrels a-workin," warned Ben.

Picking up his hat, Ambrose wished he had that copper kettle to wave, as a flag of truce.

Ben, light and limber as a scampering schoolboy, took the lead as the men dashed across a road, passed beneath the leafy arch of elms, then sprinted the home stretch to the middle of Huffman Prairie. Ben looked back at the Missus: fifty yards behind, she marched with the iron determination of Scorched-Earth Sherman, her patchwork apron churning above her angry knees. Behind the sight on the musket glared her fiery eye as the distance narrowed between wife and husband.

He looked toward a barn at the far end of the pasture. In front of the barn was a long box with a white top and bottom, but all its sides were missing. Near the Whatever-It-Was stood two men in white shirts and black ties. Neither one seemed to be wearing angel wings.

Ambrose, gasping for breath as he peered back at the Missus, discerned that the bore of her barrel was aimed slightly to his left. He glanced at Ben, then moved discreetly two steps to the right.

He heard a motor start. Looking up the length of the pasture, he watched as Wilbur, the bald brother, climbed inside the construction of horizontal stripes and vertical struts. Orville braced a wingtip. The airplane, a hundred yards from where Ambrose stood, pointed straight at him.

The Missus stopped in the middle of the road and cocked both hammers. "Ben! Ambrose! If you two ain't home this minute t'dig that privy pit, I'll be diggin' fer a twin funeral!"

"Hold yer fire!" hollered Ben. He pointed toward the airyplane and added, though with scant belief in the substance of his offer, "Yer invited to watch too."

Now something moving caught her eye: something, but almost nothing, for she could see right through it. Yet a man lay flat inside it. With a growing roar, it skidded on runners across the pasture like a sled without snow. Baffled at the lack of horses to pull it, though it was moving now as fast as a horse could gallop, she wondered what nonsense these two fools had come to see.

Ambrose, about to be shot or run over or both, had half a mind to strike out for California. But he stood his ground, for as that mechanical bird with its twin whirling propellers roared toward him, he refused not to believe in the Future.

The runners bounced and bumped and jounced and jumped; the box shivered and shook, as if the earth would punish the prideful men who sought to climb the invisible air.

Then ever so gently, as if rising before their eyes from reality into a dream, the two stripes of white cloth lifted the runners from the ground, and the man staring fiercely forward inside his clattering contraption suddenly floated on wings.

Ambrose's jaw dropped to his knees.

Ben called exultantly, "Sarah, now look there!"

She watched something so delicate, yet so determined, advancing with such unfettered grace, that it awoke a feeling from her wedding day. She had worn white muslin, (though she had dreamed of silk,) and now she recognized two bolts of muslin spread across the powder-blue sky by some sort of magic, floating confidently forward . . . as once she had floated on her father's arm down the aisle.

Emlie-Lou drew up beside her mother. She straightened her gingham dress, thinking that maybe someone was going to pick her up here on the road and take her away forever. She searched up and down the lane in both directions. Then she glanced behind her: Yesl The boy on the butterscotch horse had followed.

Reassured that the airplane, rising at a steady angle, would pass well over his head, Ambrose focused on the pilot. Between the circular blurs of the propellers, their burr growing ever louder, Wilbur lay on the hip cradle, his hands on the levers, his face lifted, his eyes staring into the sky ahead, his necktie and collar neatly in place. Just the day before, Ambrose had spoken with him, a quiet though congenial man who had made a pot of fresh coffee with his new copper coffee pot, then shared a cup with Ambrose. Now there he was, twenty feet up in the air, sailing toward him as irrefutable proof that if a man could dream, he could do.

As the flying machine glided overhead with both a mechanical roar and an ethereal whoooooosh, the pilot called down, "Good morning, Benjamin!"

Ben blinked with surprise, for the flyer knew his name. Then he turned to Ambrose and cheered with triumph, "Ten dollars is mine!"

But Ambrose's eyes were fastened on the man who climbed even higher into the sky. Though witness in his time to many marvels, he stared, his face buffeted by the blast of propellor-driven wind, with a welling respect that even his silver tongue could never articulate.

The airplane sailed in a straight line toward the far end of the pasture. Ambrose held his breath, waiting, for even this wonder was not yet enough. Twenty feet off the ground, yes, thirty feet, all right, but would it . . . could it . . . ?

The wings tilted. Like a hawk on a lazy summer day, the airplane turned in a long sweeping curve. Those tandem wings were able not only to go up and stay up, but to maneuver once they were up there. The airborne man completed half a circle, then his wings leveled again and Wilbur was heading back up the pasture. "That's it!" proclaimed Ambrose. He threw his top hat into the sky. "That's flying!"

Suddenly the airplane lurched from its path; Wilbur shouted down toward the road, "Don't shoot!"

The Missus lowered her musket, the barrel of which had followed her duck hunter's eye.

Wilbur straightened the airplane's evasive wobble. He flew the full length of the pasture, and then his wings tilted a second time. The airplane pivoted around the barn and completed the first loop in the history of human flight.

Orville whooped from the ground, "Yahoooo!"

Wilbur cruised to the middle of Huffman Prairie, then

banked into a circle with Ambrose and Ben at its center. Exuberant, the two men waved, witnesses to the promise of the newborn century.

Emlie-Lou, sitting behind the boy on his butterscotch horse, cantered across the pasture and joined her father. She and the lad turned their faces together as they watched the day's second and slightly less exciting miracle.

The horse whinneyed skittishly as the Missus stomped to the middle of the pasture. The musket over her shoulder, she shook her fist at Ben. But then she too looked up and watched a marvel not even the governor's wife had seen. She hooked her arm through Ben's, as on their wedding day.

Now the circling aircraft leveled its wings and followed a tangent toward the barn. It drifted down, hovered as if reluctant to touch the ground . . . then landed with barely a bounce on its runners.

As the five spectators hurried toward it, Orville held up a stopwatch and announced, "One minute thirty-five and two-fifths seconds!"

The inventors shook hands with their witnesses and thanked them for coming. Orville informed them that the *Dayton Gazette* would contact them shortly for verification of the flight.

Ambrose discreetly slipped ten dollars into the hand of the head of the household; Ben discreetly slipped the ten dollars into a pocket of his overalls. Though great was the unspoken delight in his eyes, greater still was his gratitude.

Ambrose touched the battered brim of his hat with a silent, You're welcome.

Then Ambrose and Orville disappeared behind the barn, where proceeded a bit of business.

Wilbur walked quietly into the hanger, brushed off a dusty calendar and drew a circle in the square of September 20, 1904: a triumph only nine months after their first flight at Kitty Hawk.

V

Whistling, Ambrose walked alone across the potato patch. The cabin was empty when he entered it. He acted quickly.

Emlie-Lou's clodhoppers stood by the door. He stuck a dollar bill into each boot: her tuition.

That left eight dollars in his hand. He was three dollars in arrears to himself from the sale of the tea kettle; granting himself a dollar's profit, he owed himself four, which he pocketed. The remaining four bills he laid in a fan on the rough plank table. Then he wrote a note that none in the household could read.

Before he stepped out the door, he paused to gaze at the copper kettle on the stove, a golden hen peacefully roosting. He thanked it for his life.

In the farmyard, he saw Emlie-Lou on the butterscotch horse. Her arms were wrapped around the boy who, in the heat of the day, had taken off his shirt. The horse was breathing hard, its ribs heaving.

The tin peddler tipped his hat. When she took the note to school and learned what was written in it, ("Hire a hand to help on the farm",) she would know just who.

He hitched his mule to the wagon. Then he wheeled the bicycle out of the barn, bits of hay falling from its spokes. With a white handkerchief, he dusted the vehicle until it dazzled in the morning sunshine.

He walked the bicycle to the edge of the hog wallow. The dozen flop-eared inhabitants twitched their dripping snouts. Brewster sat on the one and only branch he ever sat on. Ambrose tossed a small cardboard box to the boy. Brewster caught it with a snatch of his hand, thumbed open the box, then gaped with astonishment when he discovered, "Fishhooks!" He grinned at the hooks of all sizes that poured in a glittering heap onto the mud-smeared palm of his hand. For that's what he wanted, that's what he needed, and never had a penny to buy one with: a fishhook of his own.

He called across the mire, "Mister Smith, I shore do thank ye kindly."

Ambrose touched his hand to the brim of the remnants of his top hat. "Good fishing, Brewster."

Then he mounted the vehicle of the Modern Age. The hogs, horror-struck, (being creatures of comely flesh with bones unknown within, and thus mistrustful of a beast so startlingly skeletal,) squealed with zeal their porcine peals of panic, while Ambrose pedaled with skill and pluck the circumference of their pungent muck. He completed one full orbit, then followed a tangent down the driveway. The mule clip-clopped diligently behind.

Down the road came Ben and Sarah riding a red two-seater bicycle, their balance flawless. Sarah, in front, steered as if she rode a splendid steed. She no longer looked longingly at the world, for she had joined it. Despite the ruts and potholes, the handlebars floated as gracefully in her grip as those white wings had floated over the pasture.

Ben, perched on the seat behind her, sang an old ballad of newborn romance. He was hopelessly in love, his heart tender and giddy. For he had no more than received into his hand the ten dollars from Ambrose, when he noticed the Missus staring at some red mechanical contrivance leaning against the barn. It had two wheels, and two seats, and a price tag, $9.95. He had felt proud to be able to pay for it, and pocket the nickel. Now he sang with jubilant joy, his faith in a just Providence restored.

Ambrose, his course a teetering zigzag, emerged from the end of the driveway as Sarah and Ben came gliding down the road. Sarah's soft gray eyes shone upon him with gratitude, though she pulled far to the side of the thoroughfare to give him plenty of room.

Ambrose lurched in a sudden swooping loop, then leveled out beside the gliding pair. Admiring their scarlet tandem, he declared, "My, but she's a spanking beauty!"

Ben guffawed, "Dang ifn you don't look like a two-legged horse."

His top hat fetching and yawing like the mast of a ship in a storm, Ambrose replied, "I've just . . . got to . . . get the hang . . . of it."

Ben grinned as he bragged a little, "Sorry about them ten bucks!"

"Oh, that's . . . all right." Ambrose almost added, though he kept the transaction to himself, "Orville bet me twenty you'd never make it."

A Portrait of America

from the novel "A JOURNEY OUT OF DARKNESS"

Anna Sofia is a spirit, the ghost of a young Norwegian woman who died in 1917. Michael is a Norwegian-American from Florida, now living as an English teacher above the polar circle in northern Norway.

Anna Sofia is visible only when she absorbs and radiates the natural light around her. As she responds to natural light, so she responds with sensitivity to Michael's emotions.

During the last week of September, after I had hacked and slashed with my red pen through a briar patch of translation exercises, I decided to recuperate with a bowl of popcorn in front of the fireplace.

Anna Sofia soon appeared. "I would have come down earlier, but I don't like to be around you while you're correcting papers. I never got so grumpy."

I offered her the rocking chair, then drew up a chair for myself. "You never had to read forty business translations about 'foreign quota of capital shares' and 'extendable option bonds tendered for purchase'. Ooof! My brain becomes a boiled cabbage."

She scowled, unconvinced. "A teacher should always maintain a positive attitude toward his job." Then she peered into the big wooden bowl in my lap. "What is that?"

"Popcorn."

"Popcorn! Is that what it looks like? How pretty! What does it taste like?"

"Well," I laughed, "not like ordinary popcorn. You see, I boil codfish, and later I pop popcorn, in the same pot. I wash the pot as best I can, but still, the popcorn tastes like codfish and the codfish tastes like popcorn."

She wrinkled her nose. I stuffed a handful of cod-flavored popcorn into my mouth.

Settling back in her chair, she gazed as peacefully into the flames as if she sat before a campfire. Then she turned to me and asked, "When did your ancestors sail for America?"

"Ooo-ooo oo-oo-ooo."

"Please do not speak with your mouth full."

I chewed and swallowed, then told her, "Eighteen eighty-five. During the peak of Norwegian migration. But I don't know much more than that. Nobody in the family speaks Norwegian anymore."

"Where did your ancestors come from?"

"I don't even know that. They might have come from Oslo or Bergen, might have come from some little village up in the mountains. They might have been farmers, might have been fishermen. My last name is Lanes, Michael Lanes, which doesn't sound Norwegian at all. I think that when my great-great-grandfather arrived in New York, he adopted an English name."

Anna Sofia reached for an iron poker, then rearranged a log on the fire. "I'll find out."

"You'll find out? Is there some sort of historical register in Norway?"

"Tonight, while you sleep, I'll try to visit your great-great-grandfather. Do you know his name?"

"You mean, you're going to take a trip," I pointed, "up there?"

She began to rock in her chair, which squeaked with a slow rhythm. "Yes, up there. I have permission to go back and forth. Not often, but I can."

"Permission?"

"What was his name?"

"Eric Lanes. My father is Eric Lanes the fourth."

"Why aren't you the fifth?"

"That's my older brother. I'm just Mike. Good ol' American

Mike."

She gazed into the fire. "All right, Michael. I'll try to locate Eric Lanes the first."

* * *

The following evening, I came into the dark house with a bag of groceries in each arm. I was late getting home because I had attended a faculty meeting, which was, to my dismay, a dismal dreary drawn-out affair during which 529 points, sub-points, and petty particularities of all pertinent and contingent issues were duly discussed. I just barely survived by excusing myself, twice, to stand with my head out a hallway window so I could breathe cold clean air which had not been used to formulate words on any subject whatsoever, unlike the stultifying air in the conference room, which had been inhaled and vented as verbiage so many times by so many people that it contained little if any oxygen, though a great deal of point-of-information-laden CO_2.

So by the time I dragged myself into the dark house, I was in a less than cheerful mood. I set the bags of groceries on a chair, then opened the refrigerator door. The refrigerator's light cast its glow into the kitchen. I picked up two cartons of milk, one in each hand, and—

"You're from Leines," announced a voice beside me.

"Yiiii!" I cried, startled, and dropped both milk cartons. One burst open; milk streamed across the kitchen floor. In the glow of the refrigerator light, I saw two brown footprints in the middle of the growing white puddle: Anna Sofia's.

"Eric the first was from Leines," she continued, oblivious of the disaster she had caused. "Leines, (she said 'Lay-ness') which apparently became Lanes in America, is a fishing village about fifty kilometers north of here. Papa and I sailed there several times."

"Oh. Do you know if there is a mop in the house?"

"In the bathroom closet. Eric's wife's name, or his beloved's name, when he courted her, was Inger."

I waded, fuming, through the milk, then left milky footprints from the kitchen to the bathroom, where I rummaged in the closet and found a mop with an attached rag that looked as if it had last swabbed the floor after the Great Mud Slide of '06. I called back to the kitchen, "Fascinating."

"They were married in the church in Leines on the day before they left Norway. He had great difficulties in convincing her to go with him to America."

I swabbed the kitchen floor, then wrung out the rag over the sink; swabbed and wrung; swabbed and wrung. The process was encouraged by my fantasy that the rag was somebody's neck.

"Are you going to leave the refrigerator door open?" asked Anna Sofia. "Won't everything get warm?"

I stomped through the swamp to the kitchen light switch and flicked it on. The milk had streamed beneath the refrigerator, and had pooled under the table, and one white tributary was snaking toward the netherworld beneath the stove. I was staring at a down-on-your-knees job, tra la. Sloshing back across the kitchen, I closed the refrigerator door, while keeping all pertinent and contengent remarks, in the presence of a lady, to myself.

"I prefer no modern lights," Anna Sofia informed me as her invisible feet splashed across the kitchen floor to the sink. "Please, kerosene or a candle." The door to the cabinet under the sink opened, and out came an ancient sponge which, when I first moved in, I had found too brittle to use. The sponge vanished in her hand, but not the milk which she sopped up under the table: the milk crossed the room in a little white cloud, then, when twisted, dribbled into the sink.

Slightly mollified, I lit a candle and set it on a corner of the table, then I turned out the kitchen light. True enough, she glowed with the candlelight as she helped me clean up the mess. "Your great-great-grandmother was in love with Eric," she explained, carrying another white cloud of milk to the sink, "but she was also in love with her beach. And her mountains. And her waterfalls. I have been to that very beach with Papa. Inger had an extremely difficult choice. Michael, do you have a map of the coast north of here?"

What I really wanted was dinner and a cold beer and bed. But at the same time, I was curious about my family history. So, with a silent growl, I went into the living room, sorted through a pile of maps on a bookshelf, and returned to the kitchen with a map of Nordland County. I unfolded it on the table, then set the candlestick in the middle of the map. "Will this one do?"

She put her pale yellow finger on our village, traced her fingertip west along the fjord to Bodø, then she traveled north across the sea, as she and her Papa would have sailed in his boat, to a peninsula with an exceedingly irregular coastline. "Here is Steigen," she said, circling the peninsula with her finger. Leaning closer, she circled her finger around Steigen's southwest corner: a piece of land that looked like a left-handed mitten. Then she pointed at a village on the tip of the thumb. "Here is Leines, where Eric lived."

Moving the candle for better lighting, I peered, with genuine interest now, at my family's hometown. In 1885, Leines must have been a very remote village, probably accessible only by boat.

She now pointed at the shore north of the bay cupped by the mitten. "Here was a cluster of houses called Brennvika, where Inger lived. And here," her finger traced the crescent-shaped bay, "is the beach Inger loved, Brennvikasanden."

I looked up from the map to a calendar on the wall. "Today's Wednesday. What do you say we pack our camping gear into the car and head north on Friday evening? I don't have classes on Monday. We'd have three days in Eric's town, and on Inger's beach. I could take some pictures to send to Mom and Dad. They'd be thrilled to see where the family had its roots."

"In the *car.*" Anne Sofia looked at me with a mix of disbelief and delight. "Michael, I've never ridden in a car."

* * *

Lit pale green by the dashboard lights, (which she found pretty and seemed willing to reflect,) Anna Sofia marveled at the speed of cars and trucks as they whooshed past us in the night. She stared at the startling sight of a row of windows that, racing parallel to the road, caught up with us—she could see people inside the windows!—then gradually drew ahead of us. I explained, "That's the train from Bodø to Trondheim." And she gaped with astonishment at the neon-lit buildings and interweaving streams of traffic in downtown Fauske, a small town from my point of view, a metropolis rivaling Paris from hers.

But though she approved of most everything she saw, she was shocked, as we drove north up the coast, by the tunnels through the mountains. That these eternal mountains, which had stood against even the crushing power of the glaciers, should now have holes poked through them, was to her profoundly upsetting. When we drove through the first tunnel, with its overhead lights, telephone boxes at regular intervals, and giant fans sucking in fresh air, she protested, "It's like building a road through a church!" As we drove in and out of another half-dozen tunnels, she folded her arms and glowered at the ugly gray walls that arched over the car. "Why can't people go where they want to go by boat?"

"Too slow, I suppose. The world races around on wheels today. Folks don't have time for the majesty of mountains. They want to get where they're going."

She brooded, unconvinced. "I'll bet when they get wherever they're going, they don't see it any more than they saw what they didn't see while they were going there."

Not one to pass judgment on modern Norwegians, for I was a guest in their country, I offered no opinion.

Despite the giant ventilation fans, the air in the longer tunnels smelled of car exhaust. My own car was pumping out its share, I knew. I didn't want to upset Anna Sofia any further, so I said nothing, but certainly the few holes which we blasted through the mountains were far less destructive, and disrespectful, than the blanket of poison which we wrapped, perhaps one day like a funeral shroud, around the entire planet.

When we turned off the main highway and drove west on the Steigen peninsula, we soon approached a tunnel which was, according to a sign, over eight kilometers long. I glanced at Anna Sofia; she sat with her eyes closed, her face set with grim resignation, as if she were about to be shot. "Please let me know," she said, "when the mountain is a mountain again."

I wondered, as I drove through the tunnel, its amber lights passing overhead, if there was a song I could sing which she might know, so she could sing along with me. But the busy week at the college, and the long drive and late hour were catching up with me. Try as I might, as I drove beneath those hypnotically pulsing amber lights, blip . . . blip . . . blip . . . blip . . ., the only melody which I could nudge from my sleepy brain was 'She'll be comin' 'round the mountain when she comes.' Groggy as I felt, I knew that was not the right song.

"Michael, does anyone in your family play the fiddle?" Her eyes were still shut, though she had turned her face toward me.

"Yes, as a matter of fact. Well, yes, and no. When I was a boy, I found an old violin up in my grandparents' attic. My father's father said he had found it in *his* father's attic. Though nobody ever played it, the instrument was a family heirloom and therefore never sold or given away. It just went from attic to attic. Well, I took a shine to it and asked my father if he'd buy some new strings, which he did. He soon regretted his error. For the next two years, I practiced diligently every evening in my bedroom, creating the shrieks of cats boiled alive in the key of E-flat. I knew my career as a virtuoso was coming to a close when my teacher suddenly clenched his hand around the neck of my violin and asked me why I didn't play baseball like all the other boys. I think he and my father were in cahoots, because when I went home that afternoon, Dad met me in the driveway with a new baseball mitt."

Anna Sofia was smiling now, that pretty smile which I loved to see, though her eyes were still closed.

"So the fiddle is up in the attic in Florida. And in my bedroom, on the dresser, stands our Little League trophy. I played shortstop, batted .285. My violin teacher retired and moved to Alaska."

"That fiddle belonged to your great-great-grandfather Eric."

"You mean that fiddle came originally from Norway?"

"Can I open my eyes yet?"

"Not yet. I'll tell you when."

While those eight kilometers of amber lights continued to blink overhead, she explained, "Eric played his fiddle at weddings and dances up and down the coast. He had his own style of music. Yes, he knew the local tunes, but he could improvise as well. At a wedding party, after he had fiddled the dancers to exhaustion, he would play a song—not a song really, more a musical portrait—about the bride, and about the groom, and people marveled that he could paint such a true picture of them. He caught their laughter, their way of talking, the busy clicking of a woman's knitting needles, the swing and chop of a man's axe. Sometimes, for a game, Eric would play without saying whom he was describing, and the dancers had to guess."

I was pleased to learn about such a colorful character in the family tree, although I laughed ruefully, "I sure did insult his poor violin." As we cruised on and on through the bowels of that endless tunnel, I asked, puzzled, "Why did someone so apparently successful in Norway decide to emigrate to America?"

She nodded, as if I had asked the right question. "Like you, he had two reasons. One that compelled him to leave his homeland, and one that beckoned from across the sea."

I was intrigued by this parallel between myself and Eric.

"Why did they all leave back then? Too many people, too little land. Eric was the eleventh of twelve children, born where the mountains marched right down to the sea. His family struggled to find enough good earth between the rocks where they could plant their potatoes. But of course, every other family in the region was looking for a spare acre where they could plant *their* potatoes."

I had read about that bleak period in Norwegian history,

when poverty and desperation had forced nearly a tenth of the population to leave home.

"Eric could have tried his luck in Oslo. Perhaps he could have found a job as a seaman on a freighter. But Eric was no common laborer. He told me that he had a special dream. And that dream was more than his own farm somewhere in America. It was more than plowing a hundred acres of fertile land, and putting a roof over his head, shoes on his feet and money in the bank."

"He told you all this? While you were," letting go of the steering wheel with one hand, I pointed, "up there?"

"Can I open my eyes yet?" she asked with impatience.

"Not yet." I checked the odometer. "Another three point seven kilometers." The amber lights glided by, blip . . . blip . . . blip . . . blip . . .

"Eric's dream beckoned. He told me that he wanted to play a portrait of America."

"A portrait of America? You mean, with his violin?"

"What was this country, he wondered, this Soria Moria beyond the Atlantic, that compelled people from every nation in Europe to leave a farm, a village, a city centuries old, so they could become Americans? *If* they survived the voyage. If they learned a new language. If they found work, if they found land. If they were willing to leave all and to risk all, they could help to build a new nation. It was the same, Eric said, as when people centuries ago had gathered together to build a new kind of church, a loftier church, a far more beautiful church than had ever before existed. A church which people called a cathedral. Yes, your Eric wanted to be there during the building of America, and he wanted to portray her builders with his fiddle."

Anna Sofia now faced forward, eyes closed, and said nothing more.

I imagined a man who watched, with a keen eye, the other immigrants aboard his ship. And the people of strange races on the streets of New York. The coach drivers and innkeepers and railroad men as he traveled west. The store clerks and preachers, the established farmers, and the fellow pioneers who erected houses of sod on the prairie, and sowed their seed, and gathered on a Saturday night to hear the fiddler play his square dances and reels. And then, no doubt to their great pleasure, they heard the man who spoke but broken English play a strange song, an intriguing song which stirred their souls, as if, even as they heard his strong and striding cadences for the first time, his music sang the songs of their own hearts.

Those songs, Eric never wrote down. They glowed as vibrantly as the setting sun glowed over golden fields of ripening Dakota wheat; then like the sun, they vanished. And when, his years completed, he laid down his plow, and laid down the fiddle, the plow was perhaps auctioned, and the fiddle found its way to the attic.

The more I thought about Eric, the more . . . blip . . . blip . . . blip . . . I turned a critical eye upon myself. For what dream did I have?

But what dream could anybody have today, in that crazy place?

A portrait of America. What would Eric portray, I wondered with my ready cynicism, if he could return to America in this day and age? Could he render with his violin the gunshots and hypodermic needles, and the snores in front of the TV? Sirens in the night would certainly be a part of his repertoire. The sudden shouts of rage, and the silent screams of despair. The ghetto rap and the government whitewash. If he wanted to play the songs of the American heart, he'd learn to play an anthem to a broken promise, a bloodied dream. America, lighting the way for the rest of the world? Or clutching her sputtering candle while the rest of the world passed her by.

I shook my head. No, I didn't want to get all that going again. I rolled down the window for a bit of fresh air, but caught a whiff of truck fumes lingering in the tunnel and rolled it up again.

Wanting to think about something else, I asked Anna Sofia, "What about Inger? Did you talk with her too?"

I saw a wisp of a smile. "Wait. Not yet. We have to be there."

"Be where? On her beach?"

She asked with irritation, "Please, can't I open my eyes yet?"

I peered ahead, and could see the end of the amber hyphens. "About half a minute more." We rode in silence until the car emerged from the tunnel's mouth. Suddenly mountains loomed above us to the left, and an expanse of dark water lay below us to the right. "Okay. You can open your eyes now." I rolled down my window and took breath after breath of the fresh air sweeping through the car.

Anna Sofia looked out the windshield, then out her side window. "Yes, this is the way it was when Eric courted Inger."

Despite the chilly wind, I yawned wearily. Soon I would be too sleepy to risk driving any further. "I think we ought to find a spot where we can roll out our sleeping bags."

"Good," she agreed. "Better to wait for daylight before we drive through such a beautiful place."

We soon approached a roadside turnoff overlooking the fjord. My headlights swept across a picnic table: a perfect spot for breakfast. But even better, when I stepped over the curb at the edge of the asphalt, I discovered, to my delight, a bed of thick moss.

We stretched out in our bags beside each other, our feet slightly downhill toward the water. The Polar Star shone high overhead.

"Good night, Michael. Tomorrow will be a wonderful day."

"Good night, Anna Sofia. Yes, I think so too."

I looked forward to the coming day, for after five generations, I was about to complete the circle: I was returning to the home of my ancestors.

Mingled with my excitement, however, was the unavoidable question: Who are you to walk the streets of Leines?

I felt unworthy.

* * *

While I ate a bowl of oatmeal at the picnic table, Anna Sofia, glowing early morning yellow, explored the rocky shoreline of the fjord. She brought back three pieces of driftwood. As she laid them on the table, she told me they looked like a sparrow, a witch, and a "nøkk".

"What's a nøkk?" I picked up the odd-shaped piece of wood, in which I could see no particular figure.

"A spirit who lives under a waterfall. He enchants people so they can play the fiddle."

I set the piece of wood on the table. "Tell your nøkk that with regard to Michael Lanes, he shouldn't be too over-optimistic."

She frowned at me. "Tell Michael Lanes that with regard to Michael Lanes, he should not be so pessimistic."

We rolled up our sleeping bags, then drove west along the Steigen coastline toward Leines. Whenever the road curved around a bay, we looked down at fishing boats that slept quietly at their moorings. On the other side of the fjord, the mountains bragged that they were just as rugged and photogenic as any mountains we had on our side. We passed several farms; some had big new barns with corrugated aluminum siding, some had paintless tumbledown barns with sod on the roof. We stopped for lunch near an abandoned house, and while exploring the old farmyard, we discovered a rusted stove standing outside in a thicket of rowanberry trees. The clusters of festive red berries, although they would soon wither and drop from the branches, briefly embodied nature's eternal fruitfulness, while the stove beneath them, slowly corroding over the decades into incremental flakes of rust, would eventually succumb and be no more.

Toward midafternoon, we drove into the village of Leines, where snug houses with tidy yards overlooked the sea. I pulled to the side of the road so we could look at the white church where Eric and Inger had been married on the day before they sailed for America. The belltower stood above the village rooftops, and tended, like a watchful shepherd, the headstones of a well-groomed cemetery. Driving on through Leines, we saw no vestiges of nineteenth century poverty. A collapsing garage, a crumbling stone wall, an old fishing boat left to rot in the weeds, these seemed more the remnants of my own century than Eric's.

I admired the picturesque homes, but I felt no special bond with the town. I was not overwhelmed, as I had anticipated, by any feeling of homecoming. I had no compelling desire to stop the car, swing open the door and set my feet down on the very earth where my people had come from. I could have walked along one of the short seaside streets where Eric no doubt had walked. But the families of his time, who raised twelve children and grew their own potatoes and caught their own fish, and who probably read the Bible on long winter nights, had been replaced by families who bought most of their groceries at the supermarket, and judging from the abundance of television antennas and parabolas, probably did pretty much the same thing that American families did in the evening. Two boys riding bicycles toward us wore bluejeans and denim jackets. One wore a baseball cap, backwards. The other wore, I saw as he rode past the car, an earring.

I asked Anna Sofia, "Is Eric's house still here? We could swing by so I could take a picture for my parents."

She shook her head. "Eric received a letter from his brother, telling him the old log house had been torn down to make room for a frame house with a slate roof. Do you want to visit that house?"

I considered. "Do I have any relatives still living there? Would they be glad to meet an American cousin?"

"I don't know. We can stop and ask."

We drove past a man washing his silver-gray Volvo in the driveway. He held a green hose, dipped his sponge into an orange plastic bucket. He probably had a bottle of Turtle Wax, its instructions in Norwegian.

"This is the village Eric left," said Anna Sofia. "Shall we go now to the place Inger and Eric took with them?"

"A place they took with them?"

"In their hearts."

I had learned to trust my guide. We hadn't yet gotten to where we were going, and she was about to take me there. I agreed. "Let's go."

Returning to the main road, we backtracked a couple of kilometers, then, at a sign indicating the turnoff to Brennvika, we headed south on a winding lane with houses scattered along it and mountains looming above it. Anna Sofia stared ahead, her eyes sharp to every detail. Peering up at the towering peaks that stood guard over the tiny homes, I felt a growing excitement. Whoever Inger was, she surely came from a village where the mountains were almost a part of the family.

At the end of the valley, the lane branched into the driveways of a cluster of houses. Wrapped around the hamlet were grass-tufted sand dunes. Beyond the dunes, according to my map, was the beach.

We parked where the car would be in no one's way, then walked along a well used trail through the dunes. Though as a Floridian I had seen many beautiful beaches, they had almost always been straight, and hemmed in by an endless row of hotels and condominiums. So when I walked past a bluff of sand, and suddenly could see the full sweep of Brennvika's beach, I stood on the threshold of a realm more magnificent than I had known could exist. The broad crescent of sand was well over a kilometer long, with not a building in sight. The mountains rising shoulder to shoulder behind the beach, every peak with its own distinct features, seemed like spectators high in the bleachers of a vast arena: the gods had gathered here to watch us mortals as we sported, or courted, on that crescent of golden sand.

Anna Sofia gazed up, her eyes lingering on each mountain before she looked at the next, and at the next, and the next. For her, this was a reunion with old friends. "Papa and I could have been here yesterday," she said with delight. "Nothing has changed." She pointed at several ribbons of white froth cascading down the steep mountain walls. "There, and there, and there, you have your choice of waterfalls."

Much as I wanted, after long hours behind the wheel, to stretch my legs with a walk along the beach, I glanced at the late-afternoon sun veiled in clouds over the mouth of the bay, and decided we had better set up camp first. We surveyed the dunes until we found a perfect place to pitch our tent, a little valley between two dunes, sheltered from the brunt of a southwest wind should it begin to blow, yet a spot from which we could watch the waves that rolled and broke with a long sideways rush of foam. Rather than use the remaining daylight to search for firewood, which was damp anyway from a recent rain, I decided to cook dinner later that evening on my butane camp stove.

With our gear securely stowed in the tent, we had just enough time before sunset for a walk on the beach. Anna Sofia scampered ahead of me toward the water. When I caught up with her, she was examining a long thin razor clam. "Look at this, Michael." She held the shell as a teacher would hold some specimen for her pupils to inspect. "At one end, you can see very clearly the outline of the original baby clam. And see here: distinct growth ridges along the length of the shell." Her finger counted the ridges, then she announced, "Ten! Do you think this clam was ten years old when . . . She guessed, "An otter ate him? He washed up in a storm?"

Her pupil queried, "Have you ever seen a razor clam longer than this one?"

"No, this is about as long as they get."

"Then I'd say he probably reached a ripe old age, and then his gills or his gizzard gave out, and he went to clam heaven."

She handed me the razor clam. "Will you hold him? I'm going to get a bag to put him in."

"Sure." Carefully, I took her treasure.

She skipped like a schoolgirl across the sand to our tent, and soon returned with an empty canvas sack that had held her sleeping bag. The sack, like everything else from her era which she carried or wore, faded to virtual invisibility, though it glowed, as did she, pale apricot from the setting sun. The razor clam, however, like everything else from the present day, remained fully visible. As we proceeded along the beach, her growing collection of purple mussels, a white seagull feather, curious bits of driftwood, and a piece of polished blue glass, floated in an aggregate in her ghostly sack. Had we passed anyone else on the beach, he would certainly have been stunned to discover a traveling amalgam of clams and snails, hovering about three feet above the sand, apparently impervious to the forces of gravity.

We walked as far as a stream that cut a serpentine path across the broad beach, and there we paused so I could take a picture of the sunset over the bay. I waded back and forth to find the right angle. The water rushing around my rubber boots had but minutes before come tumbling down the mountain as a waterfall. Perhaps the nøkk took notice.

An hour later, we sat in the dark on a small bluff of sand—our bench at Brennvikasanden—while a pot of carrots and potatoes boiled on the hissing stove. All I could see of Anna Sofia were her boots, which were close enough to the stove that they glowed with the same blue as the butane flame. The rest of her, however, was in the shadow of the pot.

Speaking to where I thought her face would be, I said, "I don't know how anyone could ever leave such a magnificent place. Even for America."

She did not answer. I didn't know if she was looking at me, or at the bay, a broad expanse of dark gray water beneath the clouded sky. But the waves answered, as they rolled with a sustained roar and washed onto the pale gray beach, "Noooo, nooooo, nooooo one could ever leave usssssss."

Anna Sofia's blue boots shifted in the sand. "Inger heard the waves breaking while she lay in her cradle. When she was a girl, she opened her bedroom window, summer and winter, so she could hear them. As a young woman, she dreamed and pondered, and debated with herself, to the sound of those waves."

We listened to evenly-spaced breakers that roared in defiance along their length, and then gasped and sighed as they succumbed. We heard the mighty Slap! of an ocean-roving comber as it pounded the shore in protest of its death.

"Inger's house, like Eric's, was torn down long ago. A new house, though today you might call it an old house, stands in its place in Brennvika. Perhaps her cradle is in the attic, or in the nursery."

Listening very carefully, I could also hear, high on a black mountainside behind the beach, the deep whisper of a waterfall. Yes, in Brennvika, the cradle should always be near a window.

I lifted the lid off the potato pot, stuck a fork into a potato: they were done. When I took the pot off the stove, Anna Sofia, now lit by the ring of blue flame, began to glow, faintly at first, pale blue. So I had a choice, whether to leave the stove burning and thus be able to see to whom I was speaking, at the expense of butane fuel; or to turn off the stove and speak to someone who wouldn't even have boots. "Say, isn't there some way I could see you while we sit here in the gloom of night? It's sort of unsettling, talking with you when I can't see the expression on your face."

With a smirk, she stuck out her blue tongue at me.

"C'mon, I'm serious. I don't want to run out of butane and have to eat goat cheese sandwiches for the rest of the trip."

"Turn off your stove. I'll get Papa's pipe."

"You brought your father's pipe?"

"Yes. Whenever we walked along this beach, he would stop to sit on a log and smoke his pipe. So I thought I might smoke it and remember him. Will you tell me how good it smells?"

"Did you bring your Papa's old tobacco too?"

"No, I couldn't find any. So I picked up a bag of Tiedemann's Red when we stopped at that gas station in Fauske."

I was shocked. "You shoplifted?"

She was insulted. "Certainly not. I set the package of tobacco on the counter with the milk and cookies you bought. The clerk put the tobacco into the bag with everything else. You didn't notice. You were staring at that blonde who bought a newspaper."

"I was not staring. I may have glanced. But I did think those cookies were awful darn expensive."

"Tiedemann's Red is the best. Thank you very much. I'll be right back."

She disappeared into the tent. I turned off the stove. A minute later a small black package and an even smaller box hovered in the darkness beside me. The flap of the package opened, and I smelled the aroma of fresh moist tobacco. Out came a tuft, which formed into a cylindrical plug as it was stuffed into what must have been her father's invisible pipe. The box opened and out came a match. It scraped on the box and a flame appeared, protected from the breeze by her cupped orange hand. Now I could begin to see her face as her cheeks sucked and the flame bent down into the plug of tobacco, igniting its top layer. She shook the match and the flame disappeared. Then she settled back against the bluff and contentedly puffed her pipe. "How's that?"

"Perfect." I could clearly see her eyes watching me, eyes filled with the peace and happiness of a camping trip. Gradually her curls became visible, and her sweater with the embroidered collar and silver clasp, and then her wool pants as far down as her knees. When she took a good strong puff and the tobacco glowed brightly, I was able to discern her orange-tinted boots.

I told her, "That tobacco smells great."

"Does it?"

"Mmmmmmm."

"Thanks."

"So tell me," I said, settling back against the cool sand beside her, "about Eric and Inger."

She smiled, that beautiful smile I fell in love with every time I saw it. "He played his violin for her while he courted her. And who could resist? However, to marry him, that was one thing. But to marry him and then sail away with him to America, leaving behind her family, whom she would never see again, and her friends in the village, whom she would never see again. . . . And to leave her beach and her streams, and the mountains that greeted her every time she stepped out the door, . . . No, for her to leave Brennvika was impossible. These were the mountains she had climbed, higher and higher each summer as she grew up. And when she had reached the top of one, there were still so many others. 'Are there mountains in America?' she asked. Eric told her, for he was an honest man, that he would be looking for farmland, not mountains."

I peered over my shoulder, but tonight the dark giants were hidden by clouds.

"So Inger told Eric that though she loved him, she could not leave Brennvika. He would either have to stay here with her, or leave without her. Oh, he argued with her, protested and coaxed and even wept. And she walked this long beach more than once, wondering if she wasn't throwing away her life's best chance, for he was a good man, she knew, and he promised her all the blessings the New World could offer. If she stayed behind, alone, what would she have? Try as she might, thinking of this man and that, no one caught her fancy. Certainly no other man kindled her heart the way Eric could. She would have to settle for second best: some fisherman competing with all the other fishermen to earn a few crowns. She imagined her gaunt children around a sparsely set table. Children too busy grubbing potatoes and cutting wood to spend much time with their schoolbooks. Whereas in America, every child had a chance, to become President even! And yet, had she not so often dreamed of teaching her children to climb these mountain peaks? How else to make them strong, how else to give them courage, how else to enable them to understand that some land is for farming, and is therefore useful, while other land, the slopes and ridges and the windy summits . . . other land is not for farming, but is no less sacred."

Yes, I heard myself thinking. Yes.

Anna Sofia puffed her pipe, her face pensive. "Then one evening, inside her farmhouse with her parents and two brothers and a sister, who were divided about evenly as to whether she should stay or go, she heard Eric playing his fiddle outside. She went out the door to meet him, but he said nothing. He kept playing as he led her—and she followed—down the road, then along the trail through the dunes, to the beach. Along the broad beach they walked on that warm moonlit evening in spring. Still he said not a word, but with his fiddle he made her a promise, for he gave her something which he could give her again, and again, whenever she might ask him for it: a portrait of her mountains. A portrait of her beach. A portrait of the sea."

The tide must have been out, for I just then caught a strong whiff of kelp exposed to the air. I took a deep breath of brine.

"Yes, he knew those peaks as well as she, and he proved it to her. His bow glided back and forth and his fingers danced on the strings as the notes ascended a slope, climbed a cliff, jumped an octave to the summit . . . then descended slowly, half-note by half-note, along a jagged ridge. Eric could make that violin laugh as the waterfalls laughed, throwing their spray into the silver moonlight. His stream came snaking down the slope, flowed into the quietude of a pool, trickled out again through the meadow where nesting birds chirped, and where the cuckoo called, where the breeze whispered through last year's brown grass, and this year's fresh green blades . . . to the beach where the stream rippled over the sand, and flowed at last into the sea where it was swallowed, swallowed, swallowed by the insatiable waves."

Anna Sofia looked at me, and I knew from her probing eyes that she was not simply passing the evening with a tale; she was guiding. And wherever we were going, my job was to get there.

"Eric portrayed the cloudberry flowers blooming in springtime, tiny whorls of white. The flit and flutter of the first yellow butterfly. The impatient, imperious cries of seagulls that follow a fishing boat. The silent majesty of an eagle soaring on the wind that sweeps up the slopes of her beloved mountains. He played for her the shivering of birch leaves: a soft rustle in springtime, a fluttering in summer, their dry shivering in fall, and their flight on the chill October wind, each leaf sailing away, one by one, like the minutes of time that never return. And when the tree stood bare, he knew how to play for her the sad rains of November. Rains that became, with a touch of winter's wand, flakes of sifting drifting snow."

Here was a man who loved, I thought. Could ever he have loved her so much, could ever she have loved him so much, had they not both been taught how to love by the mountains?

"Eric played and played, as he portrayed for Inger the battering winds and the pounding surge of a storm driving into the bay. He played for her the sigh of a quiet sea breathing beneath the fog. And he portrayed the moon, the moon on that springtime evening when he wooed her with his music, the moon peeking, and rising, and now sailing over the mountain, looking down to see what she would decide."

Anna Sofia paused. She stared across the dark beach, across the dark bay, toward the ocean that once had divided the Old World from the New, and divided as well a lifetime into two parts linked only by memory, and perhaps, once a year, by a letter. News of a birth. News of a burial.

"She sailed with him to America."

I felt a shiver of admiration. Here was a woman who truly loved. For I knew that my ancestors had settled on the Dakota prairie.

"And now you know," Anna Sofia turned to me, "about your violin."

"Yes. What I did to that poor instrument. It certainly deserved better."

She placed her pipe, containing a last ember, in the sand, then she stood up. As the ember disappeared, so did she. I continued to sit, and so her voice spoke to me from above me, out of the darkness. "Then I suggest that tomorrow we visit the nøkk. Good night." A moment later the tent flap opened, and closed again.

I called to her, "Good night." And then I listened, for quite a long time, to the music of the waves rumbling along the shore.

* * *

On Sunday morning, as we were preparing to leave camp, Anna Sofia said to me, "Bring your cup."

My cup sat on the sand by the stove. I picked it up, shook out the coffee grounds, then hooked its handle onto my belt loop. "Okay."

While we explored the beach, Anna Sofia with her sack of treasures, I with my camera, we were watched by the council of mountains. The jagged towering peaks peered down to witness what we, in our tiny moment of history, might do with our lives.

Reaching the far end of the beach, we followed a path worn through the heather above the bay's rocky shore. We passed occasionally through stands of birch where the upland forest made a successful foray down to the water. Surely Eric and Inger had walked along this path, seeking privacy beyond the open beach. Perhaps among the slender white birches, they had shared a first kiss.

When we came to a stream that wove around boulders into the bay, Anna Sofia turned from the shore and, without a word, led me uphill along the rushing water. The foot of the mountain became steeper, the terrain more rugged. Here and there in the woods I could see enormous chunks of rock that had broken off, ages ago, from the cliffs above us.

I could hear now a waterfall further up the mountain. "Are we going to visit your nøkk?" I called in jest to my guide, walking a short distance ahead of me.

She did not answer.

After half an hour's climb, we reached the falls. A sheet of white water raced down a black cliff, as if a ribbon of lace were being drawn from a spool hidden behind the precipice. The birches and boulders, and soon my uplifted face, were wet from the spray.

"Your cup," she said, watching me closely.

I unhooked the handle of my cup, then knelt and dipped the cup into a churning pool. While I drank the cool water, I searched for the nøkk, but water sprites are a cunning sort, and any nøkk hiding behind the curtains of white froth did not oblige me with even a glimpse of an elfin eye. In any case, I had with me no violin.

When I had emptied my cup and turned toward Anna Sofia, I discovered that she had already started to hike back down.

Looking up a last time before I too departed, I spotted an eagle circling on the mountain-scooped wind. Its overlapping loops progressed along the ridge until it disappeared behind a neighboring peak.

Anna Sofia and I spent a quiet afternoon on the beach. She collected her shells, I took my pictures. At dusk we walked to the serpentine stream, where I composed a photograph of the subdued sunset. Clouds, gray and faintly yellow-pink, floated over a silver sea.

No matter how many slices of bread with goat cheese I ate in the course of a day, they never seemed to be more than a brief appeasement to the beast above my belt. I suggested that we return to camp for a proper pot of potatoes. Anna Sofia, now that the light was fading, could smoke her pipe.

While I ate dinner, she disappeared into the tent, then emerged a short time later wearing a full-skirted dress with lace at the collar and cuffs. Pretending to ignore my surprise, she stood atop a nearby dune, puffed her pipe and looked up at the moonlit pinnacles. The moon itself would soon rise over the mountains.

The beast above my belt replete, I sat back against the bank of sand. Had I had the chance to shut my eyes, I would quickly have drifted into an after-dinner nap.

But Anna Sofia called down from the dune to inform me, "There's something of yours in the tent."

"Something of mine?" I asked, looking up at her mysterious smile and watching eyes. "In the tent?" There were a lot of things of mine in the tent, but clearly she meant something other than rain gear and spare socks.

"Take your flashlight." She pointed at the flashlight which I had placed in the sand beside me, so I would be prepared for the coming of darkness.

I clicked on the flashlight, stood on stiff legs, unzipped the tent flap and shone the beam inside: there in the circle of light, to my astonishment, lay the violin case which I had thought was in the attic in Florida. On the case was the sticker of our high school mascot, a grinning pelican. I reached my hand and tentatively touched the worn leather case: yes, it was solid. Apparently real. I picked it up by its handle: it had weight, more weight than that of an empty case. The violin must be inside!

I carried the case out to where Anna Sofia stood, puffing nonchalantly. She took the pipe out of her mouth long enough to ask, "I trust you haven't forgotten how to play it?"

"Well, I . . ." I knelt and laid the case on the sand, opened it, then shone the flashlight on what was unmistakably the same dark brown fiddle I had played as an optimistic teenager. There were even the familiar nicks in the wood near the bridge, made before my time. And yes, there was the bow, and smudgy box of rosin. I looked up at Anna Sofia for some explanation, but she observed these proceedings as if she witnessed nothing more extraordinary than finding a broom in a broom closet.

"Is it tuned?" she asked.

I lifted the fiddle out of its case. Then, my left hand knowing just how to hold it, I laid the instrument on my shoulder beneath my chin. In my right hand I took up the bow, and with all the debonair grace of a virtuoso standing in the footlights of Carnegie Hall, I applied the bow to the strings. No, that was not myself I was hearing! Such a tone I had never managed before. Stunned at the clarity of my F-sharp, I tried a B-flat: superb! I glanced at Anna Sofia. Her mysterious smile was gone, replaced by a grin of delight. "Michael, you are full of surprises. Let's take a walk."

The moon must have been just at the brink of rising over the ridge, because as my guide led me toward the beach, I with fiddle and bow, we walked first across sand dark in shadow, and then across sand bright in the glow of moonlight. Anna Sofia's curls glowed like a nimbus around her expectant face. She set her pipe in the sand, then unlaced her boots and stepped out of them.

I knew what was expected of me, but I could not believe that I would ever be able to live up to the talent, and the passion, of my predecessor. Oh, I had enjoyed the day on the beach, and our hike along the stream, but what was that compared to having grown up among these mountains? If ever there was a flatlander, it was me.

And yet, Anna Sofia would be sorely disappointed if I didn't scratch out a tune or two that mimicked, rudimentarily, a mountain pinnacle. Maybe, with a lot of imagination, she could envision from an apprentice's efforts the rolling of a wave. All right, then. For Anna Sofia, I'd give it my best.

My best before had never been even middling good. But that nøkk must have mustered his powers to the utmost, for the old violin sang into the night with a resonance that reached to the mountaintops.

I played the song of an eagle's spiraling flight, its broad wings buoyed on the upwelling wind.

And the song of the tiny pink spiral inside a snail's broken shell.

A musical portrait is drawn less from the eyes than from the heart. As Anna Sofia danced in her moonlit dress along the shore, she and the mats of foam washing around her lively feet the same lambent white, my heart sang with a passion no longer pent up inside me.

She loved this beach. And so my gift to her, whom I loved, was to love the beach as well. As in Eric's day. I played a song of love for the moon-glinting sea, and for the graceful pale crescent of sand. For waterfalls like silver threads, and for mountains reaching tall into the realm of the moon.

Plucking the strings, I portrayed the patter of the first drops of rain that pock the sand.

Sweeping the bow across the strings with increasing strength, I rendered the proud resignation of the wave that rolls from the sea into the bay, rises to twice its height as if better to survey the shore, then casts itself upon the sand with a splendid splash.

I told the tale of the last sad butterfly, wondering as it flitted and floated over the path why its companions had vanished.

I played the song of the slow majestic voyage of a cloud. And of the cloud's shadow as it creeps up the hills, climbs a ridge, insists on darkening a summit, with the hope that from that height it can join the cloud itself. But the cloud marches haughtily past, not far from the peak, just out of reach, and the shadow, forlorn, must slide alone down the mountain's other side.

Now the bow is lifted from the strings, and the instrument is released from under my chin. Anna Sofia, her dancing done, comes to join me. We walk quietly together along the shore, for my heart has spoken, and she has heard. And her heart has spoken, and I have heard, and we need say no more.

* * *

When I awoke the next morning and peered out from my sleeping bag, I searched the inside of the tent and saw that the violin was gone.

Stepping out of the tent, I gazed up at a dusting of snow on the tallest peaks. Sometime during the night, old man winter had passed overhead; his trailing robe had brushed the summits.

The air was exceedingly clear. I basked the full day long in bright autumn sunshine. Scarlet rowanberries, green moss, yellow birches, and the withering, fire-orange leaf of a lone cloudberry plant: all flaunted their colors before my camera.

I basked as well, the full day long, in Anna Sofia's reflected happiness. While she collected her shells, or sat on a driftwood log and smoked her Papa's pipe, she sang old sea ballads that she had learned from her Papa years ago. Her clear soprano voice drifting across the beach seemed to blend in perfect harmony with the *basso ostinato* of the waves.

Descending toward the sea, the sun, unsatisfied with a perfect day's work, stretched forth his wand and turned the snowy peaks pink.

With a final flourish, the great magician showed how easily he could mix water with fire, for the water rippling in the serpentine stream turned copper-gold.

His blessings bestowed, the most trustworthy of gods departed.

* * *

As we drove home Monday evening, Anna Sofia, lit pale green by the dashboard lights, closed her eyes without comment from the moment we approached a tunnel until, emerging from its other end, I told her, "Okay."

Once we had passed through Fauske and were certain of no more tunnels, she reached into her bulging bag and began to arrange her treasures along the dashboard. The heater was on, blowing warm air up the inside of the windshield, and the car soon grew fragrant with the effluvium of brine-soaked driftwood and strands of kelp. One of the snails had recently, and no doubt reluctantly, gone to Snail Heaven; still in possession of a goodly portion of its odiferous innards, it began to take its vehement revenge.

But I did not complain.

The great-great-grandson of Eric and Inger was feeling, with the help of my guide, a little less unworthy.

MILLY AND THE GEESE

from the novel "DANCING WITH SAMUEL"

What a gift this was after all the years of letters and phone calls: to have time on a rainy summer afternoon to sit on the porch and simply be together.

Rocking comfortably in her chair, Louise asked me, "Samuel, you have been so many places in the world, and yet you keep coming back here. What is it about the Adirondacks that you love so much?"

Rocking comfortably in my chair, I answered, "I'm not an orphan here."

We had sat long enough in silence, had merged sufficiently with the rain on the lake, and had opened so completely to each other that Louise did not need to ask what I meant, nor did I hurry to explain. I would speak, after that patch of dark rippling water, the footprint of an otherwise invisible downdraft, moved like an amoeboid creature past the dock and into the now bobbing lilypads.

"My earliest memory, the very first thing that I can remember in my life, is a burst of orange, a fluttering of scarlet. Tall billows of colors, as bright as big happy noises." I paused to savor that memory. Then I laughed. "If I had never returned to the lake after I was three years old, I might never have figured out what it was that I remembered so vividly."

I sipped my strong hot coffee. Louise sipped hers, both of us rocking gently enough that we could hold a mug in our hands.

"But I was lucky. More than lucky: blessed. Because when I was four years old, and then again when I was five, my grandmother insisted that I stay with her at camp until late September. Three years in a row, she bundled me up in a wool sweater and a lifejacket, then told me to sit still on the front seat of her canoe. She paddled up the long narrow lake, passing close to the trees along the shore. Trees that were no longer green. Instead of candy, I was a kid hungry for colors. She must have watched me as I stared up at billows of gold and maroon, at ghosts of pale yellow, at wind-rippled red. And highest above us were bursts of orange that gave the sky its truest blue."

"Don't you see?" Louise interrupted sternly. "There's your calling. At three years old, an artist was born."

"True. And if that's all I were, life would be much simpler. But since then, other parts of me have been born as well."

"You've let yourself become too complicated."

"Well, let's not get sidetracked. You asked me why I love the Adirondacks."

Complicated! How many times have I wanted to just sit here on the porch, watch the rain patter on the lake and not think. Not think.

"Your grandmother. Is she your mother's mother, or your father's?"

"My mother's. Her name is Milly. She's what folks around here call a 'corker'."

"A corker?"

"Listen. When I was six, I was supposed to start school in Illinois. But Milly got into a huge battle with my parents. She insisted that I stay at camp until the end of September. She wanted me to see those red maples one more time, before school swallowed my Septembers for the next umpteen years." I remembered my astonishment when Milly stood up to my father; she was the only person I knew who wasn't afraid of him. "Being Milly, she won. And the geese must have known it, because they landed on the lake that September by the hundreds."

"The geese?" Louise gazed out at the misty gray-green lake, as if a flock might be paddling somewhere along the opposite shoreline.

"No, you won't see them now. Late September is the time, when most kids are in school." Remembering not a three year old's blur of colors, but a six year old's sharp detail, I smiled, "Oh, we saw them, you bet we did! Hundreds of geese honking above us while they circled, as if they were angels laughing at the lower edge of heaven. They landed so close to our camouflaged canoe that I could hardly sit still on my seat."

And ever since, the first sound of their honking in an autumn sky brings me to a complete stop. Or better, to a sudden start, because I put down my book or my paintbrush, then dash out the door and stare up at those September voyagers who honk with exuberant pity at us dull groundlings. They are not bound by the tethers of earthly trappings, nor by the weight of old baggage. They embrace the sky, their journey taking them over the curve of the earth.

"In early October, Milly rode with me on the train all the way to Chicago. My parents met us at the station. I began first grade a month late, but I've always been of the opinion that whatever I missed, the other kids missed Lesson Number One."

Louise nodded. She had found an ally. "So your grandmother insisted."

"Yes, Milly insisted."

Just that once. And once was enough.

"When I was seven, and under orders from the board of education to be in my seat in September, Milly and I had to paddle our canoe in the summer when the trees were green. But that was all right. In July, the channel meanders through a carpet of purple pickeralweed. Those trips became our tradition. Every summer, Milly and I never missed our annual picnic in the big purple garden."

"Your grandmother insisted on that too."

"Absolutely. She insisted on a canoe trip with each of her grandkids, at least once every summer. That's camp. That's the Adirondacks. That's what it's all about."

"But, you missed the red maples in September. For how many years?"

"Right. All those orange and scarlet leaves that I didn't see during my dreary Septembers in grade school, in high school, my Septembers in college. Heaven help me, even four years of graduate school. Leaves that fell and turned brown on the ground, or black at the bottom of the lake."

Much like the years without Louise.

"Milly must have had her eye on me, because for my tenth birthday, she gave me a box of watercolors. My grandfather built an easel that fit onto the gunnels in the bow of the canoe. During that summer vacation, I painted a clump of blue iris growing on the shore. And tufts of yellow bladderwort blooming on a bog. Milly sat in the stern, pointing the canoe in just the right direction. She tillered now and then when a breeze came along, while she kept an eye out for turtles and the heron and all her other friends."

I recalled the day a hummingbird landed on her paddle; but that was another story.

"Louise, I had that box of paints for sixteen years before I painted a single red leaf. When I finally finished the doctorate, I was twenty-six. I was supposed to become a teacher, but I was sick to death of school. So I was kicking around California, taking odd jobs here and there." Chasing a multitude of short skirts and catching too many of them. "My father was angry and my mother was worried. Mom must have phoned her mother, because Milly phoned me. She found me sleeping on a sofa at a friend's apartment in Los Angeles. After listening to me for no more than two minutes, she ordered me to drive across the country, nonstop from L.A. to Woodgate, in time to see the maples turn red."

"Ordered you. Not just insisted. Ordered you."

"Like a buck sergeant, ordered me. 'Time,' she said, 'for you to get back to where you belong.' "

"So you drove across the country."

"You bet I did. The states went by like phone poles. Milly and I launched her canoe on the last Saturday in September, on a gorgeous morning when northern air was blowing down from Canada and the sky was royal blue. She packed a picnic, I packed my watercolors. The channel up the lake is a mile long, then it winds around an esker, a finger of the forest that reaches at right angles almost across the end of the lake. It's really a ridge of boulders and sand left ten thousand years ago by a glacier. Now, with trees growing along it, the esker forms a perfect partition. Once we had paddled around its tip, we were enclosed in the last section of the lake: a pond, a perfect oval pond about a hundred yards long. The forest wraps around the pond, so it's very secluded, a private little world. And a superb studio for painting. Especially in late September when the low autumnal sun shone over my shoulder from the south. The shoreline cupped in front of us was . . . Louise, those orange and scarlet maples were like a fanfare of trumpets.

"A bedraggled hippy, an academic burn-out, a perennial ne'er-do-well, I placed a fresh block of paper on my grandfather's easel. And do you know, while I was painting, I forgot to worry about what I was supposed to do with my life. Because I was doing it. While I was mixing the reds, mixing the yellows, I found my Adirondack soul."

And learned never again to lose it, no matter where on the earth I wandered.

"When I had finished the first painting that I had ever done of those red leaves, I turned carefully on my seat and held the picture in the sunshine so Milly could see it. She nodded. Just that, a firm, definite nod. But I could tell by the glint of approval in her eyes that I had gotten the colors just right."

Louise rocked in troubled silence.

Until I asked, "What's the matter?"

"When was that? When did you get the colors exactly right?"

"Well, that was the September after I finished my thesis." Recalling the date, I calculated, "That September was . . . twenty-one years ago."

I wondered, What, my beautiful Louise, were you doing then? A bottle of pink champagne on your twenty-first birthday had been the last of anything between us.

She stared at me, a lifetime of regret in her eyes. "On the tenth of October, twenty-one years ago, I promised myself to

Tony until death do us part."

One card, thanking me for a bottle of champagne. One card might have made all the difference.

"Well," I said, "we're not here to dwell on our regrets. We're here to see if we can paddle our way toward a little progress."

Whatever she was thinking, she covered it with a brave smile. "So Milly was your pal."

"Yes, she was my pal. Forty-five voyages, I as a child, a boy, a man, with no other destination than to the end of the lake and back, and with no other purpose than to share the trip. As she grew older, into her seventies, we traded positions, she in the bow and I in the stern. She was so light that I had to ballast the bow against a headwind. I put three round rocks in front of her feet." I could hear her joking voice. "She called them Roxanne."

I paused for a moment. Prayers don't always have to be sent to heaven. A prayer of gratitude can be sent to a specific person as well.

"For her eighty-fifth birthday, I gave her a featherweight paddle. But she was still the captain. Because she insisted that once a year I check my bearings, patch my sails, pump out the bilge, take on provisions, and chart the coming year's course. Often had I limped into port, leaking and listing, and just as often, one month later, I stood steady at the helm while she cast off my lines."

Yes, Louise had fired her cannonballs into my hull, had felled my masts and splintered my decks. I had all but burned and sunk. Milly told me there were other women in the world, 'other fish in the sea'. She told me too that bitterness was a poison, and she asked me why I insisted on my daily dose. She was right, except about one thing. There never was another Louise.

"Samuel, you said that you shared forty-five voyages. Now you're forty-nine. Is Milly . . ." Louise hesitated, found the right words. "Did she pass on?"

I was blessed, our whole family was blessed. For I was able to say, "Milly is still crackerjack sharp, living in a nursing home in a nice little town not far from here." I felt a pang of guilt. "I should have phoned her by now. She knows I arrived yesterday from Russia. She's no doubt expecting me to call her."

"Samuel, you should visit her. Go today if you like. Don't let me interfere."

"Would you like to meet her?"

Her eyes betrayed her doubts. "You go. She doesn't need to meet me."

I didn't argue. "I'll phone her tonight. I'll let her invite you herself."

Louise stared out at the rain. Why is it, I wondered, that some people are afraid of happiness, are absolutely sure and determined that they don't deserve it, when others insist and even demand their share of the treasures of life?

"Louise, you asked me about the Adirondacks. So what I'd like to tell you about is our forty-fifth trip. Which was our last trip, almost two years ago. Milly is on a kidney machine now."

Louise turned to me, importunate. "Then you *should* go see her."

"I will, I will. She's not going to die tomorrow." I laughed. "She's been getting calendars from a funeral home in Utica for at least fifteen years."

Reaching to the floor for the thermos, I refilled our mugs. Then I settled back to a steady rocking and told Louise an Adirondack tale that was absolutely true.

"When I was forty-seven, Milly was ninety-six. She had lived on her own for almost ten years after my grandfather died, but the time arrived when she needed medical care in a nursing home. She didn't want to stay down in Utica. She wanted to be up here as close as possible to the Adirondacks. So at the end of the summer, two years ago, my mother and I drove Milly to Sunset Home in Boonville. They gave her a room with a window that looked out on a weatherbeaten red barn at the edge of a spruce forest. She watches the spruce now, keeps her chair facing the window, for occasionally deer come out of the trees to feed on the corn.

"On that awful day when she moved into her room, its white plaster walls bare, its bed a mechanical hospital bed, the three of us could hardly talk. Nobody blamed anybody, but we hated what we were doing.

"Trying my best to be jovial, I kissed Milly good-bye. Then I hurried off to a job at a college down in central New York. She and I had agreed that I would return to the Adirondacks on the last Friday in September. I'd spend the night here at camp, then I'd pick her up at Sunset Home on Saturday morning. We'd go out in her canoe on Saturday afternoon to see the maples.

"But toward the end of September, Milly phoned me on a Tuesday evening, three days early. She said the wind had shifted, it was coming now from the north. Crystal-clear air from Canada was sweeping over the Adirondacks. Pegasus outside her window was as handsome as she had ever seen him. Tomorrow, Wednesday, would be the perfect day. Saturday would surely be too late.

"I explained to her that I had classes on Wednesday. She explained to me that the doctors had heard a murmur in her heart. I was left to understand that this September might well be her last. She did not want a hazy Saturday, nor an overcast Saturday, and certainly not a rainy Saturday and Sunday, when we'd have to sit here on the porch and watch the wind and rain take down the leaves until the trees stood bare above the gray lake. No, she wanted to go on Wednesday, tomorrow, for it promised to be the perfect day.

"So . . . What could I do? . . . I phoned the dean and gave him a long and absolutely truthful explanation of why I wanted to play hooky. After I told him about her heart murmur, he asked, 'Who am I to say no to a ninety-six-year-old wood nymph?' He said he'd cover my classes himself. He loved Robert Frost and would gladly return to where two roads diverged in a yellow wood.

"Well, much relieved, I packed my woolies and my watercolors, then headed north. I reached camp a little after midnight. True enough, the stars were spectacular. Standing down there on the end of the dock, I inhaled crisp Adirondack air and exhaled clouds of classroom chalk dust.

"The night was so beautiful that, wearing layers of wool underwear and a knit hat, I slept in my sleeping bag right there on the dock. When I woke up at dawn, the bag was white with frost, and so, I think, was my nose. A thick mist covered the lake, for the water was still much warmer than the air. The mist was drifting, I was glad to see, from north to south: the weather was holding steady. A stripe of color lay like a radiant mantle along the opposite shoreline, where the sun lit the round bushy tops of the maples. I watched the bright orange above slowly overtaking the dull orange below. Milly had been right: today was the perfect day. The sky over the entire length of the lake was pearly blue. Not a cloud at either end. If I bundled her well and paddled in the sunshine, she would stay warm for at least an hour out in her canoe."

Drinking coffee as I rocked, I savored the misty orange beginning of that gift of a day.

"I arrived at the nursing home at ten o'clock sharp, as we had agreed. When I looked in through the open door to Milly's room, I saw her sitting in a wheelchair, dressed in a green wool sweater and her khaki slacks, her red plaid jacket folded in her lap. She was clearly ready to go, but she was arguing with a doctor, who was telling her, sternly, that under no circumstances would she be allowed to leave. '*You* tell this worthy physician where we're going,' she snapped, pointing at me in the doorway. The doctor turned and saw me, shook hands as I introduced myself, and then he launched into a long list of symptoms, the cumulative effect of which might lead to deleterious consequences should Mrs. Baxter become tired and chilled. Couldn't we, he suggested, chat together in the TV room?

"Well, I was in a fix. Milly insisted that I wheel her 'out of this prison', while her doctor insisted, with equal vehemence, that she calm down and take a reasonable view of things. But she was not about to calm down. Nor was she afraid of any deleterious consequences. 'I'll sign a legal release,' she declared to the doctor, 'stating that if I die of frostbite, you, sir, are not responsible.'

"The doctor explained with growing impatience that since she was a resident in the home, she herself could not sign such a waiver. 'So,' she snapped, pointing at me again, 'let *him* sign it.'

"Me? I understood immediately that if I assumed responsibility by signing such a paper, and then if she *did* die out there in the canoe, it would be me who would have to bring her body back to Sunset Home; me who would have to phone her daughter, my mother; and me who would be looked upon by the rest of the family, gathered at her funeral, as the fool who had killed her.

"Milly glared at me, her soft wrinkled face stern with determination. Her usually cheerful blue eyes were as hard as Adirondack granite. 'Samuel, you sign a release stating that nobody in this overheated hothouse is responsible if God gives me one more perfect day and then calls me home. And I will sign a release stating that you are not responsible for getting me out of here before I die of bedpans and boredom.' She turned to the doctor and ordered him, 'Now you write that up. Get sixteen witnesses if you want. What are you doing inside anyway, on such a beautiful day?"

Louise said with a smile, "She reminds me of Mama."

Yes, your mother. *She* knew we would have been happy.

I mused further, Too bad you never met Milly. Really too bad. If you two had spent an hour together twenty-five years ago, we'd probably be on the honeymoon of our silver anniversary now.

Never mind, never mind.

I continued, "Yessir, Milly was fit as a fiddle, but I was in a cold sweat as I signed that document releasing Sunset Home from any and all responsibility. Milly signed a second document, releasing me of any and all responsibility. She signed it 'Mildred Baxter' as big as 'John Hancock'.

"Then, most cordially, she shook the doctor's hand and told him she would be back sometime after dinner. He protested, poor soul, nearly at the end of his tether, that she *must* be back by two o'clock in the afternoon. Four hours was certainly enough for a woman in her condition. Glaring up at him, she informed him that she was going to have huckleberry pie at the Hulbert House, 'and not another bowl of your tasteless jello for people without teeth.'

"So I wheeled her—she rode like a victorious queen—out of her room, down the corridor and out through the front door. She lifted her face with a defiant smile to the dazzling sun. I was wishing that I'd had sense enough ten minutes ago to phone my mother to ask her what to do. So that even if I did what I was now doing, she would have concurred that what I was doing was the right thing. Never had I been responsible for anyone so delicate and precious as my ninety-eight pound, five-foot-three, white-haired grandmother. Louise, never in my life had I known such a sense of overwhelming dread.

"My hands wet on the plastic wheelchair grips, my eyes staring down at the gray sidewalk ahead of us, I almost turned her around and wheeled her back so I could phone my mother.

"Then she looked over her shoulder at me, her blue eyes jubilant as she asked, 'Got your paints?'

" 'Yes,' I answered, my mind barely registering her question. 'They're on the table at camp.'

"Good! The maples are waiting.'

"And with that, I was suddenly no longer afraid. We were going to have a wonderful time. I was taking her home, home to her camp, to the woods, to her lake. Home to the cabin where, if we could have found a nurse to stoke the fire through the winters, Milly would live to be a hundred."

"Samuel, one thing I don't understand," said Louise. "How did you get her from a wheelchair into the canoe?"

I held up my hand with a smile. "Wait. I'll explain. When we arrived here at the lake, she got out from the car into her chair, then I wheeled her through the camp and out to the porch. She didn't want to sit in her wheelchair, but in a rocking chair. So she stood up from one and sat down in the other. We sat right here in these two chairs, I in mine and she in yours, with the bedside table between us, and we had a mug of tea. She likes peppermint tea with honey. While she rested, we looked with anticipation at the blaze of maples across the lake."

I paused, to let Louise absorb for a moment a bit of Milly's spirit. Some of her courage, to take with her in the canoe on our own voyage into the Adirondack wilderness.

"When Milly was ready, I helped her to put on her red jacket. She tied a green wool scarf over her white hair, and pulled on a pair of blue wool mittens. Then she announced, 'I'm going to walk.'

" 'Can you?' I asked. Last summer she had stood up and walked around her kitchen, bracing herself on the table and stove. I didn't know what she had done more recently at Sunset Home. But in any case, the walk down the steps to the dock was not easy.

" 'Who says I can't?' she snapped, gripping the arms of her rocking chair and pushing herself up.

Acquiescing despite my apprehension, I stood up from my chair, took hold of her thin arms and helped her to stand. Gripping my arm as I walked beside her, she shuffled through the camp and out the door, then around the corner and down the hill, her leather walking shoes pushing through the first of the maple leaves that had fallen. We rested at the top of the steps, then down we went, I walking backwards in front of her, holding her shoulders as she let herself down step by step, always reaching with her left foot, to the dock.

"Once there, we talked it over and developed a strategy. She stood at the edge of the dock and faced her seat in the bow of the canoe; I stood beside her with my arms spread behind her; very slowly she leaned back into my arms and I picked her up. Then I knelt on one knee and lowered her until she sat on the edge of the dock with her feet in the canoe. I steadied her as she shifted her bottom from the dock down to the wicker seat.

'Good!' she declared, immensely pleased to be in her canoe again. I helped her to put on her orange life jacket, then I wrapped a gray wool blanket around her and tucked it under her feet. I would do all the paddling today. She would sit in the bow and stay warm while she watched the world go by."

"As you had done, bundled up in the bow when you were a child."

"Yes. As I had done, forty-four turnings of the earth ago."

Who would I have been without her? Would I even be?

"I backpaddled away from the dock, swung the bow like the needle of a compass to the north, then began to paddle up the long narrow channel. The lilypads, bug-chewed and tattered at the summer's end, had turned from green to shades of red and rusty orange. Baby maples, old enough to hold a dozen small red leaves, stood scattered on the bogs along the way, mimicking the big guys on shore.

"Snug in her blanket, Milly stared to the left and to the right, hungry for colors. I tillered close to the western shore so she could stare up at sunlit orange against the blue. Just as I had done nearly half a century ago, she gazed down at the water where the same colors rippled as if on a blurry pallet.

"At the end of the channel, we hooked around the esker and entered the oval pond, fringed with bogs and wrapped by the wreath of the forest. Today the pond was royal blue, wrapped by a wreath of orange.

"Milly liked to glide along the edge of the pond so she could peer into the forest where she couldn't walk anymore. So that's what we did. I paddled slowly past a fluttering wall of autumn colors. Though my paint box and folded easel were at my feet, and though my eyes feasted on deep maroons, I wouldn't do any painting until we had paddled at least once around the pond. The first part of this voyage was purely for Milly.

"We glided past a beaver house, a dome of sticks plastered with fresh mud. Looking down into the water, we could see a broad sheaf of alder branches, with green leaves at one end and gnawed white points at the other. The beavers had cut and stored the branches as a food supply beneath the coming winter ice.

"Further along the shore, I listened to a gathering of chickadees fluttering about in the branches of a big hemlock. Chickadees spend the entire winter in the Adirondacks, whereas most of the other birds fly south. These chickadees were discussing with delight their good fortune, for soon they would have the forest all to themselves."

Now I stopped in the middle of my story. Leaning forward in the rocking chair, I looked out through the screen at the gray day. Turning my head, I cupped my hand behind my ear as if listening to something in the distance, high above the northern end of the lake.

Louise heard nothing, I was sure, but the rain on the lake and the rain on the porch roof.

Now I moved my head slowly, cupping both ears toward something passing over the opposite shoreline.

"Samuel," I heard her ask, puzzled, "what do you hear?"

I cupped my ears further and further to the south, looking now right past Louise. "Nothing now." I sat back and continued rocking. "But I certainly did hear something on that Wednesday afternoon in late September."

She looked at me, waiting, until finally she laughed, for she realized I was teasing her. "So what was it?"

I reached for the thermos and held it up. "More coffee?"

"Samuel!"

I grinned.

"Samuel, *tell* me."

I set down the thermos, then rocked, rocked, rocked in my chair before I continued. For time, the passage of time, is part of all tales.

"Milly doesn't hear very well. She uses a hearing aide in each ear. One thing she regrets is that, even with fresh batteries, she isn't able to hear the birds. Those chickadees: though she watched them, she couldn't hear them. Not a peep.

"So she did not hear what I suddenly heard, high above us to the north: the steady, exuberant, unmistakable honking of geese. Staring up, I searched the blue sky, until Yes!, there they were, a big V of geese coming south, high over the forest ahead of us. I laid my paddle across the gunnels, cupped both hands behind my ears and listened to the sound of angels laughing at the lower edge of heaven.

"Then I spotted another flock to our left, a ragged V with a long straggling strand of flapping specks, as if a bunch of amateurs hadn't yet decided who was supposed to lead.

"Milly was still peering into the forest. Watching a chipmunk, maybe. I didn't want to call to her, didn't want to make any noise, so I did what I sometimes do: I bounced on my seat, just enough to shake the bow. She turned in her blanket to look at me, her face pink in the cool autumn air. I pointed with my right hand at the first flock, and with my left hand at the second.

"Turning forward, she looked up, nearly straight up as the big symmetrical V sailed high overhead.

"I picked up my paddle and began to pivot the canoe so she could watch the geese fly over the southern end of the lake. But she whispered over her shoulder, 'No. Take us in between the bogs.' Working one arm out from the blanket, she pointed her blue mitten at a cleft of water between two bogs just big enough to back a canoe into. Two rows of tamaracks, golden yellow now, grew along the edges of the bogs, providing a perfect blind. The canoe, as you will see when we take it off the sawhorses, is camouflaged with shades of brown and green. It once belonged to a duck hunter, until Milly bought it from him and saved the ducks from any further trouble. So once we were tucked behind the tamaracks, Milly, in her gray blanket and green scarf, and I, in my green flannel shirt and brown vest, would be virtually invisible from the sky.

"While I backpaddled into our hideaway, I saw Milly's arms working beneath the blanket. I grinned, for I knew that she was reaching into a pocket of her red jacket, and I knew what she was reaching for. By golly, she had come prepared!

"Peering out from behind the fuzzy yellow trees, she faced

the pond. I didn't know if she still had enough strength in her lungs, and we certainly couldn't be sure that a flock of geese would fly low enough over the pond to hear her. But if they did, and if they were willing to pause for lunch in the middle of the day, then perhaps the maestro had a chance to call them down. Milly had never in her life shot a goose, which is why she had learned to converse so well. Over the years I had heard several of their conversations, though they were later in the afternoon, toward dusk, when the geese were more likely to land."

Louise put her hand on my arm. "Wait a minute. Your grandmother talks with geese?"

"Absolutely." My pride was not a whit diminished when I explained, "With a goose call." Curling one hand into a tube, I simulated the instrument used by hunters, "Hooonk, hooonk, hooonk!"

"You're kidding."

"No, I'm not kidding. She's a virtuoso. She not only calls them down, but, yes, she talks with them. Not to them, *with* them. She sits in the bow of her canoe, as invisible as an Indian, and she honks until a flock has splash-landed on the pond. Then she picks out a particular goose and says hello. And except for the fact that she sits in the bow and that goose is paddling thirty yards away, I cannot tell them apart. Not only that, but when she starts to mimic another goose, it's different! Different tone, different cadence, different pitch. She can replicate what they're saying so perfectly that now this goose, and now that one, is answering back."

"So," Louise smiled, "on her last trip out in her canoe, Milly called down a flock of geese."

I took a deep breath, hoping to steady my voice. "Yes, but not all the way down. I don't think she wanted them to settle on the pond. She just wanted to say hello."

Another breath, but even so, when I spoke, my voice trembled. "Or to say good-bye."

I had to stare out at the rain on the lake.

Louise's hand, still on my arm, squeezed me gently.

"Milly loves those geese," I said, looking at her. "Part of her is as wild as they are. And of course, if they came close enough, they were the only bird she could still hear."

Louise and I rocked slowly in tandem, breathing the damp tannic Adirondack air.

"Wrapping her blue mittens around the walnut tube, Milly pointed her goose call toward the sky. With a steady, exuberant, unmistakable honking, she began to beckon them. The first flock was well past us, a tiny V sailing away over the southern end of the lake. The second flock was passing behind us. Though it was lower, it never wavered as it headed south. But Milly kept calling up to the empty blue sky, with less wind than she had once had, less volume, but with no less certitude that someone up there would hear her."

Certitude. Faith. Unremitting belief.

"And they did. I heard them before I saw them. Looking up through the yellow branches, I spotted them over the forest to the north, one strand of the V a little longer than the other. Their flight would not take them over the middle of the pond, but neither would they fly much further away than above the opposite shore.

"Now Milly spotted them. Pointing her goose call, she honked with a double measure of enticement. The lead goose wavered. A ripple went half-way along one strand. She honked steadily as they passed in the distance in front of us, her wrinkled face turning slowly toward the sun. The sun shone on her white hair curling out from under the green scarf. And it shone on her blue mittens, the same blue as the sky.

"Now I could hear, from the geese themselves, a change in their honking. A discussion was going on. Some were for maintaining their momentum. Some were for seeking out the lone goose that greeted them. The lead goose, a dark mote with a long neck and steadily pumping wings, now drew the others down in a descending curve that hooked west over the esker, and then to the north along the shoreline behind us. For a while I couldn't see them, only hear them. We didn't want to twist around in the canoe and possibly frighten them. Moving just our heads, we saw them again to our left, winging in a broad curve beyond the end of the pond.

"Milly glanced back at me with an exuberant grin, and I knew that now she could hear them. Their raucous nasal call had reached her ears.

"The geese hooked into a second descending curve that took them into what became a circle over the pond itself. Honking tirelessly, Milly brought them down low enough that we could see the sun shining through their pinions. I could hear the rich interweaving of their wings as they passed in front of us, not more than a hundred feet up.

"Then Milly surprised me. She stopped honking. Even though the geese hadn't yet splash-landed on the pond, she lowered her hands to her lap.

"The flock of fifty geese circled above the wreath of orange and scarlet trees, filling the royal blue sky with their wild, jubilant, overlapping clamor.

"Sitting behind Milly, watching the left side of her pink face, and now the right, in shadow and in sunlight, while the geese circled once, twice, and a third time over the pond, I saw that she was smiling.

"With a triumphant smile that I can only hope one day to achieve.

"Then the geese began to rise. One bird took the lead as the V reassembled and sailed due south on an incline over the esker.

"A long minute later, though the tiny specks disappeared beyond the treetops, I could still hear their faint voices.

"Milly twisted around in her blanket, shaking the canoe slightly. Her blue mittens wrapped around her goose call, she smiled at me with a century of wisdom in her eyes."

Louise and I rocked in perfect tandem. Over the lake, the rainy afternoon was darkening.

She said quietly, "So you're not an orphan here."

I answered quietly, "No, I'm not an orphan here. Because there's something here I can believe in."

Other books by John Slade

DANCING WITH SAMUEL

A JOURNEY OUT OF DARKNESS

THE NEW ST. PETERSBURG

GOOD MORNING, DADDY!

A DREAM SEEDED IN THE EARTH

CHILDREN OF THE SUN

Available from
WOODGATE INTERNATIONAL
P.O. Box 190
Woodgate, New York 13494

315-392-4508